## Praise for Emma-Claire Wilson

'Beautiful, emotional and hopeful, but have tissues to hand.'
**Liz Fenwick**

'Tragic but ultimately uplifting.'
**Katie Fforde**

'*This Child of Mine* is an emotionally-charged, beautiful, and poignant story that will stay with me for a very long time. Wilson had me sobbing from the very first page, and I couldn't put the book down. An absolute triumph of a debut.'
**Natali Simmonds**

'Right from the first pages, the reader is plunged into and emotional and heartrending story... wondering what they might do in a similar situation. This book cannot fail to move the reader.'
**Janet Gover**

'A highly emotional read. Both harrowing and hopeful. Wilson offers a subtle, raw and tender exploration of what family means and how grief can ultimately open up new strength and unknown paths to happiness.'
**Sarah Jost**

'I spent my Sunday devouring this heartfelt, emotional, charming and gorgeously-written debut. With many unexpected moments, great characters, and a satisfying conclusion, I was lost in the story. Highly recommended.'

**Louise Beech**

'Gripping, timely and important, *This Child of Mine* tackles something that is all too often swept into the shadows: the heartbreak that can come with starting a family.'

**Katie Allen**

'Heartbreaking, unexpected and necessary. This book is just stunning.'

**Emma Cooper**

'A beautifully written story of love and hope that will capture readers' hearts and minds. Emma-Claire is the real deal – a writer to fall in love with.'

**Ally Sinclair**

# this child of mine

Born in Scotland, Emma-Claire travelled the world as the child of military parents. After almost twenty years in Spain, she returned to the UK with her husband, two daughters, and rescue dog, Pip. Emma-Claire worked as a journalist for English-language magazines and newspapers in Spain and in 2015 launched The Glass House Online Magazine. When not writing emotional fiction, you can find her dreaming up new book ideas or wrapped in a blanket with a book in her hand. *This Child of Mine* is her debut novel.

@ECWilsonWriter

# this child of mine

emma-claire wilson

avon.

Published by AVON
A division of HarperCollins*Publishers*
1 London Bridge Street
London SE1 9GF

www.harpercollins.co.uk

HarperCollins*Publishers*
Macken House, 39/40 Mayor Street Upper,
Dublin 1, D01 C9W8
Ireland

A Paperback Original 2023
1
First published in Great Britain by HarperCollins*Publishers* 2023



A catalogue copy of this book is available from the British Library.

ISBN: 978-0-00-860808-8



Typeset in Sabon by Palimpsest Book Production Limited, Falkirk, Stirlingshire
Printed and Bound in the UK using
100% Renewable Electricity at CPI Group (UK) Ltd

This book is produced from independently certified FSC™ paper to ensure responsible forest management.
For more information visit: www.harpercollins.co.uk/green

*To my own mini miracles, Tabitha*
*and Matilda*
*. . . and the man who made all my*
*dreams come true.*
*Thank you. X*

Content warning:

THIS CHILD OF MINE, although fictional, tackles many issues that some may find distressing. Throughout this novel, grief, miscarriage, baby loss and cancer are all discussed at length.

# CHAPTER ONE

It was supposed to be the happiest day of my life.

I was supposed to bounce out of this chair and follow the sonographer into a room for a follow-up scan and to hear the sex of our first child. This was supposed to be the day all our dreams came true. I was supposed to have a grin on my face and a heart full of joy and love.

But that's not what happened. My heart knew it was coming before anyone else did. Somehow my body knew it too. I could feel it. My heart wasn't racing. In fact, I think it all but stopped. I couldn't feel anything. My body slipped into self-protection mode and I was simply numb. From head to toe.

'Ms Jackson. Mr Jackson. Come right through.'

I tried to rise from the plastic bucket chair, but my legs didn't want to respond.

I stood and adjusted my skirt, the hem pricking at the skin on my thigh as I hazarded a last glance towards the girl sat on one of the remaining seats, a little further down the corridor. Her faithful partner perched, just as James had been, like an eager puppy on the very edge of the chair. Her face was so full of hope, a twinkle in her eyes like Christmas had come early. Her dream was just beginning.

I had the distinct impression all mine were about to end.

I couldn't look towards James. I didn't feel in control of my own body. I knew I was in the room, but felt like I was watching the scene play out from overhead. Detached from a situation I never imagined I would find myself in. Maybe it was self-preservation. I didn't want to see the remnants of hope in his eyes. I knew the panic in mine would kill every prayer he's made these past few weeks.

I shuffled forward, not floating, but dragging my terrified body towards the door of doom. I stopped at least three paces short of the door, where my feet hit glue that stuck them to the spot. My eyes were unable to move from the clock on the wall. A tiny piece of Sellotape was stuck to its edge. Gold shards of plastic tinsel were splayed out at messy angles, a nod to a Christmas past. The air con made the small strips flutter in time with the ticking of the clock.

'It's August! Don't you know it's bad luck to leave remnants of Christmas decorations up after January?' I said.

'Well, we can't have bad luck here, can we,' Dr Li replied with a conciliatory smile. 'I'll make sure the receptionist takes it down.'

Too bloody late for me though, right?

I studied his face for any hint of what he might say.

He wasn't giving anything away with his tone or body language. I couldn't sense a lightness. I was so desperate to see him smile. Something, anything to suggest my fears may be unfounded.

I could feel James's hand on the small of my back, gently trying to ease me forward. I wanted to tell him that I didn't want to go in there. That I wanted to stay out here, where all our dreams were still possible. The pressure from his hand increased but I stayed rooted to the spot as he manoeuvred around to step into my eyeline.

'Come on, Steph, we've got this.'

As he guided me through the door, I couldn't shake the image of that damn tinsel from my thoughts.

I had sketched pictures in my mind, ready to add colour and bring to life, of all the Christmases to come. Our perfect little family sat on the sofa staring at bright, twinkling lights and children's toys wrapped with care beneath the tree. I had been so relieved; we had finally made it this far.

I wished I could close my eyes and go back in time, to feel that depth of hope and excitement again. Instead, I squeezed my husband's hand as he guided my lifeless body into the room. I couldn't quite understand how he was holding it together.

As I passed through the doorway, I noticed the air change. It was colder. The open window let in the breeze from outside, fluttering the blinds ever so slightly as I lowered myself into the armchair in front of Dr Li's desk.

This is the most terrifying bit about being pregnant. No one will tell you that. They will tell you they are worried about the pain of labour, or something going wrong during delivery, but the truth is, *that* moment right there was the one we feared the most. The moment when a doctor's face betrays them and lends credence to a silent worry that something might happen that you can't control.

That's the hardest part of pregnancy, not the sleepless nights and heartburn, but the ever-present niggling fear that lives in the shadows.

Fear is so much more paralysing than pain.

James lowered me into the chair, and I released my grip on his hand. Just before letting go, he squeezed twice in quick succession and I raised my gaze from the whites of his knuckles to his bloodshot eyes. That little pulse was our way of saying 'I love you' in public. Our own secret language.

He is still the man I love. He is still my protector. He is still here. I am not alone, no matter how lonely I feel right now. I need to remember that.

He took his seat beside me and placed his hands in a prayer-like fashion between his knees. He tilted his head back, eyes focused on the ceiling as if some heavenly prayer would somehow save us.

I returned my gaze to the man behind the desk. My judge and jury.

He looked tired – not like he did the day we first met him. I wondered if it was my case that had left him sleepless, or if I was just one in a long line of unfortunate mothers-to-be he had dealt with this week.

For the briefest moment, the world seemed eerily calm. There was no clatter and chatter. No movement or bustle. Only stale air that my thoughts and fears tumbled through, hoping to be caught, held and reassured.

As I looked into his eyes, I knew. I think I always knew.

He spoke softly and used words I didn't understand and seemed to smile at what felt like the right moments. But just seconds after the words stopped colouring the room around us, I stared at his lips.

Was he finished? Had I heard him right?

'Are you sure?'

I felt the air shift between my teeth and heard the impact as waves of sound created words that bounced around the room.

As much as I could feel the effect, I wasn't sure that the sound hitting my ears was my own.

'I'm afraid so.'

Afraid so. Afraid of what? Should I be afraid?

That tone must be rehearsed. Did they receive training on the correct voice to use with patients before they were allowed to wear a white coat?

'But what does that mean? I don't understand.'

Nothing made sense. The small part of me that hoped this was all a big mistake was now long gone, and the fog that had surrounded me for the last week grew thicker, tightening around my temples and pushing the air from my chest.

'Ms Jackson. Let me see if I can explain it a little better.' His chest puffed out, as if he was consuming the air I so desperately needed, using my life force to feed his explanation.

I hated him.

I hated every inch of him that was taking up space in my perfect world.

Hated that he was taking up space in our story, a story he was never invited into.

'The procedure we will need to perform will most certainly impact on your pregnancy. Of course, we could postpone the treatment and the operation until after delivery, but the risks are so incredibly high that I really do recommend you look at all possible options.'

The tapping of his pen on the folder cut through my concentration. I tried to focus on his words, but the dull thumping got louder with each strike.

'The problem is—' he lowered his upper body to catch my eye, looking at me with a tilted head in the way a parent would at a confused child '—we have no idea how aggressive it may be. If it does indeed turn out to be a cancerous mass, the hormones in your system could speed up its growth.'

He didn't move. I swear I didn't even see him blink, like a statue, concrete in his repose, steadfast in his resolution. Where was the compassion? All I felt from him was duty.

He continued to *tap*, *tap*, *tap* against the paperwork, waiting for my response.

'How do you mean impact? Exactly?'

Brains are clever things, aren't they? Working for us when we think we have no ability to form a sentence.

'The foetus is unlikely to survive the procedure, Ms Jackson. The risk of miscarriage at this early stage is incredibly high.'

There they were, the words I feared the most, given life by a stranger.

He paused, just a beat. Something in my expression must have reached him, as he pushed the box of tissues towards me. His words rattled around my brain, taking a moment to form a picture in my mind. The life I had planned, the family I had dreamt of, all the dreams I had painted dissolved, as if the glue on the back of the images on my mood board had flaked away, each small snapshot plummeting to the ground, one by one.

A paralysing punch hit me hard enough for the remaining air to leave my chest in the most horrifying way. Not a scream, not a gasp. That reaction, that fear, had a sound all of its own.

As my body continued to react, my mind searched for something to ground me.

An indentation on the table in front of me glittered, speckles of liquid dotted on the surface. Were they tears? Spit? Mine or someone else's? Faint lines of a signature marked forever into the cheap wood of the clinical desk. As I reached forward to grab a tissue and traced my fingers across the curves of the impure tabletop, I couldn't help but wonder what this person had signed away. Would I be expected to sign something? Was I expected to sign away my child's life? My own?

He was still talking. Had I missed something? His lips were moving. I could see the whites of his teeth and I watched as his tongue flicked across his polished veneers, making shapes with his mouth, but I couldn't hear the words at first.

'. . . and if you don't have the operation and the mass is cancerous – well, if you wait another six months, we can't guarantee the prognosis will be positive for either yourself or the foetus.'

As I scanned the room looking for something to throw up in, I tried to avoid the glow of the lights behind the MRI images on the wall. Negative spaces that once meant nothing now appeared like ghosts of my future in the shape of cancerous masses.

I tried to tear my focus away and caught sight of another pair of distressed eyes.

With a million thoughts running through my mind, not one of them had yet included him. I watched as his eyes, staring intently at the doctor across the table, glazed and filled with tears. His fists clenched around the metal of the chair frame. My fingers twitched but for some reason I didn't reach out and take his hand in mine.

Conflicting emotions battled to take over my body as I looked at the man I loved. If I thought about how much this would kill him, if I considered for one moment how this would affect him too . . . I couldn't. It made it too real. Too final. This all felt too much. I walked into this building filled with a sense of foreboding, but I knew he walked in here with hope in his heart. He was convinced this was all a mistake. I knew better.

Suddenly I didn't want him here. I needed to figure out how to fix this, to fix me. I wanted to fix it all before he even knew it was broken. I couldn't be the one to shatter all the dreams we had built together.

A voice broke through the awkward silence. Gruff and so far removed from the smooth, soulful sounds I had loved for so long. I could hear the constriction of his throat as he pushed out his emotions, his words measured, slow and calculated.

'Are you saying that if we choose to . . . what did you say? "Remove the mass"?' He paused just long enough for me to look between him and the doctor, watching as a consolatory smile and slow nod reassured my husband of his understanding.

'Right. Mass. If we remove the mass . . .' his voice was stuck, as if the words were fighting against being released '. . . could we, um . . . are you saying we could then get treatment?'

'Wait.' My words came out as a whisper, not strong enough to battle the loudness of the room.

'Wait,' I said again, a little louder, but still the men carried on mouthing words to each other, discussing my fate. I couldn't hear anything, couldn't focus, couldn't breathe!

'Wait a minute,' I said again, not a shout, but enough to have them finally hear me. Their eyes were now firmly on me, as if I had shouted *fire* in the middle of a crowded room. They were staring at me, waiting for me to say something profound. As if my body knew exactly what I needed of it, in that one moment, it found the volume button on my voice box and my words hurled towards them with a life of their own.

'Just wait. Stop. Just . . . stop for a minute will you. Both of you.'

My eyes were locked on to my husband's face. I didn't want to hear the answers to the questions he'd asked. I wasn't in any way ready to start rationalising this.

My face burned with anger as I looked at the man I had trusted with my life. The man who was this very moment discussing the possibility of our lives without this baby. This baby that we had tried for years to bring into existence. This baby that we had both painted into our future with such precision.

'Could we try for another baby a little further down the line?' James questioned as my brain tried to make sense of the scene playing out in front of me.

'What do you mean, James?'

He turned, eyes filled with fear and face as ashen as his charcoal jumper. 'I mean, I know it's been hard, but this isn't the first time we've lost a baby, Steph, and if we can try again . . .'

His voice trailed off, and my heart couldn't settle on what to say first. I wanted to reach out for him, hold him, hug him close and tell him I was sorry, again. But I couldn't. I hadn't lost this one. Not yet. This baby was still alive in our future; I still had a chance to fix this.

'We don't need to try again. Not yet. There's still a heartbeat, right, Doctor?'

Dr Li looked between us, deciding who to address first. He landed on James.

'Yes, depending on the treatment plan, there are many other options for you to explore to have a child of your own.'

I didn't like the way he phrased that. Not one bit.

'Stop. STOP. Stop talking. I need to . . . I can't . . . just . . .'

As I uttered the last word, my stomach gave up the fight and that morning's breakfast made its way onto the crisply ironed jeans of the man I have loved for over a decade.

James leapt from his chair towards the sink at the side of the room, pulling at the paper hand towels in the dispenser, as if helping me mop up the mess could fix it all. He held out a crumple of tissues, but I turned away. I couldn't look at him. I couldn't face him, scared to see the reality of this situation staring back at me.

I grabbed a fresh tissue from the box on the desk and mopped the sick from the side of my mouth.

'You should take some time to talk this over together,' said the doctor.

I stared at him.

'These decisions are never easy. I will make an appointment for you to come see me before the end of next week and we can talk things through further.' He dropped his pen onto the table before typing on the noisy keyboard in front of him. One irritating sound replaced with another. I could feel the scream building inside me.

'You're at sixteen weeks' gestation now. We'll need to make the decision quickly, but I want you to really take the time to consider all options. I'll put you in touch with our support workers. They can help you with any questions you might have in the meantime.'

He had decided that our time was up. The ticking clock stilled for a moment as he drew our meeting to a close. All I wanted to do was run for the door. To run and keep running, fast enough to spin the world backwards and reverse everything he'd said, but James wasn't running anywhere. Now his feet were stuck in the glue that had refused to let me enter, his own body refusing to let him leave and face the truth.

His clenched fists gripped the sides of the sink, his shoulders shaking, head bowed low. I couldn't hear the words the doctor was muttering to him, but the gentle tapping of his hand on James's shoulder was making me unreasonably angry. It is the one thing this pregnancy has given me so far that I enjoy the least: an inability to keep my emotions in check.

'Excuse me!' I growled. Teeth gritted and eyelids shivering as I narrowed them, my anger was directed at no one and everyone. 'Sorry, can I just check – am

I the patient? Correct me if I'm wrong, Doctor, but I'm pretty sure it's me you just informed that I have ovarian cancer!'

The sight of my husband being consoled had tipped me over the edge, and with nowhere to flee, it seemed I was choosing to fight. I was angry with myself for losing it. I felt like an unreasonable teenager in the middle of a hormonal episode, but I couldn't stop rage from rising inside me.

'I am so sorry, Stephanie.' Dr Li faced me now, but still rested his hand on my husband's shoulder. 'I'll give you some time to catch your breath alone. The nurses outside can help you with anything you need when you're ready. Take your time.'

'Take my time?' I spat my words at him; I could see small flecks of saliva shooting in his direction like heat-seeking missiles. I was entitled to lose it, surely?

'Take my time! I thought I had five more fucking months. How much time do I have now?'

The indentation on the table in front of us was now clearly soaked with droplets of my visible anger.

James finally turned to face me, his eyes a shade of red even darker than before, his face wet with tears and his shoulders now still, but almost wrapped around his ears. I never swear. It's not really in me to curse. Even after a few drinks I don't swear, but even his shock couldn't stop the words from tumbling out of me.

'What the fuck has just happened, James? What am I supposed to do now?'

# CHAPTER TWO

I counted each footstep along the corridor as we made our way out of the hospital. I had done so well to keep my tears at bay, but each step I took I felt like I was fighting a losing battle. I focused on the joins and seams of the ill-fitting vinyl as I tried to squeeze all the mismatched pieces of my life back together, but the world seemed somehow changed. Unfamiliar.

The sharpness of the luminescent strip lighting bounced off the shiny surfaces and burned my eyes. I blinked hard and fast, but the pain seared deeper and stung my brain.

An instant migraine.

I clutched at handfuls of sweat-soaked fringe. My nails searching through the skin to find the irritation, desperate to remove it.

I was accustomed to pain – my whole life had been filled with it – but this was like a constant, unwelcome companion. Always in the wings waiting to pounce and knock me off-guard. Just another reminder that my hormone-unbalanced, broken body would and could betray me at any moment.

'Why don't you wait here; I'll go grab the car. Sit here and I'll message you when I'm outside, OK?' James said.

It took all the strength I had just to nod at him. My head felt heavier with each passing second, lead weights pulling down my eyelids and a vice crushing my temples.

I lowered myself into the chair and rested my head back against the wall, closing my eyes. I tried to deep-breathe past the nausea. I knew it was a battle I would likely lose, but I needed to stave it off until I got home.

A familiar smell hung in the air like an invisibility cloak following me down the sterile corridors. The first time we came here, that cloak felt like safety. As if I was shrouded with the love of those I missed, walking in step with me just out of sight but there to share my journey.

Today, that same cloak took the shape of an ominous, faceless character following me around with a scythe held high.

Cancer. For most, that word felt like a death sentence. How could I plan for the future on the same day as being told I might not be around to see it?

I stroked my belly and allowed an image to form in my mind of my tiny little peanut.

'Don't worry, my baby, everything will be fine. I'll make sure of it. We've waited too long for you to lose you now. Hold on tight, OK?' I whispered to the air, to the universe. To my unborn child.

'Are you all right, sweetheart?'

A soothing voice broke my thoughts, and as my eyes

readjusted to the light, a beautiful old lady passed me a handkerchief and gestured to her cheek. I hadn't even noticed I was crying, but sure enough, my own cheeks were soaked. I took the cotton hankie from her and wiped my tears.

'Thank you. Just a tough day. I'm so sorry, I may have ruined your handkerchief.' I tried to rub at the black mascara stain left behind on the pure white cotton. 'Seems I'm good at ruining things today,' I muttered as she rested her hand on my knee.

'Oh, sweetheart, I'm sure it's not as bad as you think.'

She smiled sweetly at me and all I wanted to do was hug her. Instead, I cried. Hard and loud. Folding into myself, it was a relief when she put her arm across my back, rubbing circles and singing 'there there' into my ear.

My phone buzzed in my bag. I had almost forgotten about James.

'That's my husband,' I said, as I looked out of the doors to see him waving from the car parked outside.

I stood, maybe a little too quickly as the world spun before me. Spots flashed in my eyes, like specks of glitter dancing in front of me, turning the doorway of the hospital into a Snapchat filter. Losing my balance, I landed heavily on the chair, my eyes refusing to focus.

'Oh dear, you really aren't very well. Here, shall I help you outside?'

The little old lady stood up, and gestured to help me rise. If I fell, I would crush her – she was so fragile and slight – but she wouldn't take no for an answer.

I took small steps towards the exit. As the doors opened, a rush of salt air hit me smack in the face, but the unexpected cooler breeze on a warm summer day was a relief. I needed cold, everywhere, and quick. My core temperature had shot from normal to volcanic in a matter of moments, and the sudden change mixed with the cooler breeze made the acid in my stomach churn as it coated and burned the inside of my throat.

We were only two steps shy of the front door when my knees hit the hard ground without warning and my stomach emptied itself again, Jackson Pollock style, onto the grey concrete canvas beneath me.

The little old lady crouched over me, rubbing my back again. All I could hear was the loud ringing of tinnitus in my ears.

'Oh, love, she's really not very well. Best you get her home and tucked up in bed,' I heard the woman's voice explaining through the chorus of screams in my head.

My husband's hand replaced hers on my back as he lifted me from the floor.

'Come on, Steph. Let's get you in the car.'

His voice was calm and measured. How did he do that? My world was spinning, literally, in front of my eyes, and his voice sounded like a reassuring grandfather reading a bedtime story.

He carried me, like a child, to the car. He set me down and opened the door.

'How are you staying so calm about this?'

'I'm not calm, Steph. I'm absolutely terrified, but right now, I need to get you home. We can talk about it then. One step at a time, OK?'

He stroked a tear off my cheek and smiled at me with his head tilted. I was going to have to get used to that. That sympathetic nod-smile. The one you get when everyone knows you're going through something terrible. I've seen that look before. I'd hoped never to see it again.

'Lie down in the back. Use my coat to cover your eyes.'

Normally I would chastise him for giving me orders, but as I peeked through my fingers at the broken shell of a man in front of me, I loved that I didn't have to explain or protest.

He placed his gym bag under my head and handed me a jacket to shield my eyes before he closed the door as cautiously as he could.

He would make a good dad.

I pushed the scratchy material of the jacket further into my eye sockets, convinced I could block out just a little more light.

'God, Steph, I'm sorry.'

He reached round from the front seat and squeezed my wrist lightly, unable to get to my fingers as they dug into my eyes.

That one touch did it – it reopened the floodgates and I sobbed.

I rocked back and forth in the back of the car as I counted each of the corners in my mind, tracing my way home from memory, praying we didn't get stuck in the weekend traffic along the seafront.

It wasn't long before we slowed to a stop in front of the house. He didn't jump out of the car immediately; instead, he sat for a moment longer than I expected.

'Shit. I'm so sorry, Steph.'

'Stop saying sorry!' I spat back at him.

It felt like the most redundant word. Sorry for what? It wasn't his body killing my baby. Killing me.

'No. I mean. Just . . . wait here, OK? Don't move.'

I sat up in the back of the car and tried to squint through the safety bars created by my fingers. Even through blurred vision I could see why he was apologising. Stood on the pavement outside our house was Helen.

She knew I had another appointment today. I hadn't told her the worries the doctor had voiced at the twelve-week scan, only that I had been scheduled extra follow-ups to monitor the pregnancy more closely this time. As far as Helen was concerned, this was just the sexing scan.

After decades of friendship, I had never outright lied to her. Omissions maybe, a few times I had bit my tongue, but never an outright lie. Not until now.

She was the last person I wanted to see. As a fertility specialist, she had seen it all over the years. After our second miscarriage, it was Helen who sat down and explained all the steps. I didn't want her answers or advice right now. I'd hoped we would be cracking open a bottle of non-alcoholic champagne, celebrating that everything was OK and finding out the sex of our baby. I wasn't sure I could handle her sympathy. James took one look at the expression on my face and nodded.

'I'll deal with it,' he said, as he pulled himself out of the car and walked towards the one person who would probably be able to give the very best advice.

I just didn't want to hear it.

I didn't move. I sat in the back seat and pressed the coat against my eyes, wishing I could drown out the inaudible but clearly recognisable tones of my best friend's reassuring voice.

Time seems to defy all logic when you have a migraine. It plays tricks with you. You're never really sure if it's moving by quickly, or if everything is happening in slow motion. Your brain can't function normally, and reality shifts and flows like the tides. I had no idea how long he debated with her, but when he returned, the solitary voice of my husband was a comforting sound.

'I told her you've got a migraine. She asked about the appointment but I told her that you'd talk to her later. She's gone home but says she'll call you in the morning.'

'Did you—'

'No, I haven't told her anything else.'

Right on cue, I heard the unmistakable 'ding' of my mobile. I knew it was a message from Helen, but I could barely make out the features on my husband's face, so reading a text message was impossible. Later, it could all wait until later.

James slipped his arm behind my back and lifted me out of the car with ease. As he led me up the driveway, I could hear the sound of Helen's car driving away. Never, in my entire life, had I been so grateful to not talk to my best friend.

'Can you grab the stuff for me? From the medicine cabinet . . .'

I hadn't even finished the sentence before he stopped me.

'Shh. Don't talk. You sure? I thought you'd decided not to take it during the pregnancy?'

I opened my eyes and looked at him, his shoulders sunken and his face a greyer shade of pain.

'Now you're worried? In the doctor's office you were discussing me getting treatment that's far more dangerous,' I snipped at him.

'Steph, that's not what I—'

'Stop, James. Just . . . not now.'

I followed him up the stairs, clinging to the banister for stability as I crawled towards the safety of our bedroom.

I had stopped the injections the moment I found out I was pregnant, and even as I heard him shuffling around in the bathroom next door, I wasn't sure I wanted to risk it. But my heart and head were hurting simultaneously, and I needed something so I could think clearly.

As I slipped off my trousers and pulled the jumper over my head, I couldn't help but stroke my belly. You couldn't see much, a small mound that could be mistaken for a 'food baby' maybe. Helen had remarked more than once that I was 'lucky' to have such a slim frame. That she was already the size of a bus by the time she was sixteen weeks with her second. My body seemed to still be hiding our little secret from the rest of the world.

I stood at the foot of my bed, shoulders hunched over, hands cradling my 'neat little baby bump', and sobbed some more.

Before I knew it, James was in the bedroom. He placed the jug of water on the bedside table next to a packet of pills. He guided me towards the bed and pulled back the duvet.

The cold of the sheets and the cotton cover were a welcome relief. Every inch of me was on fire. The pillow felt cold beneath my cheeks, and I sighed at the single moment of relief it offered me.

I lay still, scared to move, my hand on my stomach and my eyes closed tight.

I felt the familiar sting of the needle as James gave

me the shot. Regular painkillers had never done the trick, and it wasn't until the specialist prescribed me migraine pain relief injections that I found any kind of reprieve.

I felt his hand shaking as he tried to stroke my forehead, the dampness of my skin tugging at his fingertips, his breathing laboured.

'Get some sleep,' he whispered into my ear before lightly kissing the top of my head and leaving the room.

But I wasn't alone. I never felt alone now. My little peanut was with me. This tiny little life I was growing inside me. I didn't feel lonely, but I was scared. I gripped my stomach and let out a sob into the muffling depths of my feather pillow. I cried myself into a pain-filled sleep.

# CHAPTER THREE

It was the smell that woke me from my slumber, a smell that toppled a small rock inside my stomach and set off an avalanche of a rumble, so loud and fierce that I smiled at the thought it might have woken my sleeping peanut.

It was a smell I recognised as love – his version of it, anyway. I knew what it was without taking one single step down the stairs.

As I approached the kitchen, I could hear him humming to himself. He always sings when he cooks, and he's so good at it. The cooking as well as the singing. Both soulful and full of heart.

I used to find him singing a happy tune, bouncing around to something on the radio, swaying his hips and practising his 'dad dancing' while he poured his love into the dishes he created. According to James, food tastes better when you sing to it, as if you are injecting it with love and passion. It's something his mother used to say when he was a child. Not that day. Instead, he was listening to classical music – mournful, sad – and he wasn't singing, but humming. No words.

'Hey, you.' I interrupted his quiet time and he turned in my direction. His eyes were puffy and his skin blotchy.

I rushed towards him and cupped his cheeks in my hands.

'You've been crying.' I wiped the silty residue from his skin and leant in to kiss his cheek. His frame stood tall beside me. He wrapped his arms around my waist and pulled me in, nuzzling his forehead into the crook of my neck and squeezing extra tight. He wasn't breathing. Not even moving. I took in a deep breath and released it slowly, then again and waited as he mirrored me. We shared three big deep breaths and as I felt his heart rate steady against my own, I pulled away. His lips brushed mine, like a whisper against my skin, tentative and tinged with salty tears.

'That smells amazing. What have we got in here?' I placed my hand on his chest before turning to peer into the enormous pot on the stove. I could feel his heartbeat against my palm as I watched the vegetables dance in the stock below.

'A bit of everything really. It's called 'Cancer-Fighting Soup'. So, it has all the ingredients in it that your body will need. Apparently.'

I stirred the concoction in front of me, carrots and celery dancing to the surface, bright bursts of orange fleetingly showing themselves before surrendering to the bubbles and riptide below the surface.

'It's almost done actually. I was going to bring it up to you in bed. Are you feeling well enough to eat?'

I took the spoon from beside the hob and tasted the

volcanic liquid, burning my lips and tongue in the process. The strong aromatic smells sent my stomach into some kind of internal Mexican wave, but I was far from celebrating, as the ever-present bile and nausea rose once more.

'I'll try. Fancy bringing it into the front room? I don't want to spend all day in bed.'

He nodded and returned his attention to the soup. I wasn't sure what to say to him, or how to act. I could see he was hurting, but he'd never been good at talking about painful emotions. He shuts down – it's always been his way. We can chat until the cows come home about dreams, plans for the future, but if it was painful it lived in those silent spaces between the words.

It had been the same each time we miscarried. Simple gestures linked our emotions: the hand squeezes in the middle of the night or the kiss on the tip of my nose every morning. We knew, but we didn't say. We understood but didn't voice. We mourned but never admitted.

I took myself into the front room and grabbed my favourite blanket. I knitted my legs underneath me and reached for the TV remote.

I was still endlessly scrolling through the millions of channels when James joined me with a tray laden with a steaming bowl of soup and a chunk of crusty bread. He placed the tray on my lap and took the remote from my hand, switching the TV to a smooth-chill radio station.

Lifting the edge of the blanket, he sat next to me on the sofa, facing me, feet up like a child waiting for a bedtime story.

'Are you going to sit there and just watch me eat? Where's yours?'

'I'm not hungry. I'll grab some later.'

'OK,' I replied as I dipped my spoon into the lava-like liquid and hoped my nausea would back off for long enough to keep some of it down.

'How are you feeling?' he asked me tentatively.

'Tired, a little sicky, but I can see again. I'm foggy, but I think the migraine is mostly receding.' I took another slurp of the soup and something went down the wrong way, causing a coughing fit that made my eyes water.

James jumped up and grabbed the tray from my knees before passing me a glass of water.

He bent down in front of the sofa, looking up at me as I cleared the tears from my eyes.

'Are you OK?' he asked.

'Yes, of course I am. Just went down the wrong way, that's all.' Relief washed over his face. 'James, I'm fine. I'm not suddenly going to collapse and die on the floor in front of you. Relax.'

The emotion on his face changed, but I couldn't place the angle of his eyebrow arch with any of the memories of his face I had stored in my mind.

'I'm not stupid, Steph. I know that's not how it works. I'm allowed to worry about you, you know!'

Snippy James. That side of him didn't come out often; it wasn't his style.

'Hey, listen to me. I'm going to be OK. We're going to be OK. It's not the 1960s anymore; doctors know so much more about these things nowadays and I'm sure it'll be fine.'

I didn't know this, of course. I wasn't even sure I believed it at that moment, but I was so taken aback by this new side of my husband that all I could do was switch to protective mother mode, and the irony of the moment was not lost on either of us.

'I'm sorry, Steph. It's me who should be reassuring you. My head is a mess. I'm spinning in circles.'

He sat back on the sofa and stared at the chimney breast. Our wedding pictures stood in frames on the mantelpiece, our heads tilted back in laughter, his arms around my waist. Our happiest of happy days.

'Listen, there must be something we can do while I'm still pregnant to keep stuff at bay until we can start treatment. I can start hunting tomorrow on the internet and see what I can find.'

He turned his head slowly towards me. 'Steph, you need to have the procedure. You can't put it off. Have you seen the stats for ovarian—'

'I know far too many stats about far too many types of cancer. I also know that those stats change year on year and that treatments develop just as fast.' The knot in my chest tightened. I leant forward to grab the bowl of soup from the table. 'Anyway, as long as you keep filling me with all this stuff, I'm sure it'll be fine.'

The pause between us stretched into an awkward silence. I continued to slurp away at my magical concoction while James picked at his nails, staring at the wall.

'I know this is hard to talk about. I understand why you don't even want to entertain this. But . . .'

It seemed to have taken all the air in his lungs to push those words out and he looked exhausted before the end of the sentence even found its way from his brain to his tongue.

'But, Steph, I can't lose you – you know that. This is so serious, and I don't want to wait a single moment. I want it out of you now. I want it gone.'

His words were sharp enough to burst the protective bubble I was creating around my own heart, and I felt the sting.

'You want our baby gone?'

'No!' he shouted, jumping up from the sofa and kneeling in front of me on the carpet. 'No. I don't want our peanut to go anywhere. I want the threat of losing you to be gone. I want that gone. I want you to be OK.'

I wasn't, though, was I? I wouldn't be OK either way. I wouldn't be OK if I gave up this baby, but I wouldn't be OK if I chose to continue with the pregnancy, either. No matter which way I turned, my body, my mind and my soul were destined to suffer.

'I *will* be OK. *We* will be fine.' I shook my head and took another slurp of soup.

'Stephanie. I can't lose you.'

'James, you won't. But I can't lose another baby. I have to try.'

He stayed put, his eyes boring into me as I tried to focus on the soup and not the nausea.

A few minutes passed before he sat back on the sofa again. The rest of the evening passed in silence. Not awkward or painful, just mutual acknowledgement of our very full heads and edge-of-a-precipice emotions.

The world didn't feel real. It never really did after a migraine. Everything feels fuzzy around the edges, not tangible in any way. I used to describe it as if I were watching my own life through a fairground optical illusion mirror. I couldn't think straight at the best of times with a migraine, but with all the added emotion and worry, all I could process was that something was trying to kill my chances of growing our family, and

I had to fight with everything I had to stop that from happening.

I fell asleep in front of a reality show, slipping into a less-pain-filled world as the raised voices of pseudo-celebs filled the room around me. All the stimulation got too much, and my body shut down. When I woke, the TV was off, the living room was dimly lit and an extra blanket had been placed over my shoulders. The muffled sound of my husband's voice came floating through from the hallway.

'I don't know. I can't get away right now. I need to be here.' Other words bookended the one-way conversation, but I couldn't make them out.

I tried to shift my stiff and aching bones to a sitting position and reached out to prise open the door a little wider.

'It's not that simple. I can't just pop out. She'll ask questions, and we've got enough on our plates. Please give me a few days.'

An uneasy feeling washed over me.

I readjusted the blanket and sat bolt upright. When James walked back in the room his face drained of colour.

'I didn't realise you were awake.' His voice betrayed him, wavering at the edges of each syllable. He was hiding something.

'Who were you chatting to?' I tried to ask the question with as little suspicion in my voice as possible.

'No one, just work. I asked if I could take the day off tomorrow. Told them we had a family issue to deal with, that's all.'

'It didn't sound like work?' I crossed my arms over my chest but tried to soften my expression.

'No. You're right. It was my lover in Edinburgh checking I hadn't forgotten our anniversary.' He laughed, trying to make light of the subject. He joked, but I didn't feel like laughing.

'Were you dreaming about that bloomin' show we were watching? I'm pretty sure half of those couples were split up before they pretended to do counselling on national TV.'

He didn't look at me; instead he fussed with the cushions on the chairs before switching off the lights.

'Come on, let's go up to bed.' He reached out his hand to take mine. There was an uneasy feeling settling into the very depths of me, but as I watched him fill the space in front of me, I chose not to push. More out of self-preservation than anything. I wasn't sure I could take another upheaval today.

The hallway and rest of the house were in darkness, save the light at the top of the stairs, leading us up to comfort and slumber.

I tucked my hand into the back pocket of his jeans as I followed him up our rickety staircase, our remodelling taking far longer than the year we had anticipated, but then this year hadn't exactly gone how we'd planned. I traced the paint swatches on the wall as I ascended and wondered if I'd be around to see the restoration complete. It was the first time I'd considered my own future in all this. Sleep was dangerous, bringing down my barriers for long enough for me to feel fear.

'It's all good, babe. I don't mind you having that other woman in Scotland. After all, you might need someone to help you change nappies soon.'

Not many people understood our dark humour, but it was one of the things that drew us to each other in the first place. When your life has been filled with tragedy, dark humour becomes your armour. Maybe it had been what our souls recognised in each other when we first met.

He stopped, three steps shy of the top landing, and turned to look down at me. 'That's not even remotely funny, Steph. Not even a little bit.' His face was tight, lips drawn into a perfect thin line.

'Neither is lying to your wife,' I answered back. Coldly. Maybe I wasn't joking.

We stood on those stairs for what felt like far too long.

'I'm not lying. I'm sorting stuff out so we can spend more time together. So we can figure out what we're going to do.'

He'd always been clever with words, but I knew he was hiding something. He had never so much as lowered his voice on the phone around me, let alone taken sneaky calls in an unlit hallway.

'James, you have a huge project to deliver in the next few weeks, and if you want to win the contract for the new development, you can't be taking time off work.'

He turned away from me and resumed his climb towards bed, his words drifting behind him as he did.

'They're going to have to get used to me taking time off work, Steph. You can't fight this on your own.'

I didn't respond. That was a battle for another day.

It wasn't until I lay in bed listening to the small puffs of sleep escape my husband's body, my mind more awake than it should be at such a late hour, that it hit me.

I had cancer. I might actually die. But then plenty of people recover from cancer every day, right? It's not like it was fifteen years ago. It's only twenty-four weeks until our due date. I could last twenty-four weeks, right? How much damage could cancer really do in that time? We'd caught it early, so they said. A lucky find – in their opinion, of course.

They would never have caught it at all if my little miracle hadn't come along. Our baby, my protector. Shining a light on something that could have stolen life from us both; instead, I have twenty-four weeks to endure, get my miracle here safely, and then fight the bugger. I wouldn't die. I couldn't die. My baby needed me. I would not be that statistic.

Lying in the darkness, staring at the ceiling, the questions started to write themselves all over the walls. I took out my phone and, surrounded only by backlight, I noted down the questions I knew I would need to ask at some point. I needed to tackle this issue systematically, get over the first hurdle, then tackle the next. One step at a time.

The swirling emotions and fears kept me up all night. I tried all the techniques the therapist had taught me, back then, back when I last had these fears. I tapped each of my fingers, one by one on my thumb – 1, 2, 3, 4. Breathing in for each count. Holding for the next four beats and then slowly out to the beat of eight. Over and over and over . . . but sleep didn't come. Just more fear and more questions and more counting. At 4.34 – the last time I registered on my alarm clock – I squeezed my eyes shut and tried my tapping technique one more time.

# CHAPTER FOUR

There's a moment each day that I savour, a split second between dreaming and wakefulness where the world seems at peace. No worries, no stress, no obligations, just pure peace. I love those moments. In those moments, through half-opened eyes, the world always seems to have a hazy glow and everything seems possible.

When I woke this morning, that moment passed quicker than my heartbeat. I wanted so desperately to hold on to it and fall back into yesterday, when I had risen from slumber with only wisps of fear lurking in the shadows, when I still had hope that I might be wrong.

Reaching down below the covers, my fingertips hovered over my stomach, close enough that I could feel my body heat but not close enough to feel the softness of my skin. I couldn't make the connection. I was fearful of touching it, making it real, facing the cold hard truth. I squeezed my eyes shut even tighter, praying that if I couldn't see the world, maybe I could change it somehow.

'I know you're in there, little one. I can feel you,' I whispered into the darkness of the duvet, hugging the protective layer of feathers around my body, like a mother bird protecting her young.

I had dreamt my whole life and waited breathlessly for the day when I would feel my own child taking life from me to make it whole. But in that moment, I had never hated my body more. Never been so angry and repulsed by my own DNA.

'They want me to choose myself over you. I'm not sure I can. I couldn't live in this world without you now. It shouldn't be a choice a mother has to make. I have to fight, for us. For you. Don't I?'

As I heard the sound of the words muffled against the covers, my tears squeezed from the corners of my eyes. They trickled down my nose and I knew the moment to pretend was gone.

'My life would be empty without you.' My voice cracked and as I opened my eyes and adjusted to the morning light in the room, the sight of the crisp blue skies and perfect white fluffy clouds felt out of place. The world was still turning, but I was still.

I gripped the silver necklace that hung around my neck. The sharp etching of the cross on the back scratched at my skin.

'How much more am I expected to take?' I muttered.

I couldn't bear to keep my eyes open any longer. With the palms of my hands filling my eye sockets, I pushed as hard as I could. I willed away the pain that threatened inside my brain and hoped that with each twist of my wrist I could wipe away any trace of fear. It didn't work.

I risked the intrusion of sunlight and looked towards the chair in the corner of the room. My dressing gown, which I was sure I had discarded in the bathroom last night, was lying across the chair, my slippers sat on top. It was barely eight a.m. and his side of the bed was already cold.

I pulled the duvet over my head, pushing away the world for a few more moments.

I had no idea how long I stayed there, motionless and panting against the restricted airflow. It wasn't until I felt his weight on me that I realised I wasn't alone anymore. His arms wrapped around my body; his head rested on my torso on the other side of the duvet.

'I'm so sorry, Steph. What can I do?'

What could he do? Nothing. Absolutely nothing. It was my body doing this, unless he could miraculously switch careers from architect to surgical oncologist there was very little he could do but sit and watch.

I shrugged, in silence.

'Tell me, Steph, what can I do? Anything?'

I didn't have time to placate him. I didn't have time to mother him.

But then again, why not mother him? It's not like I would ever have the chance to mother anyone else.

My head and heart battled against each other, and I tried to wriggle free of his clutches. I pulled back the covers, ready to shout, scream and curse at him, but his eyes stopped me dead in my tracks.

Those beautiful brown eyes, the ones I looked into every day and only ever saw love and joy reflecting back, seemed changed to me now. Gone were the tiny flecks of amber that glinted when the sun hit him just right, replaced with grey scars marking pain across his irises. The red of the bloodshot veins accentuated a type of torture I had never witnessed in him before.

I opened my mouth; I felt my jaw move.

Muscle memory. The actions your body takes when it expects to respond to stimuli. Speech – that was what was expected. Words, noise, something.

Then, a whimper. A sound so slight you would be forgiven for missing it . . . but I felt it. Like the smallest whisper of hope leaving my soul for the last time.

I didn't need words.

His face contorted like Play-Doh, and I watched as sorrow carved a new crevice in his forehead. As his arms encircled my shoulders and I gave in to the pain, I allowed him to take the whole weight of my world on his chest. It was a good few moments before I realised that his sobs had aligned with mine.

His breathing had always calmed me in the most stressful of moments; our heartbeats synchronising to regulate my anxiety levels. As his sobs moved with mine in a mournful tango, I recognised a dance that made me feel safe. Less alone.

When I woke, his arms were still around me, but my head was on his lap.

'How long was I out?'

My mouth was so dry, the words stuck to the ripples of its roof.

'Only about half an hour. I didn't have the heart to wake you.' He shifted, freeing one of his legs from under me. 'Here, you need to keep hydrated.'

I could see the effort of his muscles trying to raise the corner of his lips, but the weight of his pain held them captive.

'I think my leg is dead.'

He double-tapped my shoulder before carefully unpicking his body from the tangle of my limbs.

I sat up and wiped the hair from my face, clogged and matted to my skin, knitted together with tears.

'I don't know if I can do this, James. I don't even know what it is they want me to do. But I'm not sure I can even *think* about what they're asking me to consider.'

The jumble of words that poured from my throat made no sense. To anyone else listening I would have surely sounded insane, drunk even. Rambling incoherently and struggling for breath after each word. But I couldn't bear to say the words. To hear them meant facing them and I wasn't ready for that yet. Maybe I never would be.

'I called Helen. Don't be mad. I just thought . . .'

I was stunned into silence. Staring at the carpet, I focused on the tiny stain on the rug where he had dropped his cup of coffee the morning I showed him the test result.

'What did you tell her? You had no right to talk to anyone about this. Jesus, we've barely talked about it ourselves yet . . . How—'

'I didn't tell her anything, at least, no details. I just told her that the doctor has some concerns. I mentioned she might want to call you, so you could explain. Steph, I know you're hurting, but we don't have long, and you're not in the right frame of mind to make this decision alone. Helen can help. She knows more about this than anyone we know. She can help. She . . .'

He was talking a million miles a minute. Trying to get the words out quick enough so I couldn't stop him. It was unfamiliar territory for both of us. Happy memories we could talk about all night long, but these hard, grief-filled discussions were never our strong suit.

'I don't want her help right now. What the hell is she supposed to say? She has two beautiful sons and could have been the poster mum for pregnancy. How on earth is she supposed to know how I feel? She hasn't lost anyone or had to fight for anything.'

'Steph, she's your best friend. She stood by your side when you lost Alex, and your mum. She knows you. She knows us. She's the very *best* person to talk to about all of this.'

I lifted myself out of the bed and grabbed the dressing gown from the footstool.

'That was different. It's . . . it's complicated. She'll think she knows how it feels, but she doesn't. Helping others isn't the same. You don't know until you're sat there, hearing the words. No one can help you. She can't tell me how to tackle this. She can't because she's not me.'

I wrapped my dressing gown tightly around my half-naked body and tied the knot extra tight. There was a part of me that didn't want him to see me, any of me. I couldn't bear him looking at my body; I couldn't bear to look at it myself.

'We, Steph. How *we* are supposed to tackle this.'

I looked at him, studied his face for a moment. I didn't want to have this fight. It was too raw. I knew he meant well – he always did – but it was my body going through this, not his.

'I. We. Semantics, James.'

Whipping the silk dressing gown around my legs, I strode towards the door to make my exit from this impossible discussion.

He hated arguments, so I knew he wouldn't follow me. I would make my escape and he would just sit there, waiting for me to return. That had always been his way. Passive, unwavering, non-confrontational.

'She works with couples who struggle with fertility every single day, so at the very least she can help with that side of things. With the other, the . . . well . . . you're going to need friends to help you through all of this, surely?'

I was shocked and even paused as my footsteps took me towards the bathroom. He never followed me. I have the last word in every discussion. I didn't dare turn back to look at him; instead I continued down the corridor, hoping that my actions spoke louder than his words.

'She's helped so many couples through pregnancy issues. She can talk us through our options for that at least . . .'

With that I spun to face him, my hand on the banister to steady myself. I rose on my toes to meet his eyeline as he arrived directly in the centre of my personal space.

'I don't have any other options, James, and I don't have pregnancy issues. I have CANCER.' The sound of the word stung my ears and hit him full force in the face. He staggered back on his heels, conceding to the personal boundary I was creating with my flailing arms.

'I don't have a problem getting pregnant. I am pregnant. I have a problem with the fact that our unborn child is sharing space with a parasitic killer. A killer I can't protect it from.'

I stared at him, daring him to respond.

'We,' he muttered, almost inaudibly, but the word hung in the air between us.

I could see them all, the random words dangling between us – big, intrusive, angry words clogging up the space and sucking air from the room.

I turned back and continued my solitary journey towards my sanctuary. The sound of the 'Big C' followed like a battle-axe poised to strike. Pushing the creaky wooden door open, I made for the sink. I splashed my face with the icy cold liquid that spat from our leaky tap and when I opened my eyes, I saw it.

Sat on the edge of the windowsill was a long thin white stick.

The innocuous piece of plastic that had brought me so much happiness now looked like the cruellest joke the world had ever played on me.

It lay nestled in the arms of a beautifully crafted red ceramic dragon. A silly little ornament I had stumbled across in the pharmacy when I bought the test.

My first ever soft toy from Dad was my small plush Welsh dragon, a reminder of his family roots. Thirty-four years later, that tattered teddy still occupied a special spot on top of our wardrobe. It seemed like a good omen that a tiny replica of it was sat next to the till when I bought the test.

My first gift to my child. Holding the dreams of our family in its hands.

But it wasn't a gift. It was a curse.

'Steph.'

James's body cast a shadow across the floor of the bathroom. The morning light bathed him in an orange glow. I felt guilty for the relief on his face. He thought I was softening; I wasn't. Not even close.

I closed the door on him and bolted it shut. His despondent sighs from the other side were louder than my own heartbeat. His muffled words pushed through the cracks, splintering each one.

'Sweetheart, please, listen to me. You need to talk to someone. We need to talk to someone. We can't hide from it.'

I placed both hands on the door, steadying myself as the room spun and I tasted metal.

I sat with my back against the bathroom door. I couldn't see him, but I could feel him, on the other side. The creaky wooden floorboards shifted under his weight as he sat, and the warmth of his body pushed its way through ageing wood, searching for a companion.

I couldn't face him. I didn't want to see the pain or hold his hand and feel his pulse quicken as I uttered the only words I could hear in my mind. I'm not even sure how long we sat there, but at some point, the crushing tension between us was too much.

'I don't think I can do it.'

I held my breath as soon as I said it. It was one thing to know and quite another to confirm.

'What do you mean?' His voice was steady and without even seeing his face I knew he would be biting his lip, scared of what I might say next.

'I don't think I can give this baby up. I don't think I can make that decision.'

Nothing.

Silence.

'James. I want to keep this baby.'

I felt the sigh as he let it out, felt it ripple through the wood and strain against us both.

'Steph, I know you do. But it might not be our choice to make. Even if it feels like it is. If it's a choice between you surviving this or not, is there even a question?'

I couldn't answer him.

'You have to fight to survive this, Steph. If the doctor says this is your best chance of survival, you *have* to listen to him. We can get through anything together. We always have in the past.'

'This is different. I'm not sure I could take another loss. I'm not sure we could.'

It felt like there were more words to be said, but neither of us were brave enough to say them. Instead, we sat in silence.

The door creaked against his shifting pressure. Then his warmth was gone as his footsteps disappeared down the hallway. The click of the bedroom door was all the permission I needed to let go. My tears were no longer hot and burning, my sobs no longer loud and painful. These alien tears were icy cold, trailing destruction down my face as I stared at the bathroom window.

'I will fight for you,' I said to the empty room. Saying those words out loud felt like committing a thought process to real life. I was considering forgoing treatment. James wasn't ready to consider it, and I understood why, but I had to, because sat on that cold bathroom floor, I simply couldn't imagine this playing out any other way.

If I chose to save my child, I was risking my own life. I knew that, but I simply couldn't reconcile myself to the idea of losing another pregnancy.

Mother Nature, who had woken so hopeful and full of blue-sky promise, was now crying with me, her tears tracing paths down the window, gathering speed as they fell. I studied my sullen reflection in the mirror and wrestled my hair into a tight knot at my crown before taking a length of toilet roll from the dispenser and neatly folding it to clean the sticky remnants of fear from my skin.

No time for tears now. I had to be strong. For me; for us.

# CHAPTER FIVE

The next few days were so tough. On both of us – at least, that's what I assumed. Not that I would know for sure. James hadn't uttered a word. I had always loved his quiet presence. I would feel him as he shifted around each morning getting ready for work. I would feel him as he warmed the air in the house around us. But in the days that followed, his presence was tainted with something else, something I couldn't quite put my finger on. The 'bathroom door' conversation had changed things. We seemed to be sitting on opposite sides of the fence, and I wasn't ready to join him yet. He seemed so sure, as if he'd already made up his mind. I wasn't there, I wasn't sure if I ever would be. It was the first time in our relationship that we seemed to be on different pages.

Thankfully, despite it being August bank holiday weekend, I didn't have any weddings booked in. I had an engagement shoot arranged, but a quick message allowed me to shift it by a few days. The summers were always crazy busy for work, but it seemed fateful that this weekend offered a lull in the madness for once. Maybe the universe somehow knew I needed the breathing space.

Other than the few words he'd uttered about the bid for the new complex near the marina, we hadn't spoken about anything of consequence. I wondered how much he was burying himself in work instead of facing the issues at hand. Not that I minded; it suited me not to argue with him.

Our text exchanges had ranged from the hourly 'Are you OK?' to 'Have you spoken to Helen yet? Or your dad?' The first always received a love heart in reply, the latter . . . well, the latter never got a response. Helen's multiple messages sat unread in my inbox, and it was rare to go this long without speaking to my dad, but the excuse of a migraine worked wonders in these situations. I knew I'd have to tell them both at some point, but in truth, my own head hadn't reconciled it yet, so how was I supposed to explain it all to either of them?

Part of me wished I could lock myself away for the next twenty-four weeks and figure the rest out once peanut was safe. My logical brain knew I couldn't hide from my family and friends for that long, but I wanted to wrap us both up safe and hunker down until this was all over.

I couldn't keep it a secret from them, but maybe, if I could just get through the next few weeks, we could prove to them all we were stronger than they thought. We could prove to everyone we could survive this together, and by that point the decision would almost be made for us.

My relief at having a completely obligation-free weekend was short-lived, though. Without asking me, James had booked to visit family friends in Yorkshire. When I objected, he said he hoped the trip up north would give us the time and distance away from the real world to think things through properly, but I was in no mood for Yorkshire. I wanted home comforts and my own bed, safety and familiarity. I needed my claw-foot bath in my half-decorated bathroom and the box of biscuits that always replenished itself magically in my wonky kitchen cupboards. James was the one who needed to go, and he must have known I'd say no so he never asked; he just booked the train tickets.

Maybe he was right, though. Maybe the distraction would do us both good. A break from the painful silence our world now seemed encased in felt like a good idea on reflection, even if he knew how much I stiffened at the idea of going to Yorkshire. In our entire marriage, we'd only been there together a handful of times. My mother had moved up there when I was still a teenager, when she left us. I had no reason to go and see her, no intention of seeking her out. She'd made her choice and I stayed well away. Yorkshire was her space; Brighton, that remained our safe space. But the only people in the world apart from me who meant anything to my husband lived up there, so I went when I had to.

I traced my fingertips along the torn pieces of rubber that framed the window of the train as the world zipped past in a blur. Too fast for me to take everything in, but too slow not to notice the dull rolling grey clouds as they shrouded the hills around us.

Four.

I tapped on the window as the train repeated the

noise of the grooves in the track. One two, three four, one two three four.

Everything in fours.

They say bad luck comes in threes – they're wrong. Bad news always came to me in coupled pairs. Always in four words.

I could walk back through the scenes of my life and define each just by using four words.

*Your brother has leukaemia.*

*Alex died last night.*

*I'm leaving your father.*

*You have ovarian cancer.*

I was sick of everything coming in fours. Sick of the absurd symmetry of pain that seemed to follow me.

*I'm pregnant . . . and dying.* Always the fours.

I held my phone up to the window and focused in on four large raindrops, catching them before they ran out of focus. So much for summer sun; it seemed the rain clouds followed me everywhere at the moment.

I typed out a caption. *Forever chasing the fours – #thesmallmoments #banishthepain.*

I placed my phone back on the table, trying not to catch the eye of the little old woman sat across from us. Her bright red raincoat, adorned with small yellow polka dots, brightened up an otherwise gloomy carriage.

I was in no mood to chat. James tapped away on his laptop so he had an excuse not to meet the eyes of strangers, but I felt her eyes boring into my skull through her thick bottle-like lenses. The tutting from behind her teeth only confirmed my suspicions. Why do people judge so easily? As if I had encroached on her space and taken a photo of the liver spots that speckled her face, not a few lonely raindrops on a filthy train carriage window.

'Why do you young things feel the need to photograph everything? Why can't you just enjoy watching the trees pass by?'

I felt the table creak as she leant past her own personal space and into mine, finally catching my eye as she feathered her fingers over the top of my own.

'These smartphone things will give you cancer, you know, dear. You should use technology less. It'll be the death of us all.'

The tears prickled behind my eyes and before I could say anything, James took my hand in his and gave it a gentle squeeze. I took the risk of looking up and in that moment, I caught it. Fleeting as it may have been, I saw it. Etched in the tiny creases that surrounded his eyes.

'We're nearly there.'

He didn't need to tell me not to respond to the old lady. He didn't need to ask me if I was OK. The slight pulsing of his fingers against my hand said it all.

The train slowed and James slipped his laptop into its snug case before rising to claim his space in the aisle as commuters battled to find their own place in the queue.

Without looking at the lady opposite, I shuffled into the aisle and slid past James, the heat of his body and the pressure of his hand on the small of my back steadying me as fatigue spread through me. I stood, gently rocking, against the chair. My hand found its natural protective space over my silently growing bump.

I heard James's slow and steady diplomatic tone as he muttered polite goodbyes to the old woman.

Despite the pain she'd caused me, James could never be impolite. He was never able to walk away from anyone with bad air lingering. It wasn't his way.

The taxi weaved and wound its way around the snakelike paths. Single-track roads, barely any room for one passing car at points, edging its way ever closer towards Ponden Farm. James had spoken of this place often throughout our marriage. Ponden had been his safety blanket after his parents died. Steve and Julie had been friends of his parents for decades and become more like an aunt and uncle to him. The farm was just close enough to his family home to make everything feel familiar. He had walked the hills surrounding it, even helped with the cattle in the neighbouring fields on occasion growing up, but from the cosy clutches of the property, he couldn't see his own family home, beyond the brow. It was shielded from him, keeping his pain out of sight. When he talked of going *home*, he always meant Ponden. When we visited, he pointed to the area beyond the hills where his 'family home' had been, but we never went there.

I asked him, once, why he wouldn't go near, and he simply said that his mother had once told him: *Grief and pain never leave us, but if you tuck it away somewhere safe, just out of reach, it can't harm us daily; but you know you can go and find it when you're strong enough*. He simply hadn't been strong enough yet, but it was safe, nestled among the hills. I understood that feeling. I concealed my pain the same way, locked up in trinkets, kept safely in my childhood bedroom. A safe space for me to acknowledge my grief when I was ready, instead of it living in my life like a constant reminder.

As we pulled up in front of the driveway, James drew a deep breath, as if readying himself for a difficult task. He grew up around these moors but despite his father being a third-generation farmer, James had never loved the farming 'way of life'. He never talked about the details, rarely talked about his real family. He had plenty of wistful moments, generally around the holidays when he mentioned Julie and her infamous Sunday lunches and spoke animatedly about him and Steve winning the pub quiz at the local, but he rarely talked openly about his parents, or even the aunt he moved to live with in Brighton. I got the distinct impression that Miss Hannigan would have been a better guardian.

I had managed to glean a few details, though. Apparently, growing up in Yorkshire as the son of a farmer meant you were expected to follow the same path. For James, there was no older brother to take over or share the burden, so the family legacy would be passed to him. As he grew older, though, he preferred to spend his days at the kitchen table with his mother, reading the classics and getting lost in the words that filled his head with pictures rather than trudging through mud.

In the rare moments when he talked of his past, I watched as his face transformed when he recalled the stories that had shaped his views of the world. I watched his eyes sparkle at the fleeting moments he relived with his mother in that kitchen, and I fell in love with that side of him.

Those magical moments never lasted long enough. As quickly as the smile crept over his face, it would disappear. Wiped from his world by the cruel hand of grief.

James's parents died when he was a teenager. A farm accident. One very drunken night, during our first summer together, we had been with a group of friends messing around on the beach after a few drinks. The lads we were with climbed up a stack of deckchairs, sitting on top and messing around pushing each other off. James freaked out and shouted at them all that someone could get seriously hurt. I had never seen him lose his temper, never seen him shout at anyone – before or since.

As we walked home in a drunken, confused silence, he'd explained that his dad was crushed on the farm. That was how he'd died. A stupid accident that could have been prevented. The next morning as I battled with a monster hangover, I asked him to explain in more detail, and he'd simply told me that he'd witnessed it and didn't like talking about it. Our relationship was so new at the time, and I was nervous about pushing him too far, so I ended the conversation there. As time went on, I came to accept the story he told me of his dad's death and not ask for any details. It was only when we came back here that the curiosity took over me again. Maybe I hoped that digging into his past would stop any desire to search for mine.

Maybe this time, I could persuade him to take me over there. See where he lived, where he grew up, and perhaps get him to finally open up properly. Maybe talking about his happy childhood memories would help him understand why I was so reluctant to give up my dreams for our own family.

For tonight, though, we were guests of Steve and Julie, and just like real family, I knew they would embrace us, hold us close and comfort us. For tonight at least, we could relax. Maybe all James wanted was someone to tell *him* it would all be OK. I couldn't begrudge him that.

He hadn't been back here in such a long time. As soon as he took on the job at the new firm, he had worked all the hours he could to prove his worth and make his way up the ladder. Turning to architecture late meant he was playing catch-up. He had studied English literature at university, not really falling in love with architecture until after he'd finished his degree, but an apprenticeship with a small firm saw his whole world open up in a different direction. He always said he had no idea who he really was until he moved away from who everyone expected him to be. He'd worked so hard over the last six years to prove himself and finish his qualifications. Landing the last two big clients for the firm solidified his route to partnership and meant we could breathe a little easier financially and start our family. Working most weekends as a wedding photographer meant there never seemed enough time for us to trip off together. Not that I minded of course – it was a part of building the foundations for our family together, and we'd have plenty of weekends together once the baby was here.

As we stepped out of the taxi, I watched as his shoulders lowered and he held his breath a little longer, taking in the size of him and the beauty that surrounded him as if examining a rare piece of art in a gallery. The air circulating around us seemed to mould to his shape, making him a part of the tapestry.

The taxi driver unloaded our case from the back of the car and I thanked him, paying while staring at my husband.

I couldn't imagine him as a little boy running across these vast fields. I suppressed a smile as I pictured how ridiculous he would look in muddied trousers and boots, but despite the jarring visuals, something about this place suited him. The colour of his skin suited its surroundings, his walk even. He fitted like a missing puzzle piece.

The breeze that whipped around my ankles and sent a chill up my spine seemed somehow to reinvigorate him, painting his cheeks with a pink glow and curling through his hair, ruffling it like an old friend greeting him. I watched as his smile rose from his chest to his lips, pulling at the corners to meet the blush across his cheekbones. He looked content.

I took a mental picture of the man I loved, and stored it in my 'forever-bank' in my mind. Something my brother Alex used to do when he was sick. Snapshots of life that brought him happiness so he'd remember them forever.

I could hear the whisperings of painful questions deep within me, but I wasn't ready to bring them to life. Not ready to think about how long I might have left to enjoy James's beautiful face. Not ready to wonder if he might escape back here with our child in his arms, alone, without me one day. Instead, I tried to focus on the idea that the next time we might pull up here, rather than staring into the middle distance and wondering what might have been, he'd be resting our baby on his hip while he pointed to the 'baa baa sheep' and the 'moo cows'. I wanted to stand there, a little longer, and superimpose our gorgeous child onto his shoulders and watch as he made his way down the track to the old oak tree, picnic blanket in hand and a football under his arm.

'That smell, Steph – God, I forget how intoxicating it is,' he said as he closed his eyes and made space in his lungs to imprint the muddy aroma.

I tucked my arm into his and led him towards the front door.

James knocked a rat-a-tat knock that made us both giggle like schoolkids. It felt nice to smile, to laugh, to just be us, acting like we always had. I already missed this, this normal-life feeling that we would surely have to give up when the sympathetic nods and smiles started to surround us.

I heard a clipping of heels on flagstone and could feel the excitement when the door burst open revealing a grinning Julie, clutching the door with one hand and a spatula in the other.

'Come in, come in! Sorry, you're earlier than I expected! I was just fixing dinner.'

She stepped aside and James walked in, dropping my hand to wrap Julie in his arms.

She chuckled as she tried to keep the spatula away from his clothes.

'Oh, I've missed these hugs.' My husband's voice took on a tone I only ever heard when he spoke to Julie. Each word dipped in love and gratitude.

'Oh, I'm sure you've missed my apple crumble more than you've missed my hugs!'

He took a step back from her embrace and paused for a moment before laughing. 'Yeah, maybe, but those hugs come a very close second.'

Julie pushed him gently down the hallway towards the kitchen before wrapping me in one of her infamous bear hugs.

'You, my dear, look like you could use a cup of tea.

Shall we?' Her face was so warm, her ruddy cheeks giving away the hours she spent tending to her vegetable garden and the flock of sheep they still kept in the upper paddock. Having sold off most of the farmland over the years, and with no other family to take on the property after them, Julie had convinced Steve to downsize their cattle operation and now they focused on the veg patches and their flock of prize-winning Swaledale sheep.

'I would love a cup, but I might pop and drop our bags first. I'm busting for the loo – do you mind?'

'Lord, child, no. Off you go. I'll brew us up a pot. Come through when you're ready.'

She smiled sweetly at me before planting a kiss on my forehead like an affectionate mother. I guess she had been, in a way, to James for a long time. James mentioned they were never able to have kids. I often wondered if it was a pain she carried with her. It shocked me that it wasn't until I lost my first child that I was let into the world of knowing looks and understanding smiles. The one where all the secret losses lived. So many had experienced something similar, but never talked about it. Never admitted it. It seemed we all carried it silently until the day someone with a similar pain needed to feel seen and heard. That's when we emerged, like a clandestine secret agency, ready with tea, biscuits. The *I get it* hugs and the *it gets easier* smiles.

Julie and I had never talked about it, but something in her embrace had felt a little deeper after our first loss, and I'd seen it in her eyes without her saying a single word. As if she was telling me without telling me that we shared a sacred space now, one no woman ever wanted to share. The secret grief club.

I dropped my bags at the foot of the bed, as my eyes rested lazily on small notches in the wooden posts that surrounded the pure white bedding. I was micro-focusing. Something I found myself doing more and more these days. Focusing my mind on the very smallest of details, the insignificant aspects that people take for granted. I had to. I needed the distraction.

My father's words were ringing in my ears. *Focus on the small things, darling. Always focus on the small things when you feel like the world is too big.* Those sentences had lived with me for years after Mum left us. It was the only way to ward off my demons.

I ran my shaking hand over the indentations, each splinter of the wood scratching my fingertips, but all I could see was the purpling bruise on my hand and all I could feel was that knot in my stomach. Outwardly I winced, because that's what you do when you experience pain: you wince. You react. Don't you? But deep in my gut I welcomed the stinging. I welcomed the pain. It was a break from the blanket of numbness I seemed to be surviving under.

Taking my fingertips to my lips, I bit down hard on the soft tissue that played host to the imaginary intruder. There was no splinter of course, no physical remnants left, but I could still feel something there.

The room smelled like home. It was as far from our home as he could take me, but if I closed my eyes and ignored the spinning cyclones in my stomach, I could lose myself in the familiar rose-scented fragrance.

The sound of the hissing kettle on the stove, the smell of baking bread. It felt like what home *should* be, at least the image of home I had in my mind. James was right: this place seemed to hold a strange, mystical property. We had been within the confines of its walls for less than half an hour and already I could breathe a little easier. Just enough like home to feel comfort, but far enough away from my reality that maybe I could ignore what was coming. Just for a few days. We could wander the moors and forget the crazy waves and darkening storm clouds that were gathering at the edges of the world we had created on the south coast.

A package sat silently, waiting to be noticed on our bedspread, wrapped and tied carefully with a delicate yellow ribbon. My heart pumped quicker and deep in my subconscious something was telling me not to open it. Such a beautiful gift could only harbour pain. As I slipped the satin ribbon through its loops and opened the white box my heart leapt and then shattered. It was that feeling you get when you tip right over the top of a rollercoaster. The most pristine pair of crocheted white baby booties sat on top of what looked like the smallest hat known to man.

My breathing stopped. My chest stopped working and I forgot for a moment how to jump-start my internal mechanics.

I closed my eyes and forced myself to gasp, quickly dropping a bootie and sucking hard on my now-blood-blistered fingertip.

'Steph, are you OK? What's . . . ?'

James's words drifted off as he strode right into the middle of my living nightmare. He bent down to pick up the bootie.

'Oh, Steph. I haven't told tell them yet. I'm so sorry. I didn't know how to tell them on the phone. I didn't think . . . I mean, I let slip about the baby, but I didn't think to warn them . . .'

I turned sharply to face him, the speed of my movement evacuating a tear from the corner of my eye.

'It's fine. I've got a splinter, that's all.'

'I caved in and told them before, you know, before we suspected . . . I . . .' He turned the bootie over in his hands. Tiny threads of silver weaved into the wool caught the light and made the object shimmer in his hands, like a talisman, ready to transport him to a new world, a better world, a world that I wasn't destroying for him, for all of us.

'I know we said we were waiting, and I know you wanted to tell your dad first, but Steph, I was so excited, and nervous after . . . and I . . .'

'It's fine,' I said again, sucking harder and harder at my finger. Dragging out the pain in my chest through the tiny hole in my fingertip.

'It's not. I'm sorry. They don't know . . . Maybe we should talk to them? Maybe it would help . . .'

I tried to walk past him towards the bathroom, but he grabbed my hips and pulled me back into an embrace.

'The gift is lovely. It's so sweet of them. Honestly, it's fine.'

He let go of me and placed the bootie delicately back on its bed of tissue paper in the box before he took my hand in his to inspect the damage I had inflicted on myself.

'It's just a splinter. I'm fine.'

'Fine?' he asked, one single eyebrow arched in my direction. After years of marriage, he knew all too well that a woman is never 'fine'.

'Yes. Fine,' I answered back. 'But no, I don't want to talk to them about it. I'm not ready.'

I wriggled free from his grip and retreated to my safe

zone. The bathroom. Closing the door softly, I slipped down the side of the wall and sat on the floor staring at the tiny mark that marred the innocence of the skin around it. A tiny, almost imperceptible red smudge causing so much pain and irritation around an otherwise perfectly healthy fingertip.

The irritating sound of metal on metal dragged me from my safe place, the noise pinching my senses like nails down a chalkboard. The hissing of air through his tutting teeth followed. Although I couldn't see him, I could hear the frustration building from the other side of the bathroom wall. I slid the door slightly ajar and watched through the crack as he fussed with the lock on the small wooden wardrobe, turning it left and right, the key clanking and straining against its companion. Moaning at his ineptitude. His hands were shaking, a simple task rendered impossible thanks to the overflowing emotions in the room.

I felt my throat tightening. I needed air.

I glanced towards the windows, seeing my escape so clearly. The hills in the distance, the emptiness of the moors, the solitude and silence I so desperately wanted.

I took a deep breath and controlled my voice. I couldn't let him see how much I was struggling; he would see it as a chance to 'talk things through', to win me round. I didn't need help to 'see things clearly'; I just needed some space.

My strangled words released into the forbidden air between us.

'I need to go for a walk. Can you let Julie know I'll have that cuppa with her when I get back? I won't be long.'

I didn't want him to follow me. I begged him silently

to stay where he was as I turned my back to him and walked out of the room.

I wrapped my silk scarf around my neck, wincing at the pain I was inflicting on myself. I had never experienced that before all of this, that small space between pain and pleasure, but it seemed that was where I felt safe these days.

Feeling pain meant I was still here. I should be grateful, so I was told. I had time, so they said. I had a chance. Those words didn't bring me the comfort everyone expected. I tugged once more at the scarf and held back the slightest edge of a cough.

I snatched my camera bag from the top of the case, gripped the front door handle and stepped outside. The sky seemed split in half, blue skies behind me, but banks of cloud, mist and rain rolling across the horizon to meet me.

I wasn't sure how far I had walked; I hadn't noticed as the light began to dim, but as I walked, I felt less alone.

The sky seemed to lower to meet me, Mother Nature making her presence felt. But her grey cloak wasn't menacing. It felt almost as if she too had given up. Tired of holding herself up high, she had come down off her pedestal to join an old friend in need.

Her clouds wrapped around me like a blanket. Their wet droplets disguising the tears that ran down my cheeks.

I opened my eyes to take in the glory of the moors. Nothing but haze now. No glimmer of blue or lasting imprint of a rainbow. Deep, thick cloud enveloped the hills around me. I could see nothing and no one for miles. I took a deep breath; the moss and mud coated my throat and soul.

It was as close to heaven as I could get.

Sat among the clouds covered in heaven's tears, I finally gave in to the pain and let my body sink to the mossy bed beneath me. I didn't recognise the noise at first. It sounded almost animalistic. But my howls were masked by the gusting wind.

The moors were shielding me, giving me the permission and cover I needed to give in again to the pain I was trying so hard to ignore.

# CHAPTER SIX

There was something calming about the view. Nothing for miles. Maybe that was why my mother had come back here. The solitude. God's own country calling her home in the bleakest moments of her life.

The sun had dipped below the crest of the hill, but the world wasn't yet dark. The colours that seemed painted across the sky melted quickly into each other. The rain and fog had given way, retreating into the early evening, and leaving what was left of the day to expose its beauty. Violets and deep blues were streaked with amber-tipped clouds. Like the golden wings of an angel spread wide, one last moment of beauty before the darkness of the night took hold. The setting of the golden orb spread fire across the tips of the heather that blanketed the moors, transforming them into glowing candles, swaying in the wind, a chorus to welcome the night.

I glanced down the side of the hill towards the cottage.

A light flicked on in the bedroom at the front of the house, and I could just about make out the shape of James's body, his shadow dark against the thin voiles drawn across the hatched windows.

He moved slowly, stopping at the window. Could he see the silhouette of his broken wife sitting among the heather?

I removed my camera from its case and pointed it towards the house. He remained perfectly still, as if he was posing for me, arm hitched up on his waist letting the light from the room shine through. His jumper, ruffled at the armpit, shaped the space like a heart.

I looked at the image again in the viewfinder. His dark form against the orange of the backlit bedroom was almost perfect. Like the front of a lonely book or a sad-song album cover. It occurred to me he was alone there too. We were both falling apart, in separate places.

His shadow moved as he drew the thick curtains closed and just like that, the light was gone.

A shiver rose through my spine as I pulled my jacket closer around my chest. Autumn wasn't far away now, and the heat from the summer sun faded as quickly as the light, the world readying itself for the next season. I packed my camera back into its case and started back down the hill.

I let myself in the front door, slipping off my muddied trainers and replacing them with the slippers James had placed ready for me.

I crept down the flagstone corridor into the warm, inviting room, only to be hit with a cacophony of smells. In the centre of the long wooden table, a pot of hot soup sat proudly next to freshly baked bread, the steam rising and distorting the faces of those sat at the far end of the table.

James looked up. His cheeks coloured a little as he noticed me, and he shuffled some paperwork into a manila envelope before passing it towards Steve. He walked towards me, caution in his step. 'You look cold.' He rubbed his hands up and down the length of my arms.

'I'm fine. The sun has just gone down so it's a little chilly with that breeze out there now.' He gave my arms an extra squeeze before sitting back down. 'That smells delicious, Julie. I'm sorry, did I interrupt something?' I asked, getting the distinct impression I'd walked in on a serious conversation.

'No, no, dear. Not at all. Come, sit.'

Steve slid the envelope into the top drawer of the French dresser at the other end of the table before returning to fuss with the soup, a little flustered, as if he'd been caught out.

'Roasted tomato and red pepper. Is that OK? All fresh from the garden, of course. Are you hungry?'

Despite his haste, his voice was so soft, buttery. Full of love. It didn't matter if he was speaking to me, James, his wife or even their cat, he adopted a tone of love and thoughtfulness.

In that moment, I missed my dad.

I felt that pit of dread in my stomach rise. I would have to tell him soon.

My hesitation hadn't gone unnoticed around the table. Julie shot James a look. She didn't mean me to see, but I did.

'Julie, I'm OK, really. I needed some air, and the walk back down has taken my breath away a little. I'll be fine as soon as I have some food inside me.'

My words were doing little to alleviate the worry on each of their faces.

'Anyway, train rides always leave me feeling icky.'

James moved as if to argue with me. I could see his mouth crack, but Steve quickly placed a hand on his arm, and he sat back down.

'Well, it looked like a glorious sunset. No doubt you got some beautiful pictures.' Julie was trying her best to fill in the awkward space with words.

The massive gold-encrusted white ivory elephant sat proudly in the middle of the kitchen table. Even though we were all pretending we couldn't see or feel it. We shuffled around the table awkwardly as if it wasn't in the way, making conversations uncomfortable.

This was precisely why I didn't want to tell anyone. It was clear he'd told them now. I couldn't be angry with him. They were the closest thing he had to family.

'Look. Let's not skirt around it. I assume you guys know what's going on? I did tell James I didn't want to talk about it while we were here, but I think that ship has long past sailed. Am I right?'

I couldn't take it anymore. The words fell out of me, and I had no desire to stop them.

'It's fine. I'm fine. There is nothing to worry about and we're going to get through this in one piece. I'm confident of that. So, now that's out there, can we . . .'

I stretched out and picked up a large piece of soda bread and dug a knife into the creamy butter, smug in my knowledge that it hardly mattered if I was healthy now. My stomach may well have been tumbling down a hill faster than a cheese wheel at Gloucester, but I was supposed to be eating for two.

'I am not going anywhere anytime soon. None of us

are. So, eat up and let's talk about something a little happier than the fact that I have cancer, shall we?'

The room fell silent. James dropped his knife onto the china plate and scared the poor cat half to death. 'Steph.'

James shot me a look, Julie's eyes were filled with tears and Steve sat turning a butter knife over and over again in his hand.

'What? Come on. Let's be real, shall we? We all know what's going on, and there's no point hiding.'

Something about the power of being in control of when I used the C-word made me feel brave.

'I have a hell of a fight ahead of me, and I'd rather enjoy this glorious part of the world and your lovely company while I still have the strength. So come on, tuck in.'

A gentle cough came from Steve's direction before the rest of the table joined in the bustle. Salt and pepper cellars were passed, drinks were poured and I was determined to move on.

James picked up the glass of wine that sat in front of him. He never drank wine. He preferred not to drink at all. A beer or a brandy, but never wine. I watched as he all but drained the glass before turning to Steve and motioning for more.

Steve banished the awkward silence by regaling us with tales of the neighbouring farms and village life. The conversation flowed easily for the rest of the evening, as the wine navigated its way around the elephant in the room. Each glass they drank allowed it to fade a little more from view.

We moved to the comfort of the plush sofas in front of the fire where the resident mouse chaser, Jess, curled up next to me, her head resting ever so gently on my stomach. Julie smiled.

'The last time she did that was the day before our niece admitted she was pregnant with her first child. I think they sense these things.'

The wine had obviously loosened everyone's tongues and Julie hadn't registered what she'd said until the words slipped haplessly from her lips. I saw her recoil as she realised.

'Please don't worry, Julie. It's lovely. It really is. I'm glad she can sense our peanut is in there. It's nice that I'm not the only one who can feel it.'

Words that started out as placation meant more. I found comfort in the idea that another animal could sense my perfect little secret.

'Peanut, oh, that's so cute.'

I smiled at the memory. One of the pleasant ones before all these dark ones crept in. 'When we had our first early scan, it looked like the most perfectly shaped monkey peanut. A cheeky smudge on the screen that would become our little monkey. I guess the nickname stuck.'

It felt like a relief to talk about our baby in a positive way, to smile and think happy thoughts. To have someone other than me acknowledge the life that was growing inside of me. Rather than talking about the trespasser, the parasite. The glorious little peanut that was developing, unaware of the danger. I stroked my belly, and for a moment I ignored everything else and was simply happy that I could feel it, that Jess could feel it too.

Julie stood, bent down, and kissed me on top of the head.

'It's lovely to have you both here. All of you. I'm off to bed. Enjoy the peace while you have it, my dear.'

I smiled; this warm loving woman had said the one thing I needed to hear more than anything in the world. In that moment, I was both grateful and hurting. I had never wanted or needed my own mother more.

I picked up my phone and texted Dad.

> *Hey Dad. How are you? I'm away with James for a few days, but just checking we're on for dinner on Thursday night? I love you, Dad. See you Thursday.*

We were fine just the two of us, me and my dad. We looked after each other. We were each other's support system.

James and I would be fine too. And peanut. There were too many people in this world who relied on me. Everything was going to be OK. It had to be.

# CHAPTER SEVEN

I didn't remember going to bed. The exhaustion took over at some point and I must have fallen asleep on the sofa with Jess curled up on my belly, protecting our secret. The last thing I remembered was staring at the fairies dancing on top of the logs in the fireplace. Their sparkling skirts lighting up the wood and the warmth of their crackling giggles drawing my attention away from the voices and opinions of the men in the room.

James must have carried me to bed, sleeping like a child, heavy in his arms. Even in my most drunken days at university I had never been so drunk, or tired, that I didn't remember going to bed. Hormones had a lot to answer for.

In the delicate rays of the early morning, as I lay in bed next to the man who had watched me transform over the years, I was amazed that this small bean inside me was exhausting my body to the point where I couldn't control myself anymore. I could barely recognise the person in the mirror anymore. Tired and drawn, grey and sad. Of course, it could have been the cancer but I preferred to think it was my baby, taking everything it needed to get here safely.

My black leggings were once again folded neatly on the chair next to the bed, my jumper hung over the back. James had morphed into someone else too. He was becoming the nurturing husband, the caring father-to-be.

His breathing was shallow and steady. One heavy arm draped over my hip with his hand resting on my stomach, his palm slightly damp against my hot skin, and his chest rose rhythmically against my back. He was somewhere else, silently sleeping in a world far removed from mine. No reality touching him, no fear, pain or questions. I was scared to move. Waking him meant us facing this day together; it would mean talking about our changing lives. I wasn't ready for that. Not yet.

His body twitched and jerked, and his heart rate exploded against my back as his breathing quickened.

I turned over, stirring him. I stroked his face and wiped the small beads of sweat that glistened in the cracks of memories etched across his brow. Even in his distraught state, his face remained childlike and angelic. It always did when he wasn't wearing his glasses, stripped bare of his mask.

'Shh. James. Sweetheart, wake up.' I tried to rouse him, my fingers tracing down his cheeks and resting on his lips.

He took a deep breath and opened his eyes, his instant reaction kicking in as he kissed my fingertips before letting out a painful sigh.

'It was just a dream. Are you OK?' I whispered, scared to shatter the silence around us.

His face crumpled as he squeezed his eyes shut before pulling me into him. His deep embrace more of a comfort to him than me. Musty and damp, his hair tickled my nose as his breathing normalised.

'I am now,' he mumbled.

Pulling away, I looked past him as I curled his hair between my fingers. 'These pesky grey hairs seem to multiply, don't they?'

He scoffed. Our daily ritual. Before that morning, when it all changed, I would tease him daily about his grey hairs. How each of his stresses and every grey mood seemed to explode one grey hair behind his ear into a hundred. Secretly, I loved how each one glinted against the darkness surrounding his temples.

My silver fox. Old before his time.

I once joked that he was ready to be an adult before he was ready to be born. He replied that if we were really unlucky, our own baby would take after him and be born with its first grey hair.

'And there it goes,' he muttered. 'Your smile was there for a little longer today, but it's gone again. I can read your thoughts all over your face.'

I refused to look into his eyes. 'I'm fine. Come on, get up. I'm gasping for a cup of real Yorkshire tea.'

I slid from beneath the sheets straight into the slippers that had been placed at the side of my bed.

'Steph. We haven't spoken one word to each other yet. This weekend was supposed to be a chance for us to talk. That's why I brought us here. We've got some really tough decisions to make.'

When we spoke about leaving Brighton behind for

a few days, to get some 'clarity' on the situation, I knew what clarity meant. He hoped he could make me see sense.

It broke my heart to know that with each passing day, I *had* gained more clarity, but maybe not in the way he hoped. I worried that if I opened my mouth and let my true feelings out, I was going to cause him more pain. Worried more that with each hour that passed I wondered if I already knew what I was going to do; maybe that I had always known but hadn't figured out how I was going to convince him. I needed more time.

He wasn't looking at me; instead he fiddled with a stray red thread tangled around the edge of the bed throw.

'Talk about what?' I slipped my legs into the black leggings I'd worn last night but chose a white loose-knit jumper from my case. James had always loved the way my fire-red messy waves popped against the snow-white knit. Fire and ice, he said once, the perfect reflection of the woman he loved. It didn't matter if it was the height of summer or the depths of winter, this was my go-to comfy outfit, and I had a feeling I might need something familiar to ground me.

'Steph, look at me.'

I did as he asked. I looked at him, propped up in bed with the red velvet bed throw gripped between his white knuckles, like blood flowing from his pale fists onto the crisp white linen sheets. His expression was more terror than worry.

'What do you want me to say? Nothing has changed. A new place, a new bed maybe but it's the same body, the same problems. The same me.' I gripped my jumper, tearing it away from my body in disgust. 'What do you want me to say exactly? Did you honestly think that bringing me here would change anything?'

He let the throw fall as he slid his fingers underneath the thick black rims of his glasses and pressed his fingers into his eyes. 'I was hoping that maybe some time and a change of scenery would give you the space to think. About all the options. Space to really consider . . .'

'Have *you* considered my point of view at all since we last talked?'

'It's not a competition, Steph. I hoped this would be more of a conversation than a battle. You can't make this decision alone. You can't just decide. We need to talk. We have to talk about what's best for us. We have to think about the future.'

He continued to rub away the remnants of last night's fitful sleep.

'James, we talked and talked about having a baby, made mood boards, budgets. Everything was planned. Now, I'm pregnant. This tiny little peanut is growing inside me. Can you see?' I lifted my jumper to proudly show off my burgeoning bump. It was harder to ignore when you were looking straight at it. 'I saw it on the screen; so did you. I saw its heartbeat and so did you. What else is there to discuss?'

I watched as his brain cycled through emotions, trying to pick which one to land on, his face contorting with anger, then fear, before sadness settled in.

'I can't forget about all that, James. It's not a switch that you flick on and off. I can't forget all those dreams we've been working towards.'

'Stephanie, we talked about having a baby. We designed the nursery and imagined our life together. All of us. The three of us. But taking this risk, what if . . . you can't . . .'

I turned to walk towards the bathroom.

'Don't turn away from me. Please.' His voice was still calm, but there was an urgency, an insistence from him that had never been part of our language.

Reluctantly, I turned back. 'I don't know what you want me to say. What if what? Can't what?'

Maybe I was goading him, maybe I wanted him to say it. To make those words materialise between us. I needed to hear him actually say what he was thinking for once. I didn't want to hurt him, or make him angry, but something in me wanted him to be the one who finally made it real between us.

'You can't say it, can you? Maybe now you'll understand. You can't finish those sentences, but I have to live it.' My voice was rising. I didn't want to fight with him, but my patience was wearing thin.

He was supposed to be on my side. He was supposed to want the same things in life as me. We wanted this, together, so why were we at such opposite sides of the spectrum now?

'James, if I have the treatment, we might never have our own child. Do you realise that? Do you know that treatment might involve removing *both* of my ovaries? It means freezing my eggs, IVF, injections, and cycles that might never work. Expensive cycles.'

'But we could still *have* a baby, and it would still be ours. And you'd be safe.'

'It's taken us this long, and too many losses, for a baby to stick. IVF is expensive and not a guarantee. This is our chance, it might be my *only* chance of carrying our baby.'

I tried to temper my anger, but the injustice of it all was pushing the words harder and faster through my chest.

'Steph, if you don't have the treatment, we might not ever have a family of any kind together. I'm worried you're thinking so much about the baby that you can't see the danger you're in.' He took a long deep breath.

'I know all too well the danger I'm in, James. I've seen this all before.' The thought of Alex, the pain my parents went through, was like adding fuel to a simmering fire and, without warning, something in me snapped.

'I'm not ready to think about IVF yet, or anything of the sort. I'm not ready to think about freezing my eggs or going through the turmoil of tests and injections to face the possibility of yet more losses. I want to try everything I can to keep this baby safe. I want THIS baby.'

I was shouting at him. Loud enough to shock myself, and clearly loud enough that James worried Steve and Julie might hear. He looked towards the door, raised an eyebrow, and waited a moment before getting out of bed.

I caught sight of myself in the full-length mirror at the side of the bed, like a woman possessed, hands on hips, my hair a mess of waves, spun like Medusa snakes around me. I hated what this horrible disease was doing to me, how it was changing me, that I could see the same anger on my face that I'd hated seeing on my mother's. I hated that the way I looked at James was the same way I'd watched her look at my father. It was history repeating itself in the most disturbing way. This horrible disease was controlling my entire life and sucking away the happiness that we'd both wanted for so long. I wrestled my hair into a loose ponytail before trying my best to reset my combative stance.

He took my face in the palms of his hands, looked right into my eyes and took a deep breath. My body reacted as if on cue, rising and falling, breathing my way out of the anger. His actions calmed me, steadied me, just for a moment.

'Stephanie, the doctor was pretty clear about all this. We have options. They might not be the ones we hoped to have, but we can and will still have *our* family. But I want to have this family with you, which means keeping you safe. Have you ever considered that?'

'You can't even say it, James. How can we face it if we can't even say it?'

No matter how much I tried to stop my temper from rising, I couldn't help it. My voice cracked through the barriers I was failing to keep it locked behind.

It was James's fault. He was chipping away at my defences with his *non*-words and *non*-opinions.

I removed his hands from my face and took a step back. I crossed my arms and closed my eyes. I needed to say this, but I couldn't look at him when I did.

'OK. You can't say it, so I will. What if . . . the cancer kills me? I can't . . . die? I can't leave you alone? Those were the endings to your questions, right? The words you couldn't say?'

I opened my eyes and saw the tears tumble down his cheeks, the reality of the world around us coming into focus. There was no hiding from it now.

'No, James. What if I choose treatment? What if I choose to act too soon and it means losing our baby? What if I have to live with that for the rest of my life?

If I lived out my life knowing that if I had waited, a little longer, we could have had it all? I would never be able to live with the what-ifs.'

I couldn't stare into his eyes any longer, begging and pleading him to listen to me. I searched the room for a distraction before crouching in front of our suitcase at the side of the room. Turning my back on him, I dug through the neatly folded clothes, trying to find something, anything, to give me a sense of comfort. I hoped that breaking eye contact would make him understand that I was done with the conversation, but his words continued to pound the back of my head.

'But if you choose not to have treatment now, if you wait and it spreads, I'll have to live with what-ifs alone for the rest of my life. Have you thought about that?'

I expected him to retreat, to let me have my space, like every other disagreement we'd ever had. I didn't expect him to come back at me. I stood, holding my clothes tightly between my fists, trying to find a way past him to the bathroom, but he was blocking my path. He motioned to the bed, hoping I'd sit; instead I tried to squeeze past him. He wasn't done. Far from it. He took the clothes from my hands and placed them on the bed before resting his palms, as calmly as his emotions would let him, on my shoulders.

'Life is full of what-ifs, Steph. We'll never know if we've made the right decision, but the what-if that scares me the most is what if you risk it all and I lose you both?'

I swiped at the air as if swatting at his worries like annoying gnats buzzing around my head. My rapid gestures pushed him backwards, as I attempted to reclaim my own space.

'I get that. It's a lose-lose situation. I understand that. If that's what you're waiting for me to acknowledge, there you go! I get it. But just because I understand doesn't mean I can make that choice. I can't die – you're right – but I have to at least try everything else first. Isn't that what a mother is supposed to do? Put her child first?'

He looked as if I'd struck his heart with an axe and left him there to bleed out.

'Do you hear yourself, Stephanie? I've heard you argue so many times about a woman's right to choose. Not once have you ever judged a woman for making this choice. Not once. Women are forced to make this decision every day. Why do you think your life is any less important than theirs?'

'And I stand by all that, of course I do, but this is totally different. This is me.'

He stepped towards me again, trying to pull me into him. I wanted his comfort, I wanted his safety, but I also wanted to scream and hit out at him.

'You are right though – I believe in a woman's right to choose, so if this really is a *choice*, why are you so adamant about changing my mind!'

I heard the petulance the second it escaped me and regretted it, but I had to made him see somehow.

'That's a low blow, and you know it. I would never change your mind about anything. I just want you to see it from the other side. This isn't about me trying to control you; this is about me trying to save you.'

I stared at the ground and prayed it would open up and welcome me into a parallel universe.

'I'm pregnant. I have cancer. The two are separate and I'll deal with them separately. It might not be the choice others would make, and I understand that and would support anyone in whatever decision they made without judgement, but it's the only way I can deal with this.'

With that, I ran out of steam. The painful words had stolen every ounce of life-force from me. I tried to take a deep breath and as I released it, a sob came rolling along for the ride.

'I want to have our baby,' I said, calmly, with a deliberate full stop on the end.

Nothing. No reply. His vacant stare said more than words could.

We stood, for more than a minute, looking at each other, both crying, but I kept him distanced from my heart with outstretched arms creating a barrier. I knew that if he held me in that moment, I would never stop crying.

'I need a coffee. I don't think even the healing powers of Yorkshire tea will feel anything close to enough today.'

I left the bedroom without looking back. As I approached the lounge, I saw Steve and Julie sat at the dining-room table, but it wasn't the bread or the pot of coffee that caught my attention, it was the brown envelope. The same one I'd watched being shuffled between them last night.

As I approached the table, Steve stuffed the papers back into the envelope, passing it behind his back to his wife, who promptly hid it on her lap. It was like watching an amateur magician show at the school fair. It would have been funny if it didn't feel so deceitful.

'Good morning, sweetheart. Can I get you anything?

We have decaf tea and coffee? Steve popped out yesterday to get some just for you.'

Shuffling myself into the chair, I watched as Julie's eyes flitted between me and her husband as she stuffed the envelope back into the drawer.

I made exaggerated nods between the two of them and the secretive dresser that was playing piggy in the middle.

'I'm sorry, every time I come in the room, I seem to be disturbing you. We've dropped in on you rather last minute. I hope we're not getting in the way of anything important.'

'Don't be silly, dear, not at all. We're trying to sort out taxes and stuff. You know how it is,' Steve responded, patting his wife gently on the arm as he reached for a coffee cup.

'Receipts can be a bugger at tax time if you don't keep up.'

'My God, you guys are super organised. It's only August. I wait until the last minute every year before submitting my self-assessments.' I tried to chuckle my way out of the conversation, but I knew it wasn't receipts. The papers were clearly contractual, but it wasn't my place to pry. I didn't like this suspicious feeling, but there was something about Steve's guarded attitude that left me uneasy, not dissimilar to the feeling I had the other night during James's late-night call in the darkness. My life seemed to be peppered with dangerous secrets being kept just out of my view.

'I'm just making sure everything's up to date. We shouldn't really be worrying about it while you guys are with us.'

Steve was talking at a rate of knots. His words merged

into one another as he fussed with the placemats and cutlery on the table before turning his attention to the figure in the doorway.

'James! Can I get you anything, lad? Tea? Coffee?'

Steve seemed relieved for the distraction. Wandering off into the kitchen, leaving his speculative words and worries with no home.

James shifted his gaze from me to Julie. She nodded towards the kitchen, almost invisibly. If I hadn't been concentrating, I wouldn't have even noticed. All this secrecy and half-uttered conversations was really niggling at the control freak in me. I hated being on the outside.

'I'll help you, mate,' said James as he trotted towards the kitchen to join Steve. He flicked the door behind him, but not quite hard enough to close it entirely. I was grateful it'd been left slightly ajar; I could just about make out the muffled sounds beyond. I felt like a naughty child waiting at the top of the stairs, trying to hear every word of an argument between its parents. Instead, I was a fully grown woman, trying to feign interest in the conversation at hand while craning my neck ever so slightly to catch the edge of the secret words being voiced next door.

I cut a chunk from the loaf of bread and spread it with butter and jam while Julie chatted away in the background.

I wasn't concentrating on her words. I nodded in what I hoped were all the right places, but my ears desperately sought out any distinguishable words from the next room, something to give me a clue as to what they were talking about. Tuning in to my husband's voice was easy, but Steve's voice was a much lower register and I found myself missing words. I tried hard to block out the peripheral noise to focus on the details.

'Amy . . . devastated. You know . . . happy . . . now. She won't . . . coming at all. She loves . . .' His words came in fits and spurts and I cursed my crap hearing for missing all the words that would give the conversation context.

'I know. But I can't . . . anymore. I . . . Steph now.'

James's higher pitch was easier to decipher, but words still dropped away at the edges. They were hurried and hushed, and I tried to rewind and replay to no avail. The mention of another woman confused me. I thought James would be talking about our decision but those words made no sense. I racked my brain to think of all the Amys in our circle. What didn't I know?

'You don't . . . obligations, James. You can't . . . now.'

I had never heard Steve sound so serious before.

The words became clearer as they edged closer to the door.

The door opened quickly, and James caught me staring right at him. His face flooded with colour. Steve patted him on the shoulder and encouraged him back into the room as he did everything he could to avoid my eye contact.

I dropped the slice of bread I was holding, missing the plate and sending a clatter through the muffled sounds. Julie appeared by my side and rested her palm on my shoulder as she brushed my hair away from my face.

'Stephanie, darling. Did you hear me? Sweetheart, you've gone all pale and clammy. Shall I fetch the doctor?'

Whatever it was that James was talking about, I had to find out.

'I'm fine. Honestly. I'm feeling a little off, that's all. I'll pop back to the room and have a shower. That'll perk me up.'

Nausea coursed around my body and I wasn't sure if it was what James had said, the morning sickness or the evil bastard replicating itself within my body that was causing it, but either way, I couldn't repeat my Jackson Pollock moment, not here.

I let the water caress me as it fell though my hair and trailed down my flushed skin. This was not how I imagined it would be. We had been trying for a baby for so long, with so many heartbreaks along the way. Was it possible that James had sought comfort from someone else? Never, not in a million years had I ever considered he would cheat on me. But I guess no one ever thinks the man they love will stray. No one thinks one day the doctor will be giving them 'that' news either. But James? Surely not? But then, who was Amy? Was that who he'd been talking to on the phone the other night?

I tipped my head back and let the hot water pound against my closed eyelids.

This isn't how it is in the books and movies, you know. All those glowing women with their happy husbands excited to grow their family. I never, for a second, thought that fighting for a family of our own would result in such deep feeling of loneliness, but I wasn't about to back down. This tiny human was the one thing in the world I wanted more than anything. If James had changed his mind . . . Was that it? What if he'd changed his mind? What if meeting this Amy girl had caused doubts? My chaotic and unordered thoughts were exhausting me.

The mirror reflected eyes filled with pain, punctuated with dark circles. Anything but glowing. Fading maybe, certainly not glowing.

'This is James we're talking about,' I reassured my reflection. 'He wouldn't. He wants this baby just as much as you do. This is your hormones talking!'

I shook my head to clear it, chiding myself for being uncharacteristically distrustful. The last thing we needed was to question our relationship. We already had enough to deal with. But even as I said the words to myself, I couldn't deny the seed of doubt burying itself deep in my gut.

Amy. The late-night call. The shuffled papers and secret envelope.

Shaking my head at my pathetic expression in the mirror, I took a deep breath and stepped back into the bedroom.

I had only just slipped my jumper over my head when I heard a delicate knock at the door.

I opened the door and Julie's kind smile beamed back at me. A guardian angel dressed in dungarees, holding a tray laden with self-care goodies.

'Hi, my love. I thought you might like a few bits.' She gestured towards the dressing table. 'Shall I pop these over there for you?'

'Oh, Julie. You're much too kind. Thank you.'

'It's no trouble. It's just a few things I thought might help.'

She took a steaming mug from the surrounding

objects on the tray. 'Here, it's honey and ginger, something to help your nausea.'

She winked at me as I took the mug and sipped, the pungent aroma filling my senses and warming my insides. The rest of the tray was stacked with ginger biscuits, anti-sickness wrist bands, a small oil burner and a collection of oils.

'Some of these really help, and lavender of course will help you sleep. There's even a wee thing you can spray on your pillow.' She really was the most thoughtful person.

'James has popped out with Steve, to the top field to check on the sheep. I think they both needed a bit of fresh air.'

'I think that's exactly why we came up here, to be honest, Julie. I think we both needed a bit of air. The world seems thick and heavy where we are at the moment. He seems to breathe easier here. I'd forgotten how much he suits this place.'

I gestured for her to sit down on the chair in front of the dressing table, and took my place perched on the edge of the bed.

'It's funny, really, how home always calls you back when you're in times of stress and pain. James mentioned once that your mum moved back here after your brother passed?'

It had always been something we'd laughed about, the fact that my mother moved all the way to Brighton to marry a Welshman, but still ended up moving back to Yorkshire in the end. Funny, really, that I ended up marrying a Yorkshireman who escaped his roots in much the same way.

'Yes, she did. But we don't have any contact these

days. It's been a long time since we've been in touch. I honestly couldn't tell you where she is now.'

Julie reached forward and placed her hand on top of mine, like a loving grandmother.

'That must be hard. Especially now.'

I could feel a ball knotting in my throat and tears threatening, but I didn't want to give in.

'I guess it would be nice to have her around, for the baby. I'm sure I'll tell her at some point. We just need to get our bubs here safely first, I think. I don't need the stress of a reunion right now. I haven't even told my dad yet. You guys are pretty much the only ones who know. Well, you and my best mate, Helen. Do you remember her? She was my maid of honour?'

A smile erupted across Julie's rosy-red cheeks, her bright blue eyes twinkling at the memory.

'Ah yes, lovely girl. She's a nurse, right? Have you talked to her about all of this yet?'

'She's a fertility specialist. No, I haven't talked to anyone yet.'

I picked at the red velvet throw James had left haphazardly across the end of the bed.

'Darling girl. You can't keep all of this inside. It'll kill you.'

I let out a painful huff. 'Quicker than the cancer?' She reeled back in her seat, removing her hand from mine and knitting her own together, prayer style, between her knees. Just like James. She may not be his mum, but the learned behaviour was easy to spot.

'Sorry, Julie. I realise not everyone shares the same dark sense of humour James and I do.'

'It's me who should be sorry, Stephanie. I know how much you guys have desperately wanted this. Sometimes humour is the only way you can get through a tragedy like this. James's father was a bit like that, you know, always turning a difficult moment into a laugh.'

Julie didn't talk about James's father often; it was almost like an unwritten rule.

'Really? James never mentioned that.'

'I knew William since he was a teenager. He and Steve had been friends all their lives. Their fathers helped each other through the tough old farming days. William's humour was what snagged him Margaret, actually. I've never seen a couple so much in love and have so many laughs along the way. Well, not until the two of you, of course.'

Her eyes find the white box, sat on James's bedside table.

'I didn't know, before you got here. I'm sorry. You can keep them, of course, or I can keep them here, until next time, if it's too painful?'

I realised quickly what she was trying to say, what she was thinking.

'Julie, do you think it's wrong of me to want to do anything I can to keep this baby? I'm seriously considering postponing treatment until after the baby's born.'

She stood up, picked up the box and held it delicately in her hands.

'I don't think it's wrong for you to want to. No. But I do think you need to think hard about the risks you'd be taking if you did take that path.'

I knew it. I knew that no matter who I spoke to, they wouldn't understand.

'I just don't think I can do it. Not until we've tried. I know I'll need treatment, but I'll need it either way. I can't go through the pain of losing another child.'

‘I know that pain. We both do, Steve and me. I lost, a few times, over the years. We kept trying. I don’t think there was even a day we acknowledged we’d stopped, if we ever did.’

There was a sadness to her tone, a painful mourning that coated the words she so softly spoke. So careful not to offend me.

‘I think parenthood comes to people in different ways. And not always how we expect. We were lucky to have been such a huge part of the life that Maggie and William built. We were there when James was born. Did you know that?’

I smiled up at her, drinking in the details of my husband’s life I never knew before. I didn’t know Julie was there for the birth; I guess it made a lot more sense now, the close bond they shared.

‘We were there for every party, and James came here every chance he got. We watched that boy grow up and become the man he is. He might not have been my child, but I do hope that Margaret is looking down now, comforted that we’ve been here for him through the years. We would never want to replace his parents, but being a part of his life in the way we have helped us all in different ways, I think.’

‘It’s not the same though, is it? I guess that’s what people don’t understand. When you have such a strong desire to be a mum.’

‘A child doesn’t need to have come from you to be meant for you. Family isn’t always what you’re born into, but what you choose.’

I heard her words, even understood what she meant. I just didn’t want them to be for me. I shuffled awkwardly on the bed and wrapped the red throw around my knees.

'I grew up with my aunt – did you know that?' Julie started again, this time turning to take a picture from the dressing table, an image of a young James, Julie and an elderly lady in a hospital bed. James had explained once that it was his 'adopted granny', who died long before I came on the scene.

'No. I had no idea,' I replied, taking the picture and scanning the eyes of the two women.

'My parents weren't exactly nurturing types, and when my dad died young, my mum decided she wanted to see the world. Having a daughter was a burden. So, she left me with my aunt.'

Julie stared out the bedroom window, deciding which memories to hold close and which ones to share.

'Aunt Peggy once said the day my mother left was the day she started living. That it had all made sense to her, justified why she'd never married, nor had children of her own. Her story was *meant* to be joined with mine. She honestly believed she was supposed to bring me up, that life had conspired to make sure she was living nearby when my mother chose to walk away. She believed the universe found another way to deliver her the child of her dreams.'

As Julie poured out her soul to me, the quiet sadness in her started to make more sense.

'I was angry at times – don't get me wrong. I wasn't *her* child, and I wanted to know why my own mother wasn't interested, but sometimes life gives us what we need, instead of what we think we want. Over the years, my aunt gave me everything I could have ever needed and more. I never felt lonely, always felt loved and, more importantly, I knew that I was wanted. I might not have been born to her, but she chose to spend her life raising me. It wasn't the way she thought she'd have her family, but we had a good life. A happy life. We were what each other needed.'

She took the photo from my hands and placed it back on the dressing table, smiling at a memory only she understood.

'I'm not saying you're not destined to have children – please don't think that – but what I'm saying is that I know you think this might be your last chance, Stephanie. I know it feels like you have no other choice, but sometimes what we want can cloud our view of what could be possible. Who knows what plans sit just around the corner.'

She picked up the box from the dressing table and turned it over in her hands before cautiously lifting the lid.

'I knitted these, you know. The first time I was pregnant. I think I knew, when Margaret got pregnant, that my journey wouldn't end the same way. I gave her these. James wore them home from the hospital and then Maggie put them in a box for safekeeping, to one day pass to James for his child. It wasn't how I expected them to move through the generations when I knitted them, but I was so full of love and pride when I boxed them up for her, the same pride I felt when I boxed them up for you. I don't think I could have been prouder if James were my own flesh and blood.'

A tight ball stuck in my throat; my heart ached for this beautiful woman who had been through so much, weathered so many storms, and still stood with arms open wide to share love with anyone who stepped into her world.

I watched how closely she stared at the tiny, purled

stitches, the intricate threads, knitted with such care, hope and promise.

'Sometimes a child finds its way into your heart via a path you never expected.'

She packed the booties back in the box and retied the ribbon around it, delicately, as if scared something might break. Our dreams now rested, together, in that pure white box. A shared pain, a silent mutual grief.

'But enough about me – this is about you. There are so many ways the doctors can help these days, and if you're healthy enough, there's nothing stopping you both having the child you always wanted. Don't give up hope, but don't give up on yourself, Stephanie. Your life is worth just as much. Not only to the child you're carrying, but to the people around you.'

As Julie stood up, I saw her differently – the slight roundness of her shoulders. I wondered if her grief had been a tough weight to carry. I wondered if the lines sketched across her face were born of late nights and tears for a life she never had.

I didn't resist as she wrapped her arms around my shaking frame. My body gave in to her and I sobbed as she rocked me like a child. I hadn't realised how much I'd needed that – a motherly hug.

Neither of us moved until we heard the front door bang.

As Julie and I stepped into the front room, our husbands were deep in conversation, and that damn envelope was shoved into James's briefcase. The whispers stopped and an overly animated James turned to me, wiping the grey from his face and plastering a smile in its place.

'Are you feeling better?' he asked me, as I took a seat on the sofa.

'Much,' I replied. 'What have you two been up to, eh? Sneaky little whispers in the corner, shuffling papers and clandestine walks up to the top field? Anything I should know?'

The two men exchanged a glance, before Steve jumped in. 'Boring farmer stuff, love. Don't want to worry the womenfolk with the woes of the woolly ones, if you know what I mean?' He chuckled as he took a seat on the sofa opposite me.

'If you're about to tell me that we've had another escape, I swear I'll lock them in the shed!' said Julie with a serious look on her face.

And just like that, the conversation moved on. We laughed about the recent exploits of the naughty sheep and the chasing they'd had to do in the next farmer's field. They talked about the sheep as if they were their babies. Each with a personality of their own, and one particular 'bugger' that insisted on being the very last one to come in every single night.

I put my fears aside for the night and tried to embrace the love in the room. I wanted to soak up all the happiness and live in the moment for a while, and as we passed the time, shared stories and made plans, my heart felt lighter. These were not James's parents, but they were his family. Not the conventional family, no blood links, but a love that was stronger than any I had seen. James was right. This little break away had done me good. I needed to feel unconditional love for a while, and as much as I knew I'd get that from my dad, I needed love without guilt – for a few days.

Later in the evening, just after dinner, James sat scowling by the fire, brandy in hand as he read an email on his phone.

'Steph, we might need to head home early.' He didn't turn his head to look at me. His brow furrowed and his fingers furiously tapped away at the screen in his hand, the light only serving to accentuate the dark circles under his normally beautiful brown eyes.

'Why? It's a bank holiday!'

'Is it?' He looked up, eyes frantic. 'God yeah, I'd forgotten. Um. Yeah, I still need to go back. There's an issue I need to see to. The pitch. Yeah. The, um, hang on . . .'

He looked panicked. He was hiding something. I knew for a fact that his office wasn't open tomorrow because his assistant Kerry had just tweeted she was enjoying a spa break away for the long weekend. Nothing in that office functioned without Kerry.

He looked up, shifting awkwardly on the sofa, but keeping his phone tucked close to his chest. 'Do you want to stay here and come back on the original train? I can book a new ticket and head back myself. Steve, would you be able to drop me to the station tomorrow morning?'

Steve nodded. 'Ey, lad, of course. No problem.'

'Stay on my own?' I replied, my words a little stronger than I meant them to come out. 'Sorry, Julie,' I said as I clocked her expression. 'Not that I wouldn't be absolutely happy to stay.' I turned back to my husband and furrowed my own brow at him. 'It's Alex's anniversary on Thursday. I could do with getting home and sorting stuff out myself.'

Silence descended on the room and the atmosphere chilled.

'Shit. Steph, oh my God, how could I forget? With everything, well, you know . . . it just slipped . . .'

'Why don't you come and help me dish up dinner, Steve? Leave these two to sort out their arrangements in peace?' She winked at him and Steve followed dutifully behind.

As soon as the kitchen door closed, I shot back at my husband. 'I took the time off to come here. Felicity offered me two photography sessions this week. I turned the work down – you asked me to! You said we needed time away. We've barely been here twenty-four hours and now you want to rush back to work? What's changed?'

'Nothing. It's just . . . I'm under the spotlight, for the partnership.'

'Don't lie to me, James. This isn't about work. If it was, Kerry wouldn't be relaxing in a spa. She'd be in the office firefighting before they'd even call you. So, tell me the truth?'

He picked at his nails, biting at the edges as he continued to tap away on his phone.

'Look at me, James!'

He turned to me as he ripped a piece of skin from around his thumbnail, chewing nervously while he formulated his lie. 'I am. It's just a few work bits I have to sort out. I wouldn't be going if it wasn't serious.'

He was never this evasive. I knew all about his work, every project, every person he worked with. I knew his colleagues' wives, where they went on holiday and even knew the biographies of all the people he hoped to snag as clients. But then, since all this started, I hadn't asked him once about his work. He was up for promotion before we got the news, but we hadn't discussed it since the day at the hospital. Maybe that was it? I hadn't even asked.

I was a crap wife. A crap mum and a crap wife.

If I was honest with myself, I didn't know what was going on in the rest of his life, because I couldn't focus on anything other than what was going on in my own body. I'd always been so good at multi-tasking, but at a point when I needed to multi-task more than I ever had before, I'd clearly failed.

'You know what,' I said, all the fight draining from me as quickly as it had come. 'It's fine. Like I said, I want to get stuff sorted for Thursday, and I can reschedule those photoshoots.'

'OK,' he said, distracted and probably only listening to one in every three words. 'Wait, Alex is Thursday. What day is the hospital appointment?'

'Yes, Alex is Thursday, but it's fine. If you can't make it, Dad will understand.' I wanted him to be there, but it felt like the smallest of worries in the greater scheme of things. 'He was my brother, not yours; there's no obligation.'

'Um, yeah. No. Wait, that's not what I meant. I want to make sure I book the hospital time off, that's all. I'm getting my days all jumbled up. My head is a . . .' He lost grip on his words as he continued to tap away on his avoidance tool.

'Whatever. Yes. The appointment with the doctor is Friday afternoon.'

'Have you told your dad yet?'

'No. I haven't. I'm not sure it's the right time.'

His eyes narrowed and I knew instantly what he was thinking.

'The last thing Dad needs is to be told that his only remaining offspring now has cancer. I'll tackle it after the anniversary.'

The thought of having to tell my dad had preyed on my mind. We never kept secrets from each other. He knew before James that I would accept his marriage proposal; he even knew before James when we lost our first baby. He knew all my secrets. Except this one.

'He's a grown man, Steph. I'm sure he can cope. You mother him too much.'

The words shivered in the cold air. He instantly regretted saying them, I could tell, but he couldn't take them back.

'Well, someone has to.'

My petulance was back. I was acting hormonal, unable to choose and stick to one feeling. I hadn't been on this rollercoaster of emotions since I last wore wedges and body glitter.

'It's not fair that Mum left him to deal with this alone. I have to be there. No one else will be.'

This was an old argument. A debate we had every month when I'd schedule a whole weekend to sort out Dad's finances, sometimes even turning down work. I had cancelled weekend plans with friends to help him do his online food shopping once. James didn't get it, but without me, my dad would be lost. He wouldn't cope.

'Steph . . .'

James reached out for me, his fingers outstretched, inviting me into his embrace.

'Don't. It's fine. You know what, let's not fight. It seems like all we do is pick at each other at the moment. Let's just enjoy this last night.'

'I am sorry, Steph. I really am.'

He moved closer to me on the sofa and pulled me by the waist into his side, wrapping his arms around me. I knitted my fingers into his and squeezed.

'I love you. More than anything in the world.' He exhaled.

'I know you do. I love you too. Stop worrying. Everything is going to be fine.'

The words sounded so strong coming from my voice box that I almost believed them.

His lips touched the crook of my neck, leaving the softest imprint of a kiss behind. He released my grip and shuffled to stand up. His arms slid away but the ghost of his touch remained; the imprint of our hands together left on the fabric of my jumper, resting delicately on the skin that encased our child.

# CHAPTER EIGHT

James held on to Julie a little longer than normal and the looks between him and Steve were full of mystery and unspoken words when they dropped us at the station the next day. The trip back to Brighton was a quiet one. We very rarely had moments of awkward silence; in fact, some of the most profound conversations in our past had happened without uttering a single word. It seemed like we'd saved all those awkward moments for that one trip home. I might have been reading too much into it, and of course the clandestine chats in Yorkshire and the call in the hallway still played on my mind, but something about his manner on the journey home only served to escalate my suspicion.

James sat tight-lipped with his laptop, a flurry of emails keeping him preoccupied. He jabbed furiously at the keys, beating them into submission, but I didn't dare ask why. Instead, I opened my own laptop and clicked on my latest project.

The image that stared back at me from the screen made me smile. Although an angelic sleeping baby was curled up in a ball on a deep brown shag-pile rug, I giggled at the memory of taking the shot.

I hadn't done many baby shoots before. I'd spent most of the last ten years focusing on wedding photography and model portfolios. Being on the south coast meant there were few lulls in work. People would travel from miles around to get married by the sea. But with the recent renovations on our house, I wanted to bring in a little more money during the low seasons and Felicity had asked me to join her studio as a second photographer. So, for the last year, I'd worked my new job around wedding shoots and been able to pick and choose my schedule to fit me. I'd gone from studying photojournalism to wedding photography, and then all of a sudden I was thrust into baby shower parties, pregnancy shoots and new-born baby sessions. I loved the variety, and photographing babies while trying to get pregnant felt like I was giving all the signals to my body that it might need to get ready.

During that particular shoot, and before that specific shot, little Tyler had been in the depths of dreamland, neatly curled up on a pristine white rug. An unexpected bowel movement saw the scene change drastically; both Felicity and I had rushed around to change the props and ease the poor new mother's embarrassment before her sleeping angel woke.

Photography was more than just a job; it always had been. Capturing memories was important to me. To be the one who helped others freeze a special moment in time to keep forever was the greatest privilege. It felt like performing magic every time I pressed the shutter button.

It was also the only area of my life where I welcomed spontaneity. When I gave up control and allowed the images to speak for themselves, a kind of sorcery happened, and it always seemed to result in the most unique picture.

I looked once more at the image – in no way perfect, but in all ways the perfect memory. I knew I'd have to tweak this 'outtake' too; after all, some of our most precious moments in life are those not captured on camera, and I smiled at the idea that his mum might pull this from the family album on his eighteenth birthday and laugh at the memory. Captured by me, just for them. I felt as if I'd been a part of a special moment. Those moments made this job worth it.

Felicity was great to work with and working at the studio gave me stability, which was exactly what I wanted for us starting a family. A stable job that I was passionate about, but that I could fit around our home life.

I adjusted the colour balance on the screen and tweaked the vignette. I hated that effect, something popularised by the rise of Instagram, but mothers loved a smoky, romantic edge. It reminded me of cringe-inducing Eighties prom pictures, but I wasn't the client.

Any other week, and I'd be champing at the bit to get back to the studio, but in that moment I felt conflicted. How could I continue taking pictures of other mothers as they held their neatly packaged dreams for the future, while mine was so cloudy and uncertain?

I'd have to pull back a little now, no matter what option I chose.

I'd stepped down from full-time to three days a week when I fell pregnant the last time. When we lost the baby a few weeks later, the heartache was a lot to come back from, but I was determined to push through, though I didn't go back to full-time after that.

Could I work through all of this? Would I be working my body too hard? Would I have to consider giving up my job as well as my baby and my life? How much of my world was this parasitic cancer going to claim from me?

I had always known the job wouldn't be forever. I knew it wasn't terribly modern of me to admit but I'd planned my career around my desires for a family. I don't ever remember a day when I wasn't sure I'd be a full-time mum. I honestly thought I had control over when and how I'd leave my former life behind to become a mother.

What was it my own mum used to say? *God laughs at those who plan . . .*

I closed the lid of my laptop and retrieved my mobile phone. Looking up the number for the client I had postponed last week, I drafted a text.

*Hi Danielle, I've had a change of plans and will be back in the studio tomorrow. If your darling bundle is ready, we can try and get the shots done in the morning? If you're free, let me know.*

I didn't expect a message back straight away. Danielle was a new mother with her arms full, but no sooner had I sent the message than I saw the rolling dots move across the bottom of the screen. Despite knowing a message was coming, the vibrating of my phone still startled me, and I elbowed James in reflex.

'Sorry. I was just . . . I'm trying to rearrange work,'

I muttered, speaking to my own husband as if he were some stranger I happened to be sat next to.

*Absolutely, tomorrow will work. Days merge into one another at the moment so I don't know what day of the week it is, but it works! I can't wait.*

I knew James would go straight to the office from the train. If things really were as busy as he said, he'd be home late and leave early, which meant I'd only be alone with my thoughts until tomorrow. I made a list in my mind of all the things I could do to keep me occupied. Surely if James had a secret girlfriend, there would be something in the study that would give him away. I planned the hunt in my mind.

I turned to look at the face of the man I loved and searched for any trace of deceit. Would I be able to see it on him if he had cheated? Would I know if he had betrayed me?

'James?'

He examined me with his big brown eyes, the same ones I had fallen in love with.

'Is there anything you're not telling me? Anything I should know?'

His face paled and his fingers twitched, but his lips remained exactly where they were as he closed his eyes for a beat longer than a blink. No hint of a smile or crease of a lie.

'No. Nothing.' His words came out as a sigh.

But his pause said it all and I waited for the lie I suspected would follow.

'It's just really busy at work and if I want this promotion, I need to prove I'll put the hours in.'

He hadn't blinked again yet, a dead giveaway; he was trying too hard to conceal something and I could see it written all over him.

'If there was something wrong, you would tell me, wouldn't you? We don't have secrets, do we?'

James looked around the train carriage and nodded in polite acknowledgement of the old man sat across the table from us, clearly engrossed in the soap opera playing out in front of him.

'Stephanie, I don't think now is the time to talk about secrets. Not with most of the North sharing a carriage with us. But no, nothing is wrong.'

He hadn't denied any secrets.

He was clever like that. Always so careful with his words.

'OK,' I said. Unconvinced but unwilling to push it.

He couldn't lie to me if I found proof; I just had no idea where to start. I had never been the snooping-partner type.

I returned to my laptop, eager for my own distraction. I searched out the client details for the shoot with Danielle.

Her story was one of hope, and that was exactly what I needed right now. A previous miscarriage made this rainbow baby so incredibly important to her, and I was looking forward to producing the perfect gift for a couple who had already been through so much.

My heart skipped a beat as my body tried to remember how to breathe.

I reached for the necklace around my throat, repeating a nervous tic that I'd developed many years ago. I pressed the small silver disc into the crevice of my clavicle. The scratching of the etched cross tugged over my skin. That small space where pain felt good was becoming addictive. Tomorrow's shoot would be tough but worth it. It would give me hope and a distraction.

I opened my notes.

*Feathers spread in the shape of angel wings in the shot*
*A tiny feather on the nose of the sleeping baby*
*Touched by an angel*

I wasn't overly keen on using imagery like this. Every mother wanted their child to look angelic, but I struggled with the idea of using religious symbolism. To me, having an angel in the family was a painful issue. Not a joyful one. Alex was an angel, watching over me. Whether that meant there was a God also looking down on me was something I'd wrestled with ever since losing him. But this was one case where I believed an angel had every right to be in the shot. Maybe this new baby would look back in years to come and take comfort that she too was being protected by someone special.

# CHAPTER NINE

No sooner had we stepped onto the platform in Brighton than James retrieved his mobile and called the office to say he was on the way. He directed the cab down to his office in the city centre. He didn't even ask if I wanted dropping at home with our luggage first.

As the cab pulled up, I leant over to kiss him goodbye. His phone buzzed and as he looked at the screen it unlocked, showing the start of the message.

Amy: *Please don't do this, James. Not yet. Give us a little more time . . .*

I tried not to show my shock, but James saw my face.

'It's a client. She's super demanding and I'm not sure we can give her what she wants.'

He had never lied to me before. Not that I knew of.

There were things he hadn't told me, of course, things he wasn't ready to talk about and maybe never would be. I had accepted that about him. But he had never outright lied to my face. That was twice in one day now; this was serious.

I couldn't think quick enough to respond, so I nodded and returned to my side of the cab. Staring into the back of the headrest in front, I didn't let my eyeline waver as I heard him say the standard: 'I love you, darling. See you later.'

It felt cold. He sounded cold.

The sun was low and the pier lit up the dusky sky as tourists walked along the promenade with ice-creams or chips in cones. Families were enjoying the final few days of the summer holidays. I wondered if we would ever be a threesome enjoying late summer nights like these.

Without warning, an intruder scrawled a sudden doubt across my mind space. Was James thinking the same about another woman?

The house renovation had already taken up so much of his time and I couldn't begin to imagine where he found the time for an affair, but that message . . .

It must have been the same woman he and Steve had talked about. We had no Amy in our circle of friends. Was he building a separate circle with her?

I scrolled through my contacts, ignoring the message from James at the top of my notifications.

Abigail, Alison, Ali, Anthony. No Amy. We didn't know an Amy.

As I continued to scroll, a message popped up on WhatsApp and I clicked it before even thinking.

*I can see you're online, Steph. Is everything OK? I'm worried about you. H*

Helen. I wasn't sure how much longer I could hide from her.

As I turned the key in the door to our home and pushed it open, I noticed the stack of letters on the doormat. I wasn't ready for all of that yet. Bills, real life, adulthood. I wasn't ready to be making grown-up decisions.

I wheeled my suitcase over the papers, abandoning it against the wall. Grabbing my thicker coat from the rack, I turned around and closed the door behind me once more. A walk along the seafront with the fresh salty air was what I needed. A chance to clear away the cobwebs.

As I walked, I could feel the exhaustion taking over like waves across my body.

I lowered myself onto one of the benches, the painted metal barrier the only thing between me and a glorious view of the sea. The sun was setting in the distance, illuminating the abandoned shards of the West Pier.

The way the light caught it now made the whole scene so much more dramatic. Broken and battered can still be beautiful.

This once glorious building held the dreams, memories and hopes of so many. A gorgeous monument that meant so much to those who were born and raised here. Now it barely stands. A mausoleum in remembrance of a time long past, memories lost to the sea and prayers gone up in flames.

I felt a kinship with the discarded building. Hollow, empty and falling apart. Desperately clinging on to the shifting sands of life as the waves continuously batter her from each side.

But resolute she stands. Weathering every storm,

determined to cast her shadow in the setting rays of the sun. How long could she stay standing? How long could I?

I pulled my phone from my pocket and replied to Helen.

*Not really, no. I'm actually feeling pretty battered and broken.*

I attached the picture of the pier and hit send.

Within a split second, a reply pinged in my hand.

*Give me half an hour. I'll come to you.*

I didn't have the headspace to talk to her. I wasn't ready.

*Not tonight, H. Please. Just back from Yorkshire and I'm knackered. I'll message you when I've finished my shoot tomorrow, OK?*

The rolling dots were already moving again before I hit send. They stopped and then started again.

*Yorkshire? Really? Now you're really worrying me. Promise you'll message me tomorrow, or I will hunt you down. Love you, babe xx*

I stayed on that bench long after the sun went down. I watched as the stars sparkled in the sky, fighting for space against the neon lights from the pier. I listened as the clicking of high heels passed by, young girls on their way out for the night. I watched as the world packed up its belongings and headed indoors. Only then did I slowly stand and walk back home, my shaky legs barely keeping me upright as I neared our front door.

This time I carried on straight upstairs, peeled off my jumper and leggings, pulled my hair back and slipped a nightgown on. I was too tired to be hungry and too exhausted to care about removing any remains of makeup from my face. I licked my lips and tasted the salt left behind from the sea spray and bit down hard to quell the tears. I closed my eyes and prayed I'd be asleep before my husband got home.

I woke the next morning to find James had not been home at all. At least, if he had been, he hadn't slept in our bed. His side was still cold. Pillow plump and duvet unwrinkled. Three messages illuminated the screen of my phone.

The first explained he would be really late. He wouldn't wake me when he got in. The second was a message saying he was on his way home. The third was only a few minutes later and said that he'd bumped into Paul, Helen's husband, and they were going for a drink.

I jumped out of bed, dizziness knocking me off balance. Had he stayed the night at Helen and Paul's? I padded down the stairs and I saw his shoes strewn across the floor below. As I picked them up and walked towards the living room, I could hear his snuffling snores. He was asleep on the sofa with my favourite blanket thrown over his head, not nearly long enough to cover his body.

'James. James. Wake up!' I muttered as I shook his shoulders.

He opened his eyes with a start and as he opened his mouth to speak the smell made me retch.

'Jesus, James. How much did you drink?'

I didn't need to say anything else. He looked around the room, saw the time on the clock on the mantelpiece and shot up so quickly he almost knocked me over.

'Shit, shit. Sorry, Steph. Oh my God, my head.' He gripped at his temples. Clearly he'd had more than a skinful last night. It irked me that he was allowed to drink his problems away, while I was the one facing death and couldn't raise a single glass to my own lips.

'What time did you get home?'

He fussed around the living room, picking up papers and shoving them into his briefcase. I spotted the envelope again. The same one. I recognised the curl at the edge and the scrawled writing on the front.

'I don't know. Late. Early. Shit, Steph, I'm so late. I need to go.'

He made for the hallway, putting his laptop bag on his shoulder before catching himself in the mirror by the door.

'Fuck! I look a state. Damn it!'

He ran up the stairs and I heard him crash through the bathroom door, its screech painfully loud as it strained against the abrupt early morning movement.

I followed him, hoping to find his laptop bag in the bedroom, but he'd taken it into the bathroom with him. I wouldn't have even questioned it if I wasn't already so suspicious. Maybe everything I needed was in that damn briefcase.

I sat on the edge of the bed waiting for him to come out of the shower. I needed answers.

He walked into the bedroom, dripping all over the bag and papers he held in his arms. He dumped everything onto the bed and reached into the wardrobe.

'Who's Amy?'

If he was worried, his face hid it well, but he tensed as water droplets rolled down his perfectly carved back muscles, collecting in the roll of the towel at his hips. If it had been any other day, I would have jumped his bones. That effortless shaggy look, his hair messy and skin wet. Any other day, I would let this slide and walk him over to our bed to make love. This wasn't any other day.

'Answer me, James. Who is she?'

He turned to face me, and I crossed my arms over my chest.

'I told you. She's a client. She's having a bit of trouble and I had to tell her we can't help anymore. That's all.'

He ran his fingers through his hair before drying them on his towel and picking up his shirt, wrapping it around his shoulders still glistening with water droplets.

'Why has she got your number then? Why not call the office and leave a message? Why message your personal phone on a bank holiday?'

I hated how jealous I sounded.

'I don't have time to get into this, Stephanie. You'll have to take my word for it.'

He didn't even flinch; instead, he continued to dress, picked up his papers and bag, and walked right past me.

He turned just as he was leaving the room. 'I love you, Stephanie. You know I do. We'll talk later.'

Just like that, he was gone.

I spent the next few hours looking though our papers in the study. I searched through his drawers and even checked in the attic. There was nothing, but did that mean he was simply better at hiding things than I was?

He messaged to say he'd be late again. The longer he stayed away, the more I became convinced something was going on. I needed to figure out what to say to him, how to get him to tell me the truth. I wanted answers before we saw the doctor again. I wanted to know exactly what I was fighting for and *who* I was fighting with.

I pulled down the old plush dragon teddy from the top of my wardrobe, held it close, breathing in the musty familiar smell, and allowed myself five whole minutes to let the tears out before I got ready for the day ahead.

# CHAPTER TEN

I walked to the studio. It was a fair distance, but I needed the fresh air and I was grateful for the warm breeze as I made my way down the promenade. Felicity was on a photoshoot on the South Downs with an expectant mother so I knew I wouldn't be disturbed.

The South Downs was one of the best places to shoot if weather allowed. Away from the hubbub of the city centre, the fresh air encouraged the mothers to shed their inhibitions and feel free. Felicity always sold it as being able to 'watch all your fears and anxiety about birth float with the clouds over the top of the hills'.

I could have done with the escape myself.

Taking photos of nature was my happy place and I longed for beauty, peace, space . . . freedom.

As I set up the studio lighting and lit the burners filled with lavender wax melts, I hoped that today would deliver a sleepy baby willing to be moulded into the dreams of its mother for that one perfect shot. I needed one easy day. Just one.

I placed a white fluffy pillow inside the ornate wooden crib in the centre of the space. The one James had built when we started trying. It was too painful to keep it in our house after the first loss, so I brought it to the studio. Hoping to give it a life filled with smiles and giggles, even if not from my own child.

The set came together exactly as I'd imagined. I dimmed the lights to a glowing golden and sat sorting through the tiny feathers. I was looking for the perfect one. Small enough that it would sit on the button nose of a baby without disturbing her slumber.

I picked a few bigger ones and started arranging them on the wooden floor, subtly, in the shape of angel wings.

Then I saw it, floating from the bunch, as if lifted by the air around it: the smallest and most perfect white feather. Letting it fall onto my open palm I noticed two small dark streaks, crossed perfectly over the middle of the feather.

'X marks the spot,' I whispered, to no one.

That tiny little feather would mark the kiss from an angel. It couldn't have been more perfect had I created it myself.

The hormones racing round my body were playing havoc with my emotions. I was so happy that I'd found the perfect feather, but so sad about what it truly represented that I found myself sobbing uncontrollably.

I heard a staged cough from the doorway. Holding the smallest bundle, wrapped in a yellow knit blanket, was Danielle.

'I'm sorry, Stephanie. I can come back if it's not a good time?'

The blush that covered her cheeks made her blue eyes pop against her perfectly pale skin. Danielle had looked like a goddess in her pregnancy shoot, but I had expected her to at least look a little tired now that she was fighting a new-born sleep schedule. Instead, her glowing skin and contentment made my heart ache.

'Don't be silly . . . I'm being emotional. Hormonal, I think.' I blanched at my honesty.

'Oh, really?' Danielle glanced down at my belly, but the Sixties-style smock I had chosen this morning was hiding anything that could be remotely construed as a bump.

'Is it . . . um . . . time of the month?' she asked tentatively.

I brushed my hair from my face and tightened the bobble once more around the bun at my crown. 'Well, yes. I guess you could say that.'

I fiddled with the lighting and shades. Danielle barely knew me, so seeing the lies in my eyes was probably impossible, but I couldn't risk getting into that conversation.

'This,' she announced, 'is Celeste.'

There it was. The last sign I needed that this shoot was perfect. It was a once-in-a-lifetime opportunity to capture the innocence of a new-born and the pure love and devotion in a mother's eyes. A celestial shoot for Celeste. I no longer worried about my choice to abandon the mother's request for bright pink glittery feathers and princess crowns.

'Well, it seems my instinct may be right on point, Danielle. I ditched the pink and went for a slightly more ethereal scene. I hope you don't mind?'

Danielle looked down at the collection by her feet, her eyes resting on the angel wings just off to the side.

'Oh, Stephanie. I couldn't have even . . .' Her words faltered, but her reaction was enough to give me the answer I needed.

She pulled her new-born daughter closer, taking in the scene. My chest ached; my stomach cramped. I closed my eyes for a beat and heard her whisper to her child.

'See, my darling? Your brother is watching you from above. He helped you get here, of that I'm sure.'

I could picture in my head a beautiful baby boy peering over the shoulder of the mother he would never know and the sister he would never hug, and it took all my willpower not to cry.

'Give me just a moment, Danielle. I need to grab something.'

I raced to the bathroom and tried to compose myself. How could I continue to take pictures of those who had it all, knowing that my dream was so close to shattering into a million pieces?

I splashed cold water on my face and wiped away the mascara from under my eyes. As I marched back into the room, my mother's voice was loud in my head: *Be a swan, darling. Always a swan. Graceful and poised up top but paddling like shit underneath.* Clearly, she had been great at playing the part, right up until she left us without warning, of course. I'd inherited a lot from my mother, but this was one of the few traits I was grateful for.

I paddled hard for the rest of the morning. I clicked and cooed and smiled, and Danielle left my studio with the most beautiful images of her miracle baby, looked over by her angel boy taken too soon.

I locked up and switched off the lights, head full of the memories I had made in this place. No matter what happened next, I would likely be taking a considerable amount of time off work. I wasn't sure if I would make it back anytime soon, but until now, I'd spent my days photographing the most wonderful and innocent moments life had to offer. For that I knew I'd be forever grateful.

# CHAPTER ELEVEN

I walked the length of the beach again, but after an emotional morning, I wanted to be surrounded by noise. I needed the voices in my head to be quiet and I knew the only way to quieten them was to drown them out. So I headed towards North Laine.

The plethora of small boutique shops with trinkets in the windows and smells coming from the doorways were a welcome distraction.

My phone buzzed and I stepped to one side, my back flat against the brick wall, making sure I wasn't getting in the way of the millennials and their Heely shoes and robot-looking scooters.

One of the support nurses had been informed of my 'situation' and was offering her time. She suggested meeting me for a coffee and a chat. Of course, if I wasn't yet ready to talk, I could message her with any questions at any time, day or night.

The friendliness of the email struck me. This was the

first time that someone had offered help or advice without having an ulterior motive.

I continued down the rabbit warren of streets, not really sure where my feet were taking me but knowing that the bustle and vigour made me feel more alive.

I snapped a picture outside one of the florist's. Beautiful big sunflowers stood wrapped in a perfectly neat bunch, a yellow satin ribbon hugging them close. Blushing pink dahlias sat next to wreaths of crisps white droplets of gypsophila. The smells were overpowering and despite my stomach squabbling with my resolve, I kept the metallic taste of bile at bay and bathed in the heady scent.

I lightly touched the small heads of the pure white delicate flowers. Baby's breath, my mother used to call it. When we'd discussed names for our child, Ophelia was at the top of James's list. It mattered little how far I went to distract my brain, the world continued to give me small signs of recognition.

'Can I get you anything, sweetheart?'

The distinctly cockney accent of a sweet young girl in the doorway startled me and looking up I caught sight of a familiar face a little down the street from where I was stood.

Helen.

'Um, no, sorry. I'll come back later. I've just realised . . .'

I wasn't ready, not yet. I hadn't thought about what to say to her.

I picked up my pace and tried to weave through the crowds.

'Stephanie.'

I could hear her calling my name but I didn't dare

look back. I hurried down the path, trying not to look like I was running, but walking with purpose. Two women were blocking my way, one with a double buggy and one with a toddler, both chatting with animated gestures. The toddler pulled at his mother's skirt.

My heart raced, and the sound of Helen's voice got louder, closer.

'Stephanie. Hey! Steph. Wait.'

I didn't look back; instead I smiled at the young boy at my feet, motioned him to let me squeeze through.

I spotted an open door and slipped inside, a bell dinging as I stepped over the threshold.

As I stood behind a rail of clothes, I saw her appear outside the doorway. Ducking behind a mannequin, I watched as she looked both ways for the friend she was sure she had seen. She dug through her bag and my heart raced. I quickly flicked the silent button on my mobile, a split second before the phone vibrated in my hand. I watched her searching for me, as my phone continued to buzz.

As she disappeared, air returned to my lungs. Only then did I look around at the shop I had entered.

Snoopers Paradise. This shop had been one of our favourites when Helen and I were kids, our playground. Each Christmas, we would task each other to buy the most outrageous gift. The only rule was that it had to be from here. It had been some years since I'd been back in here. Our fun teenage years a long-gone memory, replaced with trips to fashion boutiques in The Lanes, or a drive out to the retail parks in search of gifts for her kids.

This entire shop was a vintage lover's dream. Rows

of brightly coloured shirts, decorative hats, exquisite jewellery, and the most eye-catching array of trinkets.

I walked slowly towards the shelves at the side of the shop, before my magpie eyes were drawn to the glass cabinet filled with rings, bracelets and all the shiny things. For a moment, my own fears, worries and dramas faded into the background as I lost myself in the magic that reminded me of childhood. Then I saw it, sat all alone on a shelf next to an extravagant pair of velvet gloves and a fascinator that would put Cilla Black to shame. A solid silver baby rattle.

I touched my fingers lightly to the glass case and everything else that glittered paled into the background. It wasn't practical, not at all. It was cold, expensive silver. But it was lovely.

'Can I help you, miss? Is it a ring you're looking for?'

The shop assistant drew me out of my daydream. I turned to face her, and her expression dropped.

'Oh, I'm so sorry. Are you OK? Can I get you a tissue?'

I hadn't felt the tears trickle down my cheeks. 'Oh, sorry. Um.'

I looked back and forth between the pretty young girl and the rattle on the shelf before she spoke again. This time in a much gentler tone.

'That's perfectly fine. I understand,' she mumbled. Her head tipped to one side in a sympathetic nod. 'It's quite remarkable how many people are moved by some of these objects. You are definitely not the first person to cry in front of this cabinet.'

I tapped on the glass more briskly than I had intended. 'Can I have that baby rattle, please. The silver one.'

'Are you sure I can't get you a tissue?' the lovely girl asked me as she delicately passed me the silver trinket.

'Honestly, I'm fine. Thanks. Just hormones getting the better of me,' I said.

I followed her to the till and as she wrapped up the gift, I pulled out my phone and texted the number that had been enclosed in the email.

*Hi Sarah. This is Stephanie. I got your email about having a chat. That might be a good idea actually. I have an appointment on Friday but if we can talk before then I would really appreciate it.*

Leaving the shop, I looked cautiously up and down the street before heading back towards the seafront.

My phone buzzed again as I walked back past the flower shop.

*I know you saw me. Where did you disappear to? Let's have coffee, please. I'm worried about you.*

She wasn't going to give up, but I wasn't ready. I was on high alert now; Helen was like a sniffer dog. Even when we were kids she knew where to find me when I went off to hide during the 'dark days'.

I hurried out of the North Laine, hoping that the wide spaces and fresh air would calm me, but in my haste, I bumped straight into a guy wheeling his bike along the path. I screamed out in pain as his wheel rode right over the top of my foot. Cursing the rude man who walked away tutting, I locked eyes with a small girl. Her hair was as red as mine, tight curls that framed her face with fire. Her eyes were greener than any emerald I had seen.

'Here you go, lady. You dropped this.'

Her voice was so crisp and clear. Perfect English with a tiny hint of an Irish twang.

I looked up from my hunched position and nodded in recognition to the mother holding her daughter's hand so tight.

'Thank you so much, sweetie,' I said and I took the bag with my silver secret tucked neatly inside. 'You are really very kind to help me.'

I stood, steadying myself on the wall before the girl, turning her pools of emerald into lakes of jade, the shadow of my body casting a darkness over her from above.

'Mammy says you should always be kind and share a smile. You never know when someone needs it.'

With that, the mother walked her away, patting her on the head and congratulating her on her manners.

I stood stunned, watching as the beautiful child floated away from me, the very image of me in mini form, drifting out of sight.

As I made my way towards the seafront, the image of that young girl imprinted on my mind, I let the tears flow freely.

This pain was becoming too much to carry alone and I felt my body weakening with the weight of it. With James refusing to admit the fight we had ahead, I knew I would have to tell someone. Soon.

# CHAPTER TWELVE

I stood staring at the sea and wondered how best to fill the rest of my day. I wasn't ready to go home yet; I didn't want to be alone with my thoughts. I stared at the Kiss Wall, the vertical sculpture that always seemed to muscle its way into the emotional moments that punctuated my memories. The tall piece of punctured aluminium that showcased six varying faces of love had predictably been the spot where I had my first proper kiss. Not very original, but at the tender age of fourteen, it was just about the most romantic thing that had ever happened to me.

A terribly nervous lad called Daniel had once spent hours wringing his hands as we played the penny slots in the amusement arcade on the pier, before buying me hot fresh doughnuts that cost more than my pocket money and walking me along the seafront. The closer we got to the high street, the more nervous he got. Probably because he knew that's where his mum was meeting us to drive us home. When we passed the kissing post, he tapped me on the shoulder and kissed me. The butterflies lasted all the way home. Each time I passed it now, I smiled at the memories of the young naïve girl I once was, thinking that hormonal teenage boy would be the one I would marry. We lasted six months, but the memory would last as long as the structure itself.

Over the years, I had watched many special moments happen there. I even witnessed a tall, slightly anxious-looking man with trembling hands get down on bended knee in a puddle of rainwater. The poor guy seemed totally unaware of the torrential rain that poured around him as he grinned from ear to ear. I remember my heart soaring for those strangers as I watched the woman knock him to the ground with the force of her excited acceptance.

I had shared this special place with James on our first date. There was something so pure and innocent about all it represented. Love, hope and acceptance.

I picked at the ragged edge of the lid on my takeaway coffee as I stood cycling through happy memories. Desperate to smile and forget the future and all it threatened, just for a while.

'If you're going to hide from me, at least pick somewhere original!'

The voice was unmistakable, and my soul immediately recognised a life-long companion. Helen.

I didn't take my eyes off the statue; I didn't need to. She looped her arm through mine and squeezed.

'Why don't we head to The Flour Pot for a decent coffee, eh?'

She knew me too well. Our favourite coffee shop,

filled with the most amazing cakes and indulgent desserts, and with a view over the pebbles to the sea beyond. Anytime Helen needed to 'have a break from the kids' or 'take a time-out from Paul', we would meet there and put the world to rights. With an ever-changing landscape in front of us, we could sit in companionable silence and decompress, or natter away over a long lunch and sometimes even a sneaky white wine spritzer.

I turned to her, scared to see the look in her eyes. James had been with Paul last night, so Helen for sure knew all the details of what was going on by now.

'Yeah, OK,' I said, tossing away the remnants of my watery coffee in the closest bin before we walked in silence along the promenade.

The intoxicating smell of their locally roasted coffee felt like safety and my hunched shoulders relaxed as soon as I took a seat at one of the outdoor tables.

'I think the sea air will do me good.'

She looked worried as she shook her head. 'I remember the nausea. Morning sickness can be a bugger.'

I smiled at her. We both knew she knew, but she was patiently waiting for me to take the lead.

'I'm so sick of seeing the bottom of a toilet bowl, H, honestly.' I tried to chuckle, make light of the situation, but I was nervous. Explaining all of this to Helen meant facing reality, no more hiding from it.

A waiter approached the table and placed menus between us.

'Don't worry, we don't have to eat if you're not up for it. But honestly, I always found that nibbling small bits helped. The sickness is worse when your stomach is empty and drinking coffee on an empty stomach is never a good idea.'

The tears sprang from nowhere. It was the simple gesture of her treating me like a normal pregnant mum that got me. That was all I wanted. To experience all the highs and lows of pregnancy with my best friend by my side. I realised I was mourning already, mourning something I'd never had and worried now I would never experience: a normal pregnancy.

Helen got up from her chair and hugged me tightly. I lowered my head and rested it in the crook of her arm, and it was as if a pressure switch had been released. I let go. I wanted to be a teenager again, crying about a boy, not about this.

My tears were slow and quiet, but enough to soak her cardigan with my pain.

'Come on,' Helen whispered. As she pulled away to look me in the eye, she dabbed at my cheeks with a tissue. 'You don't suit blotchy. Your face resembles Mr Blobby when you cry,' she joked.

I laughed. Hard. I couldn't remember the last time I'd laughed. Maybe the night before the pregnancy scan when James came into the room with a pillow stuffed up his shirt? That seemed like a lifetime ago.

'See. Now that, my dear, is why you need one person in your life you can talk to who is *not* family. You need to laugh. Even if you think you're too sad to ever laugh again. The pain gets too much, Steph. You need a release.'

'It feels wrong to laugh,' I said. 'I'm not sure why. To be honest, I think it's the first time since . . . well . . . it's the first time I've felt anything. Everything feels numb.'

She let go of my arms and rounded the table to take the seat opposite mine.

'And, Helen, you're quite literally the only person in the world who could call me Mr Blobby and not face the wrath of a pregnant woman.'

We both laughed again and, for a moment, the air was light.

The normal questions were asked first, of course. She asked after my dad – she always did. She had a soft spot for him.

I watched her lips move as she talked. My heart rate eased and the dread floated away with the clouds as I remembered how easy it was to be around her. I had been wrong to avoid her. I should have remembered how much of a tonic she'd been for me as a teenager, always my strength through the darkest moments of my life. I had forgotten how much joy she brought into my world, so effortlessly that I never really had to think about it, but as she sat in front of me, I wondered if I had subconsciously ignored how much I needed her.

Helen knew everything. All my secrets, all my dark moments. All my pain.

She had been there the day they buried Alex. She was there when my mother walked out and had always been the pressure release when things got too much, but I never imagined I'd need to lean on her for something like this. Maybe that was why I had tried to avoid her. She was the one who helped me through the tough times, so without her, maybe I could just ignore it all and it would go away?

The waiter stopped at our table, cutting Helen off mid-story, which was a blessing in disguise, because I hadn't been listening properly. I was far too caught up in my own head.

'Do you think you can stomach anything?' she asked me cautiously.

'Just a decaf Americano with cold milk on the side, please, and a plain croissant?'

The waiter nodded as he took my order before turning his attention to Helen.

'Are you sure?' she asked, looking at me with a pleading in her eyes 'How about I get something a little bigger and you can pick at mine if you're feeling brave enough?'

She didn't wait for my response, instead she ordered a chai latte and a prosciutto, rocket and parmesan sourdough pizza.

'That sounds so good,' I said to Helen as the waiter left our table. 'Honestly, even if I wanted to eat, I don't think I can focus enough to read a menu.' I wiped at my eyes, clearing the mist created by the intrusive tears that lurked below the surface.

'I'm sorry I didn't tell you,' I offered up finally. Opening the door a crack to see if this was a conversation I could fully immerse myself in out in public. 'I wasn't sure what to say.'

She reached over and squeezed my hand hard before giving me the head tilt, only – from her – it felt sincere.

'It's fine. You needed time to come to terms with it. You needed to figure out the diagnosis yourself before I sat in front of you with all the facts.'

She let go of my hand and sat back in her chair, giving me the space to unfold in front of her, but I didn't how to respond. I looked down at the table and picked at the napkin.

'You just needed time to feel all emotional first before thinking clearly; I get it. We all need time to process.'

She gave me that look that told me she had rationalised it this way so as not to be hurt by my actions, but I knew it must have hurt to hear the news from someone else.

'Did James tell you?' I asked.

'No. Paul did. James hinted that something was wrong, but he wanted you to tell me. They went for a drink and when Paul got back, he woke me up. James is really worried about you, which in turn worried Paul, and after six pints of beer, he couldn't hold his water 'til morning. He sat up until one in the morning talking to me about what *they* had talked about.'

I couldn't help but let out a chuckle at her one solitary raised eyebrow. We had laughed over the years about the fact that when our men got together without us, we always asked what they talked about and got a 'nothing' in response. It baffled us how they could spend so much time together and never seem to talk about anything of consequence.

'It seems all it took for our men to talk about something other than football was one of their wives getting cancer,' she finished.

'Bloody cancer,' I replied. 'Coming in uninvited and changing us all into people we don't recognise. How dare it!' I tried to smile, make light of the situation, but the sting in the words bit at my throat.

'Honestly, Helen, I'm sorry I didn't tell you first.' I paused. It was time to get real and I couldn't hide from this anymore. 'I didn't know how to tell you what I was thinking. I was worried you'd try to talk me round. I needed time to get my head straight before I let anyone else's voice into my head.'

There was no point in lying to her now.

'I figured that was the case when you ran and hid in North Laine. I knew you'd seen me.' She reached over and took the napkin out of my hands. I had a bad habit at picking at them until there was nothing left and it drove her wild. 'But I knew it was you – your hair is a dead giveaway among the bleached blonde Brighton babes! I've always been able to spot your lioness mane a mile off, and I *knew* the next place you'd go was that damn statue.'

She fiddled with her own locks. She had always been envious of my hair, always telling me that I'd get all the men because I looked like Jessica Rabbit, which was absolutely not the case, but then she was such a humble soul she never believed that the boys who surrounded us during our teenage years were more interested in her than me. She couldn't see her beauty, never understood how much the size of her heart drew people towards her. I loved her, completely.

The waiter placed our coffees down on the table and smiled in Helen's direction. I winked at her as he left.

'Totally checking you out!' I said to her.

'Stop trying to change the subject, missy,' she said as she blushed. 'And no, he wasn't. Anyway . . .' She took a sip of her latte and scrunched up her nose as the steam rose to meet her lips. 'You knew you couldn't hide from me forever. We're tied together, with an invisible thread. No matter what, I will always find you.'

She couldn't look at me, and her words hit me harder in the chest than I was expecting.

'I really am sorry,' I said, again.

'I get it. I would have done the same,' she said, peering from beneath her thick fringe. She was doe-eyed like an Eighties Diana. 'I just hate to think you haven't been talking to anyone at all, Steph. This is huge.'

I smiled at her. But something in my expression must have given me away, because her brow furrowed.

'James told Paul that you're considering not going through with treatment until after the birth?'

I nodded. She nodded in return and I smiled. I was hopeful I might have found an ally.

'I'm not going to say I agree with that decision, Steph,' she said, then softened her brow before continuing, 'but I'm not here to convince you otherwise either. This has to be a decision that you and James come to together. I'll be here to support you both, no matter what.'

The way she said *both* prickled at my skin. Her words were deliberate; they felt rehearsed.

'What has he said to you?'

I hadn't meant for my tone to be so sharp, but the paranoia was back.

'Don't be angry with him, Steph.' She used her Diana eyes on me again. 'You both need someone to talk to and who else is he going to turn to? He can't wait for Paul to be three sheets to the wind every time he wants to talk about something emotional. I called him this morning but he was already at work. He didn't say too much. After what Paul said, I wanted to make sure he hadn't misunderstood or had too many beers to understand all the details.'

'Helen. What has James said to you?'

I didn't like the feeling of being ganged up on.

'It's not what he's said, hon. It's what he's *not* saying.'

I pushed my chair back from the table, my fight-or-flight reaction coming into force.

'Don't get angry, Steph.' Our conversation was interrupted as the waiter placed the croissant in front of me and the steaming pizza in front of Helen. He recognised he had interrupted something so he skulked away apologetically.

'Steph,' Helen continued, keen to restart her monologue before I got a word in. 'I'm not here to take sides, I'm here for you both. Just me, your best mate, not in any kind of professional capacity, not wearing my uniform or name badge. This is just me. Someone you can get it all out to without fear of ramifications.'

I shuffled the chair back in again and picked at the flaky pastry of the croissant. My stomach gave a low growl as I ripped off a corner and tempted fate.

'I don't know what he wants from me, Helen. How can he expect me to do it? How can he even think that I would consider it?'

'Consider what?' Helen was pushing me. Part of her training had included a stint in psychology. She would have had these conversations countless times with her patients.

I didn't want to be her patient. I'd always prayed that I would never have to be.

'You know what!' I replied.

'Stephanie. You need to say it out loud.'

'Abort. Is that what you mean? End it?'

'End what, Stephanie?'

'Our baby. My baby. Our marriage. Our dreams. Our life.'

There it was. This child meant so much to me. I had planned for this, my entire existence built around this one small factor.

My life, at least since Mum left, had always run to

a schedule. My schedule. I had 'a plan' and the day that I saw that blue line, my plan was put into action. Nothing stood in my way. Ever. I never let it.

Helen looked at me, her arms softly crossed on the table between us.

'I don't know if I can make that decision. I can't end this life and everything we have ever planned for. I'm pregnant. I'm having a baby. Yes, I'm also playing host to a devil in the same space as my angel. But I can beat this.'

There it was again. The sympathetic head tilt. The biting of the lip and the large sigh.

'There's an awful lot to unpack there, Steph. Let's take it a beat at a time, OK?'

She cut off a tiny corner of her pizza and offered it to me. I shook my head, not quite ready for the strong flavours. Instead, I picked up my coffee, cupping it with both hands, warming my fingers from the cool breeze coming off the sea.

'You don't have to make any kind of decision straight away. But you do need to consider all the options and work out what questions you have, so you can ask the right people and get the right guidance.'

She spoke through mouthfuls of food, eager to get her words out before I started arguing with her.

'You have to stop thinking that you're in this alone. The baby might be growing inside you, but you can't beat this disease on your own. You're right, the two things are separate, but you can't separate them right now, which means you have to accept help. You can't do this alone.'

She placed her fork and knife on the table, wiped her mouth and looked at me, expectantly. I wasn't ready to argue with her. All I wanted was sympathy and understanding. I just wanted *one* person on my side.

'It's not fair, Helen. This wasn't the plan. This isn't how it's supposed to happen.'

'Life doesn't always work out how you plan.'

I noticed her spinning the gold band on her left hand, a nervous twitch.

'Look at all the mothers I treat. Some of them have lost more babies than I would ever consider possible. They go through unbearable pain over and over again and still plan for one more time. It shows just how resilient we can be, and stubborn, but it's not the only way to build a family. I've also worked with mothers who chose to abort when they were younger and then struggled to get pregnant later in life, and my God, Steph, some of them beat themselves up for *years* thinking they're being punished for a decision they made a lifetime before. Life doesn't work like that and one does not lead to the other.'

She reached over, placed her hand under my chin and tilted it in her direction.

'Listen to me, and you need to *hear* this. Every decision ever made by any woman, *ever*, was made for a reason, and no one *ever* has the right to judge what that reason might be.'

I felt my face flush with rage. James had said the same thing. Had they compared notes? I opened my mouth to respond but Helen shushed me.

'Wait, before you bite my head off . . . listen. What is the one thing that all of those mothers had in common? Each and every one that I treated has had to see that a family doesn't only form in the "get married, come off the pill, get pregnant" kind of way. Life is more complicated than that.'

She was trying to steer my rage towards process, but I wasn't having it.

'James said that too, you know. He said I was being judgemental of all the women who had chosen to have abortions. But I'm not. I know who I am, Helen. I know *me*, and I can't live with that regret. With that wondering. I wouldn't ever stop blaming myself. It's not about judgement. It's about knowing what I want and what I don't, and understanding that I know I won't cope with that pain again.'

'Stephanie.' She looked deep into my eyes, not blinking or wavering once. 'You can try again. There are so many options. But you can only try again if you're here. Ovarian cancer is nicknamed "the silent killer", did you know that? Most don't catch it early enough to recover fully. You, from what James has said anyway, can still recover from this.'

I took a long drink of my now lukewarm coffee and resisted the urge to throw up.

'But I don't know if *we* would recover. I don't know if the resentment would end up killing us eventually.'

'What resentment?'

'My own, I guess. Or towards James if he pushes me to make a decision I will forever regret.'

'Steph, we *both* know that James could never convince you to do something you don't want to do.'

'He's trying.'

'Is he? Really? Or is he trying to get you to think clearly, so you don't make a hasty decision you might come to regret? I think he's trying to save your life, not control it.'

'It's my body. My decision,' I spat, sullenly.

'Stephanie. Come on now. I know you don't honestly

believe he's trying to make you do anything. We both know him better than that. Let that anger go; it has no place here. You're being unfair, and I understand why; anger is an easier emotion to deal with than fear. But honestly, sweetheart, can you hear how selfish you might sound saying something like that to James?'

'How is it selfish?' My voice teetered precariously on the edge of a shout. 'I'm trying to save my baby!'

'He's trying to save a life too, Steph. Yours. And it's his baby too. Imagine how terrified he is.' She started again, taking a deep breath. 'There are three ways this could go. He could lose his baby. He could lose his wife and have to raise a child alone, or he could lose his wife and his baby. That's a lot to take in. He has no control over any of this, and you're pushing him away.'

'You're missing one option from that list. Or two, even,' I replied, removing her hands from me and shuffling my chair an inch further back. 'He could have us both, Helen. We could fight this and win. We could fight this and get our perfect family. The child that was always meant for us. The child that completes our family. The child we planned for.'

I paused and looked out towards the wild sea. The waves crashed against the shoreline, sending spray into the air. I watched as a father and son ran circles around each other, the seagulls cheering them on overhead.

'Or he could walk away,' I finished, reluctantly.

'Walk away? Be quiet. You are the love of his life. Nothing would convince that man to leave you to deal with this alone. You don't believe that, do you?'

I continued to watch the man as he swept the young boy up, flying him through the air into the arms of a woman sat on the pebbles below.

'No. Yes. Maybe.' The thought of Amy spun in my mind, but that wasn't a conversation I was ready to have with Helen yet. 'It doesn't matter either way. I can do this on my own.' I pulled my shoulders back and sat up straighter, trying to believe my own words.

'First off, that would never happen, but even if hell froze over and James *did* leave you, how, Stephanie? How would you raise a child and deal with the side effects of the chemo? The radiation? The surgery? Even if that man was mad enough to leave you, who would raise this child if you didn't beat it?' Her voice dripped with exasperation, the words coming quicker, faster, sharper.

'Dad would step up.'

Helen shook her head, a small smile playing on her lips. 'I love your dad. But he hasn't had to do anything for himself, ever. The day your mum walked out, you took over.'

She wasn't wrong, but my dad would help. I was sure of it. Especially if James left me for another woman while I was sick with cancer.

'He would step up; I know it. That's what parents do – they do the hard things to help their children. It's a fundamental part of parenting.'

She shot a look at me I recognised all too well. The same one she would reserve for those days when I would say: *I'll never let my kids watch TV as babies* or *I'd only feed my child organic food.*

'Parenting is about so much more than being there for your kids. Have you thought about him in all this, your dad, I mean? How would he cope if you weren't here anymore? Who would do his bills? Or pop by the house every Wednesday to make sure the bins are put out?'

I tried to avoid her eyeline, but she craned her neck to grab my attention again.

'You mother him. You have for years. He is the most loving man, but he won't be able to bring up your child if, God forbid, you're not here. Or you're locked away in a hospital recovering from surgery.'

'There is always a way, Helen. I have never met a problem I can't face.'

'And I love you for that, Steph,' she interrupted, 'more than you realise. You amaze me. But you can't push away the only person who will love that child as much as you do. Not allowing him to even have a say is only going to do that.'

She was done. She sat back, crossed her arms and dared me to respond.

I tried to pull the conversation away from James.

'Honestly, Helen. I think the decision was always made for me. I don't think I'm the type of person who would have ever been able to ignore how I feel about this. I want to keep my baby. This baby.'

I stared at her, waiting for her to reply. She remained silent.

'H, you've always said that we have the best medical professionals right here on the south coast. You were the one who told me to put my faith in science and let them help me have my baby.'

'Yes, I did. But I said that when you were ready to talk to someone about the miscarriages. I still believe you should trust in science, absolutely, and our medical professionals. That's why I think you need to consider the treatment. Because if they're telling you to think about it, it's because they know more than you do.'

Helen continued to munch away on her pizza while I pushed around the crumbs on my plate.

'What would *you* do?' I asked. I knew it was a senseless question, but I was running out of points to play.

'It's not fair to ask me that, Stephanie. I don't know. I'm not in your position and my circumstances would colour my choice.'

I raised my hands and nodded my head. 'See!' I said, hoping that I had now won the battle. That finally, someone could see that the decision I was making might be right for *me*. 'But—' I raised a pointed finger in Helen's direction '—if you ask any mother on the planet, what would you do to keep your child safe, every single one would answer "anything, everything", and I would believe them. So when do you become a mother?'

She raised an eyebrow at me, pushed her almost empty plate away from her and reached over to take both of my hands in hers, squeezing tight so I couldn't let go.

'What about all those mums who are never able to give birth?' she asked, taking a small pause before continuing. 'Those mums who adopted, or fostered, or had surrogates. Wouldn't they jump in front of a train to save the child they call their own? Of course they would. Still a mum.' I tried to pull back but she tugged my hands closer towards her. 'What about those in similar situations to you who choose their own lives so they can be there for the children they already have at home? So they can be around for the loved ones who need them? Decisions just like yours? Or what about the mothers who have the horrific decision to end a life they know will be full of suffering, those mums who are forced to make a decision like yours because their baby isn't viable? Are they any less mothers? You can't tell me that you would judge them for the decisions they made, because I know you better than that.'

I looked back at her, aghast. 'This is different!' My voice rose slightly. Anger and shame coated my throat like thick tar. 'I'm not judging anyone. I wish people would stop saying that. Everyone has a right to choose. This is my choice. So why am *I* the one being judged?'

She reached forward and took the napkin from my hand that I hadn't noticed I had been ripping into tiny pieces.

'I know, Steph, and I swear I'm not judging you. No one is, but that's why I'm saying this. No woman, ever, knows what decision she would make in this position, until she is forced to. But why do you think people like me exist? Or consultants? When you're in the middle of something like this, you can't be expected to think clearly. It's the job of those around you, the professionals and the people who *love* you the most, to help. Emotions are high; your hormones are all over the place. Switch roles, for a moment. If it were me, sat where you are, can you honestly say you wouldn't do or say anything you could to at least make me *consider* saving my own life first?'

I looked at my friend, with eyes bigger than the sea and a heart that rivalled even that. I took in the smile lines that graced her cheeks, and the crow's feet from all the laughter that her children had brought her over the years.

'Of course I would, but like you said, you're in a different position than me. You have kids who love you, who need you—'

'And you have a husband who needs you, friends who love you. Why would we fight any less to save you than you would to save us?'

For the first time I found myself getting angry with myself. Maybe she was right. I knew all the points she had laid out made perfect sense, but that was the problem – it didn't matter what I did, how many times I questioned, the good and bad points were evenly matched.

'I don't want this choice, Helen. I really don't. It's not fair to make me make it. Nothing will ever be the same again.'

She stood, pulled me up from my chair and wrapped me in the deepest hug, for longer than might have been socially acceptable in such a public setting.

'I love you,' she whispered into my ear, 'more than you will ever know. You are the strongest woman I've ever known, and you deserve your happy ever after.' I tried to back away from the hug, but she wasn't letting go.

'Wait,' she said, 'you're right. It's not fair to make you choose. It's not fair. None of this is. But I love you. James loves you. And we *will* help you get through to the other side of this. Because we love you, and we need you.'

I couldn't breathe. My world was spinning and the only thing holding me up was her.

We changed the subject, for a little while, as we sat chatting over one last coffee. She talked about her kids and the back-to-school routine, her dog Pip and his latest escape attempt, and all the banal gossip from the school WhatsApp group. By the time the bill came, I was ready to head home. Exhausted, physically and emotionally.

'Thank you,' I said as we neared the promenade again. 'I needed that. The normality as well as the kick up the bum.'

I kissed her on the cheek, and she did the head tilt again.

'Always, my love. You can *always* rely on me for a good ole dose of reality. Normality, I'm not so sure; but reality, that I can do.'

She leant in for one last hug before saying, 'Right, I have to get going. Need to collect Freddie's school shoes on the way home. Think about what I said. I'll support you, no matter what, but please think. I'm here if you need me, OK?'

As we made our way off in different directions, I didn't want to admit that her words had gotten to me, and I wasn't ready to think about what that meant for my decision. All I knew was that I wanted my bed. I wanted to curl up under my duvet and shut out the world. As I made my way back along the seafront in the direction of home, my phone beeped.

The message, predictably, was from Helen.

*Of course the store boxed up two different-sized shoes for me to collect. Bloody useless. #RealitySucks. Let me know when you get home safe, and call me if you need to talk. No matter the time.*

As I stepped into our cold and lonely house, my heart sank. James wasn't home. I didn't want to talk, or debate, but I wanted to curl up with him. I wanted to be held and rocked to sleep.

*Hey. Just had lunch with Helen. Home now. Will you be home for dinner? xxx*

Almost instantly, the rolling dots appeared, and my heart leapt. It didn't matter how long we had been together, I still felt like a soppy teenager when I waited for his replies.

*I'm so glad you've seen her. I hope it went OK. I've been asked to go for dinner with this new client. I shouldn't be late though. Wait up for me?*

The disappointment washed over me, merging with my exhaustion as I climbed the stairs towards the bedroom.

*I'll do my best xxx*

I slipped back into James's old T-shirt and slid under the covers. I was in no mood to watch anything, I just wanted noise to drown out the warring opinions in my head, so I switched on the TV and scrolled through endless channels of rubbish. I knew I wouldn't last until James got home. It was early, the sun barely set, but I was done with the day and all the emotions it had brought with it.

I slipped into a deep sleep and only briefly woke when James climbed in beside me, whispering 'I love you' in my ear as I patted his arm in sleepy acknowledgement.

# CHAPTER THIRTEEN

I loved our home. We had painted the walls, plastered the ceilings and with each stroke we added our own memories to the house that was becoming a home. Inside our four walls, we were us, and nothing could harm us. I had always been excited to come home to James. Each time we closed the door, the latch would click loudly, and the whole world beyond it would disappear. Anything held within was ours. Untouched, untainted, no stresses from outside were carried over the threshold. It had always been like stepping through doors to our own personal Narnia.

But since the morning of our first scan, the day the seed of doubt was planted in our minds, it had felt like we were living with an intruder.

I had spent the day out of the house, my sanctuary now feeling like a prison, plastered with false hope, stuffed full of dreams and aching to be filled with the laughter of a family. The smiling faces in the photos that littered our hallway made me angry and resentful. I wanted to be that happy again and wondered if I ever would be. When I had woken, a cold cup of coffee sat by my bedside next to two messages on my phone, one from James asking if I was awake yet, the other from my dad reminding me to bring the picnic basket round later.

It was so rare for me to sleep until lunchtime, but my body obviously needed the rest.

When the silence seemed only to serve as a dangerous playground for my overactive imagination, I had to escape. With the clouds in the sky creating a perfect canvas, I headed out with my camera, determined to lose myself for the day. No babies, no expectant mothers, just me, my camera and nature. I headed out to Great Wood, hoping the dappled light through the ever-moving clouds and the thickness of the tree cover would aid my disappearance. I spent the day hidden among the branches, leaning into my desire to micro focus as I committed to memory all the beauty that could exist in the shadows, in between the cracks of broken things, in the darkness.

It was the first time I had felt normal in weeks, but as evening drew near, I knew I had to rejoin the real world.

When I returned home, I closed the door gingerly, careful not to allow the latch to click. I didn't want James to hear me. I wanted a few more moments of undisturbed fantasy before I had to face him. Face us.

Stepping over the split wooden floorboard, I tried to avoid creaking as I tiptoed to the kitchen. James was upstairs. He was back to his usual routine. It was 5.45 and he would have walked in the door at twenty past, dropped his briefcase on the telephone seat next to the door and gone upstairs to shower off his day.

I stood at the bottom of the stairs and heard the water running and the low hum of the radio playing. I had at least ten minutes before the elephant followed him downstairs to join us.

I looked back towards the telephone seat and noticed that his laptop bag was missing. I'd hoped I might have the chance to sneak through his papers and find the envelope, but it seemed my husband was better at covering his tracks than I thought.

I walked into the kitchen and opened the fridge, the bottle of white wine in the side of the door taking my fancy. Its condensation glistened, imploring me to pour a long well-deserved glass.

I chastised myself: my poor little peanut was already sharing space with nasty toxins; putting more into my body wouldn't help matters. Instead, I pulled out the carton of cranberry juice and poured a generous glass.

Nausea reared its ugly head again and filled my mouth with a repugnant bitter tang. I sipped the cold juice, hoping the acidity would replace the taste of fear, but no such luck. Launching towards the kitchen sink, I emptied my store-bought lunch into the basin. I tried not to make a noise, but as I spat out the last of the bile and rinsed my mouth, I could feel his presence, his strong hands steadying my shaking frame.

He didn't say anything, and I didn't turn around; instead, he rubbed his hands up and down my spine, pressing more forcefully on the small of my back.

A dishcloth appeared in front of my hazy vision. I wiped my mouth and turned to face my husband.

For the second time this week, he was stood in front

of me wearing nothing but a towel, hair wet and dripping around his temples. Never had I wanted him more and at the same time wanted to run faster from him. Hormones were making my body react to his, but my fear and anger were blocking them at every turn.

'I could hear you from upstairs. You never were good at containing your cat squeals.'

He sounded tired. His voice low and gruff.

'Oh, be quiet. I wasn't making a sound. I'm an expert at silent sickness!' I said as I tried to lighten the atmosphere.

'No, darling, I'll let you in on a secret. Why do you think there was always a glass of water and packet of pills waiting for you when you came out of your bathroom at uni?'

He stroked my arms, up and down like a reassuring parent in protection mode.

'I don't know what you're talking about; I never had a hangover at uni. I was hardcore.' I laughed and used the exaggerated flick of my hair to back away from his grip.

'Of course you were. Still are.' His lips twitched as he said those last words. A small lift of the lip at one side, before his thoughts reminded him. The fun sparring between us was there for a moment before the panic took over and then all I could see was pity.

'I'm fine, James. It's morning sickness. I have to get used to it.'

He stepped back, looking wounded. As if I'd told him I didn't love him anymore.

'Is it, though, Steph? What if it's . . . The doctor said you would . . .'

He still couldn't say the word out loud: cancer. Until he admitted it, we'd never move on.

'It's morning sickness, James. I have a tiny human growing inside of me that's already developing a sense of taste. Clearly this little one does not appreciate the smell of cranberry and is, at the moment, craving white wine.'

James closed his eyes. I could no longer see the sad brown pools of fear. He ran his hands through his hair, spreading the wet droplets over his face before turning and walking out of the kitchen. I watched as he edged towards the stairs. With his hand on the banister, he paused.

'I have to pop out for a few hours,' he shouted back towards the kitchen. 'Are you still going to your dad's?'

He didn't move from his spot on the bottom stair. I could only see his hand resting on the wooden rail and a small section of his towel poking through the slats. I couldn't see his face or gauge his expression. I didn't want to. It was safer with this distance between us.

'Yes. I'll take the lasagne from the freezer – unless you want me to leave some for you.'

There was a beat of a pause. All those words not said, just waiting to be plucked from the air and given a voice. Instead, he tapped his wedding ring on the balustrade and mumbled something too low for me to decipher.

'Is that a no?' I shouted after him.

His hand disappeared and I heard his footsteps getting heavier as he ascended the staircase. 'I'll sort myself out,' he shouted back down, before closing the bedroom door.

He never closed the bedroom door. There was never

any need, and he hated closing it – it stuck. Was he in there making plans to see Amy while I was at my dad's? Surely not. But then what did I know? I never thought he'd be the type to cheat on a sick wife.

I grabbed the Pyrex dish full of James's famous lasagne from the freezer. I hate cooking; it's not something I am good at. I never know what is 'missing', but luckily James is the opposite. He has taste buds to rival Heston Blumenthal's.

I had already planned to spend the day with Dad tomorrow, but I had no desire to spend another evening alone with my thoughts as James worked all the hours he could to avoid me.

I popped the lasagne into the picnic basket. I hadn't packed an overnight bag, but the thought of trying to force the bedroom door open and face James's mood was a highly unappealing notion. I could sleep in one of Dad's old T-shirts, and I had more than enough spare clothes there.

I made my way towards the front door and heard the low rumblings of chatter from the bedroom. I considered going up and listening at the door, but with an emotional night ahead, I needed to focus on one pain at a time. James and his midlife-crisis hook-up would have to wait.

# CHAPTER FOURTEEN

I turned the corner and made my way down the street towards my family home. My stomach did a familiar flip. My body recognised this place as home, but happy memories were often mixed with pangs of pain. A comfortable pain. One I often embraced.

I watched as the ghost of my younger self, a sullen-looking teenager battling the pain of her mother's disappearance, skulked down the cracked pathway.

I parked in the driveway and could almost make out the phantom figures of my mother and brother sitting in the front garden, surrounded by cuttings of my mother's wildflowers; the sounds of Alex's music on the boom box. I glanced up at the front bedroom window and as I squinted, I swore I could see him peeking through the curtains. The idea used to make me cry, but over the years I became grateful that I could still remember what he looked like, what he sounded like, his laugh.

We used to laugh about what the walls would say if they could talk. The exposed brickwork, cracking under the pressure and strain of the memories it held, the bright-red-painted front door with marks from our countless slammings, even the patch of weeds growing from the front door stoop made me smile. The same patch that tormented my father every year since.

I felt the resistance as I tried the key in the lock and brushed my fingers down the marks on the doorframe, the ones Alex once made with his broken key. He was still so present in every part of my life.

I stroked my belly and looked down, noticing that it was a little more pronounced. Alex would have made a brilliant uncle. At least, the Alex he had grown into in my imagination would have anyway.

I pushed the door open and the smell of my dad's Old Spice filled the corridor, the sound of Radio 2 floated towards me from the kitchen. My father's favourite pastime was shouting at talk-show presenters, mainly because they couldn't argue back with his flawed opinions.

My heart burst with love as I spotted him stood by the stove. The shirt I bought him for Father's Day last year no longer clung to his waist. It seemed to hang loose from his shoulders. I always assumed my father would be the kind of person who would develop a beer belly, but it seemed the older he got the thinner he became. I had noticed it more over the last six months or so.

He was battling with something on the stove top, his shoulders hunched more than normal, and he seemed to be struggling to stir a sticky concoction.

'Hey, Dad. Need help?' I shouted over the top of the argumentative radio presenter.

I slid an arm around his waist, noticing the slightness of his muscles. He turned to face me. His greying complexion seemed to blush with colour.

'Ah, hi, pal. I didn't hear you come in. Careful, you'll give your ole dad a heart attack sneaking up on him!'

He pulled me into a tight embrace and held me longer than normal. I didn't pull away; he had no idea how much I needed that closeness right now.

'How are you?' he asked as he turned back to the stove. 'Risotto for dinner tonight. Sound good?'

I looked down at the picnic basket. I wanted lasagne, comfort food and a hug from my dad. But he had made such an effort that I didn't dare tell him.

He was a messy cook, not great but always enthusiastic.

I fussed around him, collecting up the remains of the garlic and onions. I leant over the pot to inspect its contents and knew instantly that half the dinner would be burnt to the bottom of the pan. I had thrown away at least half a dozen pans over the years, each one a victim of my dad's risotto skills.

He clocked my worried expression and laughed.

'I know . . . but the top is always the best anyway, the bottom half is a comfy bed for the rice to relax on.'

He winked at me, and I instantly felt like a little kid again.

'What's wrong, darling? You look like you have the weight of the world on your shoulders.'

I couldn't cry. I wasn't ready to tell him, but I knew there was no way I could get through this evening without spilling my secrets.

He stumbled briefly then steadied himself as he hung his head over the pot.

'Dad, are you OK?' I was grateful that I didn't need to answer his questions, but there was a look on his face that worried me more.

'Oh, sweetheart. Of course I am. Just taking in the smells.'

He was lying.

'Dad.'

I put my arm around his waist and led him towards the kitchen table. I noticed the ragged sigh he let out as his bones relaxed onto the wooden frame of the chair at the head of the table.

I let him take a moment to compose himself, as I fussed around preparing the time-honoured remedy for everything. Tea.

'Listen, pal, I'm fine.' Even his voice sounded weaker than normal 'It's the end of a nasty virus; that's all. I'm getting my energy back, but I can't sit on my bum in front of the telly all day.'

As I poured the milk into Dad's favourite mug, I did a mental calendar check. He was sick the day we were supposed to go to the market together. That was five weeks ago, a very long time to have a virus.

'So, about the picnic . . .' he started.

He was about to read from the invisible script, the very same play we re-enacted every year. I could recite it word for word.

With my back to him, I swirled the tea into small whirlpools in front of me, marvelling at the bubbles that danced on top of the murky brown liquid.

My lips moved along with his words. A necessary ritual he needed to steady himself and his own thoughts. I played along as usual.

'We'll leave here at ten o'clock and pass by the

florist's. I've called ahead and ordered the flowers. The pruning shears are in the gardening bag by the front door and we'll make the picnic before we leave. We should be there by eleven at the latest. That gives us time for a spot of lunch with him and we'll bring back the apples to make the pie in time for supper. Do you have the basket?'

'Of course I do.' I smiled at him. 'And actually, I already have the picnic stuff. I'll put it in the fridge so all we have to do is pack it in the morning.'

'But we always . . .' He looked crestfallen.

'Dad . . . don't worry. It's all the same stuff. I picked it up on the way, figured we could enjoy an extra cup of tea before we leave in the morning.'

I sat on the chair next to him and placed a protective hand over his. Each day that passed I felt the roles in our relationship reversing.

He closed his eyes for a moment and said, 'Or have a lie-in for a change.'

I was surprised he even knew what a lie-in was. He was up with the lark and fussing before seven a.m. every day, no matter the time of year.

'Dad, if this virus has you wiped out, we can do something here and I can pop up to put the flowers down. Maybe we could do a carpet picnic, you know, like when we were kids?' I didn't want to go alone. I never went without him, but he looked so tired and worn out.

'In all these years, I have never once missed seeing my boy. I have never not been there to comfort him. I was there that day, and I will be there every anniversary until my dying breath.'

It was a veiled attack on 'her'. My mother had never shown up. Not once.

'I vowed to always be there for you kids. It was the first promise I made the day I first held you, and one I never intend to break.' He took my hand in his and squeezed, a pleading in his eyes. 'I have made many mistakes in my life, pal. I'm not perfect. But I promised never to let either of you down. I may not be great at the practical stuff, but I would never miss an anniversary. Never.'

Before I knew what was happening, my body was shaking and I was sobbing.

'Hey, pal, come on. I know it's tough, but we get through this every year, together. Come, give your dad a hug.' My port in a storm.

I pulled myself up from the chair and knelt on the floor next to him. My dad, my hero. I snuggled into his waist, my arms around him the same way I did as a child.

'Dad, I'm pregnant.'

The words just arrived.

I never intended this to be how I announced our happy news, with sad tears collecting in my father's lap. I had ordered a T-shirt that said 'proud grandfather'. But something inside me was ready to be free of secrets.

He didn't say anything at first, simply continued to stroke my hair. As my sobs eased, he lifted my chin and his eyes were full.

'Ahh, my baby girl. I'm going to be a grandad? Are you past the three-month mark?' I nodded. There it was. Pure pride. Happiness magnified and reflected in sparkling gems dotted down the wrinkles of his face.

'My beautiful girl. My baby. You're going to be a mammy.'

I closed my eyes. I couldn't look at him as I told him. I didn't want to see his world fall apart just like James's had that day. It felt wrong that I was the bearer of such horrible news only moments after giving him such hope.

'It's not that simple.'

I opened my eyes, and like always, four words were all it took to change everything.

I saw fear, my fear, painted across his skin. I held his hands in mine, grounding us, anchoring us to each other.

We sat at that table, clutching the threads of each other for two torturous hours. The sticky risotto, long past its best, grew a crust as it cooled on the stove. The heart of the man-size box of tissues spread across the table in ruins.

All the words had been said. What remained was acceptance.

With nothing left to say, my father took my face in his hands.

'We'll get through this. We will. That little one in there is coming to you one way or another. You'll be here to give it the best life possible. I can feel it. I'll be here to help, for as long as I can. I'm here.'

As we moved to the living room, it was as if we'd reached our quota of words for the day. The little men in our heads had clocked off, all the words locked up in those tiny filing cabinets in our brains to be kept safe for tomorrow.

We sat on the sofa and instinctively I coiled myself up and slotted into the space next to him. I laid my head against his chest and for a few hours allowed myself to feel looked after.

He stroked each strand of my hair as we lost ourselves in a James Bond movie. It wasn't often that the roles between us were traditional. They would be reversed again in the morning. I'd step up and be the strength to keep him moving, but now there was an extra layer in our grief. I had no idea how to heal the pain we shared.

His daughter was pregnant with his grandchild but having his one and only grandchild could risk him losing his only living child. Life's a bitch. And then you die . . . Isn't that the way the story goes?

He understood my pain, more than most. He knew exactly what it felt like to lose a child. I was putting him in the familiar, painful situation again and there was no way for him to help me.

As Bond battled wits with M on the screen, we fell into a comfortable silence, allowing our anxieties to rest a little.

# CHAPTER FIFTEEN

A bright green glow lit up the room, highlighting the posters on the wall and etching dark shadows around the pictures tacked to the side of my childhood mirror. Waking up in this room, in a bed surrounded by memories, was always bittersweet.

I focused on the small figurine glued to the top of my white plastic childhood alarm clock, surprised it was still working after all these years.

Alex had put it there the night he moved into his own room, to keep me safe from my night terrors. Something to watch over me when he couldn't. It was battered and chipped, but it still did the trick.

It wasn't the alarm that woke me, it was the crashing of pots and pans at the ungodly hour of six-thirty that ripped me unceremoniously from my slumber.

I sat on the edge of the bed, rubbing the scratchy sleep dust from my eyes. It had been a late night but even as my head hit the pillow, I knew I wouldn't sleep. The movie had ended and without even discussing it, we'd both moved around each other, shutting down the TV, switching off the lights, locking the doors and closing all the windows for the night. We'd gone round the house in a way I would imagine an old married couple do. A routine my dad should be carrying out with my mother, had she stayed. Instead, I was his surrogate.

We'd hugged each other close as we parted ways at the top of the stairs and I'd watched as he snuck into their room, as if he might find her asleep in bed. Melancholy seemed to weigh heavy on his shoulders. He'd stripped the room bare of all her things, but nothing filled the empty spaces. It saddened me that he seemed able to move on with some areas of his life, while others remained in remembrance of her. As if he was grieving her too.

I had gone to bed and had lain staring at the ceiling, praying for sleep and being denied. I should have known better – praying does no one any good.

As pans continued to clatter downstairs, I pulled a dressing gown around my shoulders. The cold morning air caught my skin as I slid my dad's oversized slippers on. I felt like a child again as I tripped in his shoes and tumbled down the final few stairs.

I had slipped on those stairs far too many times to count. Part of me expected my mother to appear in front of me with a stern look on her face as I staggered back to my feet.

When I came home to visit after I moved out, there was a brand-new pair of slippers by my bed, identical to his. Still too big – they always would be – but they anchored me to him.

'Dad, what on earth are you doing up so early?'

My pre-caffeine croaky voice sounded like I'd smoked twenty a day for the last twenty years and I squinted to see his full frame, my eyesight blurry without my contacts in. Instinctively, my body gravitated towards the source of the heady cocoa-enriched coffee smell.

'I'm making breakfast. I can't make the lunch as you've already done that, but I need to make something.'

He sounded agitated. He didn't like change.

I had built routine and structure into his life after Mum left. She used to keep us busy to distract us, especially when Alex was sick, so I did the same. I followed her lead. Replacing my mother as the core of the family, ensuring the house ran smoothly.

'Dad, it's not even seven and you never eat breakfast.'

His movements were becoming more exaggerated, but his exhaustion was clear. He missed the handle of the frying pan and nearly plunged his hand into the oil.

'Well, I'm hungry now. I didn't sleep. I needed something to do,' he huffed, pushing the pan to the back of the stove.

'Dad. Please come and sit down. I'll do it.'

He didn't even argue, he just turned and sat at the kitchen table with another huff. I flicked on the radio and the booming voices of Radio 2 replaced the awkward silence in the kitchen.

With eggs on toast and a pot of fresh coffee now sat between us, the world stilled. We both picked politely at the yolks. The last thing I wanted to do was to eat, but like a mother leading by example, I pushed through and encouraged my dad to do the same.

The soothing silkiness of the coffee calmed me, and

as I closed my eyes and allowed the aroma to fill me, my world started to open up.

'OK, Dad. I'm going for a shower. Leaving here at ten, right?'

I knew we were; we left at the same time every year. We'd take the same route, past the same florist, the same flowers, the same parking spot. He needed the routine, today of all days. So, I followed the script.

'Yes, pal. Ten on the dot, so we have time to collect the flowers.'

He fiddled with a stray red thread on the edge of the placemat. Staring at nothing, thinking everything. I could hear the cogs turning.

'OK.'

I paused, waiting for him to say something, but it didn't come.

'Dad.'

He looked up, his eyes rimmed with red. 'Sorry, darling. What did you say?'

The script. He never forgot the script.

'Just that I'm going for a shower. I'll be down in time to leave.'

A small nod. Reignition but no words. Had he really forgotten?

*It'll all be OK* – that's what he normally said. Telling himself more than me. Always. But he didn't say it. Because it wasn't *all OK*, was it? He'd lost his son to leukaemia at age ten. Lost his wife to another man because they lost their son. Now he would either lose his daughter, or his grandchild, or potentially both. To cancer. All over again. Only this time he had no one else to lose in the fall-out. There would be nothing left to lose. Nothing would be OK. On the anniversary of his son's death, he'd be sitting by a grave with a daughter who may well suffer the same fate. You can't say what you don't feel, can you?

I was halfway down the hall when I looked back.

'It'll all be OK, Dad. Wait and see,' I shouted along the corridor.

'Love you, pal. Go get ready.'

Today was going to be tough. It always was. But this year, it felt harder.

# CHAPTER SIXTEEN

Summer in the South of England is never quite summer. A week or two where the floors feel warmer and the grass not so wet maybe, but most years we'd walk down the gravel paths dodging puddles. It had been a fair few years since we'd been able to enjoy the graveyard in full summer bloom.

Enjoy the graveyard. It was odd to think that way and I would never say those words out loud; but I enjoyed this day every year. The one day we talked openly about our memories, about Alex and the life we all had before the bombshell that ripped apart the fabric of our family.

We approached the aisle where he lay, forever sleeping.

His headstone shone in the summer light. Many of his neighbours had been abandoned over the years. Dusty headstones and flowers long gone. So many people laid to rest then forgotten. Not Alex. His grave was always well tended.

*May the angels enjoy your laughter as much as we all did.*

The gold lettering of the small quote at the bottom of the headstone stood out against the black marble. Dad had spent a fortune on it. In fact, Mum had remarked that she was sure they'd spent more on saying goodbye to their son than they had welcoming him. No expense had been spared on the balloons and bright-coloured casket they had chosen to lay my brother to rest. Mum used planning the day as a way through her grief and Dad threw money at it left, right and centre, hoping it would help fill the fractures appearing between them; as if stuffing the cracks might mean they wouldn't fall apart. It didn't work, but I couldn't fault him for trying.

I took the blanket from the picnic basket and laid it down in front of the grave. I placed his favourite book up against the cold marble next to a large bottle of Lucozade and two glasses. I unfurled the sausage rolls, laid out the peanut butter and jam sandwiches, and put the Party Ring biscuits and Jammie Dodgers onto a plate. We filled ourselves with the things he loved in the hope that we could share one more moment with him.

Next to the headstone stood an apple tree.

Dad had picked a plot at the very end of the aisle and convinced the local council and the church to let him plant a tree.

Alex's favourite indulgence was Mum's apple pie. We had a tree in our back garden, and they would pick the apples every year and make pies together. In his final days, Mum brought him a fresh hot pie, and despite no longer being able to eat, sores in his mouth making anything more than water unbearable, his face lit up at the smell of the steam rising from the bowl when she lifted the lid.

That was his last proper smile before he died.

It took six years for Alex's tree to bear fruit, and by that point Mum was long gone.

'The tree looks good, Dad. Really strong. So many apples this year.'

He had been so quiet on the drive over, and the guilt I felt weighed heavy on me. This day was already hard enough for him, but I'd burdened him with so much more this year. I should have waited. I looked at him, fussing with the clingfilm, and noticed the dark marks on his skin. Bruising.

'Dad?'

'Yes, pal? Oh, I'm fine. Just thinking about the day I planted it. It feels like only yesterday sometimes, but look how big it is. How strong it's become. The life it's lived already.'

He was definitely more melancholic this year.

He had planted the tree the day we buried him. As everyone made their way to the wake, Dad sat on the sodden soil, knees in the wet mud, and, using his bare hands, he poured his pain into the hole as he planted the one thing he hoped would live on forever.

More than twenty years later and the tree had been well maintained. I wandered over to the strong and stable reminder of my brother, stroking the bark and feeling the trunk breathe against my palm.

I reached up and plucked a solitary apple from one of the branches. Blushed and unblemished. Dad usually picked the apples, donating them throughout the season to the local church. He'd said once that it was his way of giving back, despite the fact that he couldn't face walking into the church himself; but as I looked at him hunched over by his son's grave, I wondered if he picked them so they didn't spoil. He couldn't bear to see them less than perfect.

Now, I bake the pie every year. It's not Mum's pie obviously; she didn't leave her recipe behind. She didn't leave much of anything behind.

'Look, Dad – they're fabulous this year.'

I passed him the apple and watched as he stroked it, his thumb passing over the reddening of the skin on one side, as if stroking the blushing cheek of the son he missed.

I tried so hard over the years to replicate my mother's recipe, but it was never quite right. Dad smiled sweetly each year and professed it was better, but I think he was secretly happy it tasted nothing like it. Maybe it was less painful to swallow that way.

I sat back down on the blanket and reached into the picnic basket. My eyes rested on one word: Dolly. His infusion friend. Every time he went to the toilet, he would wheel Dolly with him and talk to her. It was Alex's way of dealing with how his life had changed. He spoke of Dolly as if she were an old friend, keeping him smiling though the dark moments. Mum had insisted on stitching the name into the picnic basket so that when she took snacks to the hospital, Alex would see that the food was as much for Dolly as for him. To keep them both strong and fighting.

It worked, for a while at least.

'I thought James was joining us this year?'

I looked up to see that Dad had caught me staring at the name.

'No, he's so snowed under. A difficult client, apparently – we had to rush back from Yorkshire so he could deal with them. He's up for promotion too so needs to keep his head down. He'll meet us at the house later.'

James had always said that our annual trips were a little macabre. When I invited him to the picnic the first time, he admitted that he found it morbid. Strange that we would toast Alex's life in such a joyful manner, in a graveyard, on the anniversary of his death. Over the years he had come with us once or twice, but I never pushed him and he always met us back at the house for apple pie. Maybe James didn't quite get it, but I understood why Dad did it this way. He needed not to slip into the darkness again. He needed a small spark of light on this one day that served as a reminder of the beginning of the end for him, in so many ways.

So, we celebrated. Together.

We never worried about my mother turning up. We knew she wouldn't. She would spend the day in a church somewhere, clutching her rosary beads and praying to the God that took her son away. She would talk to the priest, confess her sins, and proclaim herself a good Catholic woman.

I would not. I hadn't stepped foot inside a church since that day.

I envied my mother for her sheer determination to be faithful to this feckless God despite all the pain and suffering he'd caused our family. Envious that she found peace and comfort in something as simple as a church.

We sat in silence for a while. We didn't talk about faith, religion or my mother. Instead, we swapped memories. We didn't mention the C-word. Instead, we sat among the headstones, surrounded by wildflowers, and flooded the blanket with happy memories.

But perched uncomfortably between the memories and the flowers sat the biggest elephant of all, so close to me I could see the rippling of its skin and the detail of its eyes. It was as real to me as the Party Rings on the plate below. But it wasn't my mother, or even Alex. The elephant in the graveyard was me. It was us. It was *it*. The *it* that I couldn't conceal or deny anymore. My unwanted guest disrupting a day and a memory it was not invited to be a part of.

'Twenty-three years. How is it possible he's been gone twenty-three years? He would have been turning thirty-four this year. My little boy would be a man. Maybe even with a wife, and . . .'

He stopped himself and looked away sheepishly.

'And . . . kids? You might have had grandkids. It's OK to say it, Dad. It's true.'

He fiddled with the plastic label on the Lucozade bottle.

'I can't tell you what to do, Stephanie. I've had more years with you than I had with your brother. I've loved watching you grow and succeed. I'm so proud of you. But it terrifies me that you might go through the same pain he did.'

'Dad. I'm twenty-three years older than he was. I'll cope.'

I took his hand in mine. Looking at the man who had loved me first, I knew I could be honest, and I needed more than anything to say it out loud.

'Dad, I can't let my baby go. I have to try everything. Anything.'

'It's OK to be scared, Stephanie. It's OK to want to hide from this decision, and the fear will cloud your judgement for a while, but you're allowed to be scared.'

'I don't think I'm scared, Dad. I think I'm determined. I don't have time to be scared.'

I knew he understood. His face said it all.

He pulled me close, the peanut butter sandwiches squashed between our knees. As he held me, I felt it all slip into place. He was resigned to watching his daughter go through this, and I knew full well I would be causing him more pain.

'When is the doctor's appointment?' he asked as he pulled away and searched his rucksack for his phone.

'Tomorrow afternoon. I'll go home with James tonight and he'll take me to the hospital tomorrow. But I'll pop round on Saturday to go through the bills as usual.'

I tried to get the conversation back on track, but he wasn't done.

'Do you want me to come with you? I can meet you at the hospital?'

His face pleaded with me to let him be a part of this tragic story.

'No, Dad. It's OK, honestly. James and I need to do this bit on our own.'

'But I know all about this, Stephanie. I know what questions you need to ask. I can help.'

I watched as he tried to find more words but was unable to form them.

'Dad, it's not leukaemia. Besides, I think I need to find out how to keep the baby safe first. Then you can help me with all the cancer mumbo-jumbo.'

He opened his mouth to argue with me but thought better of it and smiled *that* smile instead.

Despite my own worries, I still had a job to do. I would get through the hospital appointment and then help Dad with the usual chores. By the end of Saturday, his meal plans would be sorted for the month, and all the money would be in the right accounts for the bills to be paid. Cancer may take my life, but only when I chose to give in. In the meantime, my life would continue.

Small things gave me focus, structure and control. I needed that – a purpose. My child would be my purpose, but in the meantime, my father was my charge.

We packed up the picnic, straightened the nest of wildflowers on the grave and said goodbye to the boy we missed so much.

A prickling sensation swept over me as the breeze picked up a familiar scent. My body reacted before I could even put my finger on what it was that was niggling. As my eyes searched, the little men in my head were desperately seeking the connection between the smell and a distant memory. I searched the rows as we made our way out of the cemetery, but it wasn't until the breeze blew once more in my direction that the smell and the memory collided.

Mum.

I could smell my mother. Her perfume. The one she always wore on a Sunday to church. A woman had breezed past us as we left the cemetery, a big hat and sunglasses hiding her grief from the world as our paths crossed briefly, but as I stared at the back of the stranger, my body filled with a desire to run and embrace her. It wasn't her, of course. It couldn't be. It was my brain reacting to the memories of us. The mind plays funny tricks on you when you're emotional. Like awake dreaming. Seeing the faces of those you miss on the bodies of people you don't know.

She wasn't here, she was in Yorkshire with her new husband and family. Living her new and best life no doubt. My heart raced and my palms sweated. I was closer to forty than fourteen, yet the very thought of her still reduced me to an angst-filled teen.

'What's wrong, pal?' My father's supportive hand on my arm steadied my thoughts.

'It's nothing. Ignore me. I'm seeing things.'

As I unlocked the car, I glanced back and watched the older lady walk towards our aisle. Pausing at the end of the row, waiting. It couldn't be her. My mother was a classical woman. Blacks and whites. Practical and uniform. This elderly lady wore an explosion of colour. A long-flowing maxi dress clipped around the bottom like feathers grazing her bare ankles. Sandals with a wedged heel and an oversized hat. She was dressed for a carnival rather than a memorial. But there was something about her stance . . .

I brushed my paranoia aside and lowered myself into the car. As I put the key in the ignition, I noticed my father's pallor. He was struggling for breath.

'Maybe we should get you to the doctor?'

'I'm fine, pal, honestly. It's taken it out of me; that's all. A proper cup of tea and a slice of your pie and all will be right with the world.'

I smiled at his stubborn resilience.

# CHAPTER SEVENTEEN

Dad sat in the living room watching *Pointless* on the TV while I battled with the flour in the kitchen. I added a touch of nutmeg to the pastry base. Dad assured me it wasn't the secret ingredient, but I had tried almost everything else over the years. The smell from the oven was intoxicating.

My stomach ached and I felt bloated, but having had only two small triangles of sandwiches and a mini sausage roll, I couldn't understand why I felt so off. The midwife had said the sickness would ease in the second trimester, but it seemed to be taking a stronger hold. I sipped a cold glass of water, hoping to quench my thirst, but the water hitting my stomach only seemed to make the vomit monster rage.

I trotted as quickly as I could to the downstairs toilet, trying not to disturb Dad in the living room. Throwing up as silently as I could, it was as if praying to the porcelain queen had summoned a strong knight to save me. My husband's hands were rubbing my lower back in a clockwise motion, pushing harder at the base.

I knew it was him. He didn't need to say anything. I hadn't heard the front door open, and I was being so violently sick that I couldn't smell his aftershave, but I knew it was him.

I knelt down on the floor in front of the toilet, giving up the fight to stay upright, and rested my forehead on my hands. I had neither the desire nor the strength to stand.

'God this is shit,' I mumbled into the porcelain.

'It doesn't have to be this hard.' My husband's words hit my ears and struck my chest simultaneously. 'I mean the pregnancy, all this sickness . . .'

'Just part of the pregnancy journey, I guess.' I squeezed the words out in between heaves.

'You shouldn't be having to battle both at the same time, Steph. One at a time is already too much for your body.'

'It's pregnancy. You take the sickness as it comes. It'll be worth it in the end.'

I had no desire to fight with him, but I felt like we kept going round and round in circles, and my patience for this conversation was starting to wear very thin. I didn't have the energy or the brain space to consider my words carefully anymore. The only words I wanted to throw at him were expletives, and that was not going to help.

'It's more than that, Stephanie, and you know it.'

His words seemed to materialise all at once and with deep, sad sighs attached to each syllable – but a note of something else, too. A growing frustration. The anger was back and, this time, he was losing the battle to keep it hidden.

'I know one thing. If I don't get in that kitchen, the pie will burn.'

I stood and pushed him aside, stumbling past the open living room door where Dad stood just inside, clearly listening to the interaction that had just taken place.

'Don't worry, Dad. It's nearly ready.'

I looked back down the hallway. The two most important men in my life fixed to the spot, staring at each other. Not saying a word but saying it all at the same time. These two men so pained, and neither of them able to do a damn thing about it. They say you choose a man to marry who most resembles your father. In this respect, I couldn't have chosen two men more alike. Neither able to talk about emotions, neither able to admit fear. They stood next to each other, looking like bodyguards who had misplaced their charge. Both confused and lost, waiting for direction and instruction. That was my job.

We were all functionally fucked up. Able to complete daily tasks without anyone ever realising just how messed up we were, never showing how broken we had all become.

I served the apple pie into the deep dessert dishes. It was not a day for counting calories. The whipped double cream sat proudly on top of the crumbling pie lid, apple steam filling the air.

I took my phone out and snapped an image of the steam, rising and curling around the pain in the room. Something about its invisible magic warmed and soothed me. With the colourful backsplash of the kitchen painting a perfect dark blue background, the image looked almost ethereally doctored.

I focused on the smallest crack of pie crust, a corner of the cream, sparkling with hidden diamonds, a sweet sugary secret concealed within.

I added the image to my Instagram page and typed a caption.

*#JustForYouAlex #ItsTheSmallMoments #LifeWithoutFilters . . . when I miss you most.*

I wondered about all those times when we would sit in front of the priest and hear him say that heaven was the most glorious place, how all those who entered the pearly gates found everything their hearts desired. But how could they, when we were all down here? How could heaven be such a glorious place when so much of what Alex would miss was left behind?

What would I miss?

Apple pie.

These days we spent together.

My father's hugs, my childhood bed and our James Bond moments.

I would miss my husband's kiss, his smile and the way he held me in the night.

I would miss the smell of the crisp autumn air. Nowhere in the world smelt like Brighton did on the first day of autumn.

I would miss that. He was missing all of that.

I'd been so busy pottering around, I hadn't noticed what the boys were up to until I walked towards the kitchen table with the plates in my hands. They were stood in the corridor, heads bowed and hushed words being swapped. My dad's hand was on James's shoulder. He seemed to be wiping tears from his cheeks.

'Food's ready, guys. Come get it,' I shouted from the kitchen, both men breaking away as if caught in a clandestine embrace.

I placed my father's bowl at the head of the table and lit the candles. Everyone took their seats silently and waited for me to proceed.

We may not go to church anymore, or pray in the traditional way, but this was how we honoured him. This was how we chose to remember him. Our rituals may not have included saying the Lord's Prayer, but these routines were our understanding of faith and duty.

'To Alex.'

I raised my spoon and was met by the other two.

'Made with love, memories, hope and pain. Bittersweet but nonetheless enjoyed in your honour.'

They were the very same words I uttered each year, the same smiles tainted with a smidge of pain, but despite the atmosphere, the men tucked in hungrily. Enjoying every bite and professing that *this* really was *the one*. Imploring me to write the recipe down.

'I'll have to,' I muttered a little louder than a whisper. 'Our little peanut will be wanting all my secrets soon.'

James dropped his spoon, pushed his chair back from the table and walked out of the kitchen.

I continued to nibble away at the tart apples in silence, a bitter taste coating the roof of my mouth. I hoped that was nutmeg, but I suspected it may be something a little deeper-rooted.

By the time I'd cleared the dishes and put the remains in the fridge I walked into the living room to an atmosphere. I watched as my dad gripped James's shoulder and shook it in the most fatherly action I had seen him make to anyone. There was tenderness, understanding and love between them, and I wished I could bottle that moment. James would always have my dad; the two of them could raise peanut together, if the worst happened. My baby would be safe, in the strong arms of the men I loved.

'James was just saying he has a rather large presentation at work tomorrow. So, he's going to head off. Why don't you go with him and get an early night? I'm exhausted; could do with an early night myself.'

My father wasn't really asking if I wanted to. His tone was authoritative and by the look of the expression on my husband's face, this wasn't his idea either.

'Don't be silly, Dad. I was thinking of staying here again tonight to keep an eye on you. I'm worried about you.'

I didn't want to go home. I wanted to hide. I had the distinct impression that the conversation over the toilet bowl was only on pause, and I wasn't ready to hear the rest. I wanted us to all stay in this house a little longer, wrapped in happier memories, and to ignore my own fears.

'I'm trying to be polite, sweetheart. I think you guys need to go home and talk, and quite frankly, I don't think I have the energy for company this evening.'

We collected our coats and made our brief goodbyes. As I stepped outside the safety of the four walls, the cool air hit my cheeks and I took a sharp breath.

There it was. Autumn. I raised my face to the sky and could see the turning of the evening. The blue and purple hues as they blended together, getting ready to paint the canvas black for the arrival of the diamonds of the night.

'There it is,' I said to the sky.

'Autumn,' James muttered. 'Another season begins.'

I looked towards him to see his eyes closed and nose to the sky.

'Time goes by too fast, Steph. It feels like only yesterday it was Christmas, summer came and went, and already we're hurtling towards Christmas again. Time rushes past too quickly.'

'I know, James. That's why you don't think too hard. You just live with what you have right in front of you. You never know what's around the corner.'

He lowered his head, eyes still shut and his fists pushed deep into his pockets.

'Only, you do, Steph. You do know what's around the corner. You can hear the clock ticking. Ignoring it is not living.'

He walked off towards the car and I stood rooted to the path, stunned. The colour of the sky deepened, and a chill crossed my shoulders. Like someone flicked a switch, suddenly the light was gone.

# CHAPTER EIGHTEEN

The energy in the house felt different the next morning. No words had been said, no voices raised, but the whole house felt colder. He felt colder. There was no kiss on the cheek as he got out of bed. There was no morning cup of coffee sat next to the bed today, no radio playing downstairs, no joyful chatter. He was punishing me because I refused to talk to him when we got home from Dad's.

I lay in our once-warm bed and stared up at the ceiling, wondering how it had got so bad. Had the cracks in our carefully crafted world always been there but I'd been too blind to see them? Maybe our perfect little bubble wasn't so perfect after all. Maybe all it took was for one thing to break for the whole house to crumble.

Over the years, we'd had our small misunderstandings and even a few arguments here and there. Every couple disagree, even if it's only behind closed doors, but our friends always commented how tranquil our relationship seemed. We were '#goals' – but just because we didn't air our dirty laundry in public or scream at each other, that didn't mean we didn't frustrate each other.

He found me contrary. His frustration was that I could change my mind quicker than the wind would change direction.

I often found him too passive.

It frustrated him that I loved how calm he was, and how he could de-escalate any difficult situation, but would get angry at how calm he could be when I didn't *want* him to be.

But he would never say that, because he was too passive to cause a fuss. He let me get away with everything instead.

I could be so passionate about something that I knew fine well he didn't agree with, and even though I would push for a reaction, he'd always respond with 'that's why I love you'.

There were days, especially around a certain time of month, when I wanted – no, *needed* – an argument. Days when I would look at him and genuinely wonder why he wasn't more pissed off with me, when even *I knew* how unreasonable I was being.

When we first bought the house, I insisted that the grey hue we'd spent an entire day carefully and painstakingly painting the bedroom wall with was *absolutely* the wrong shade.

I cringed at the memory of sending him back out to buy the 'correct' shade. I had stood in our hall that day and tapped angrily with my fingernail on the sample selection on the colour chart.

Of course, it was the exact shade we had bought. He laughed at me when the penny dropped. I scowled. Dutifully, James went back to B&Q, bought a shade of grey just one shade lighter, and by the time he got home I'd changed my mind.

Instead of being mad, he took my hand, carefully squeezing it as he kissed my forehead, and went down to the kitchen to make tea. No huff, no backbiting or 'I told you so'. Just understanding.

It infuriated me.

I stared at the empty space in our bed. The indentation of the pillow was still warm to the touch, but a hole replaced where my calm and reasonable husband had been. I wanted more than anything to go back to the days when our disagreements were about the banal. I wanted to go back, treat him better. Be more reasonable, but more than anything, I wanted to go back and argue about inconsequential things. Back to when our fights weren't so life and death. Literally.

My phone buzzed as the morning alarm kicked in. I took in my thin frame in the mirror. My cheeks were hollow, but my stomach was rounding. I cradled it, but then that awful menace that lurked in my mind ready to pounce snuck up on me. The thought that I was cradling an intruder as well as my baby.

I tried to picture my peanut instead of a cluster of cancer cells.

'Good morning, my little one,' I whispered into the dead air. 'Time to get ready for our big day.'

The appointment was booked for one p.m. I had the whole morning to figure out what I was going to say, and to see if those thoughts were going to stick and form a decision. Helen's words replayed over and over in my head and picked at my conscience, and just when I thought I'd made my mind up, I remembered Julie and the sadness she still carried. Could I live like that?

I checked over the notes on my phone and added a few more questions from last night's insomnia session.

James sat at the breakfast bar. That bloody envelope was by his side again and a stack of papers sat in front of him. He turned to look at me before I reached him, slipping a top cover sheet over what he was reading.

'At it already? Your pillow's barely cold and you already look totally engrossed,' I said, careful not to sound too accusatory or petulant, but I was still bugging over the lack of bedside caffeine.

'It's D-Day. No time to hang around,' he replied.

I glanced down at the paperwork. There was a sheet of designs resting on top of the burning secret. It was not the right day to start a fight. I needed to stay calm; I had a bigger fight to prepare for.

'OK,' I tutted. Apparently, this is a fabulous and little-known side effect of pregnancy: the sudden compulsion to become a moody, mardy teenager with no sense of reason. Because we all *loved* that stage the first time around.

'Well, what time is your presentation? I have my appointment at one p.m.'

I walked past him to the coffee machine, pulling out only one cup and deliberately not offering to top up his. Juvenile, yes, but I couldn't help it. Our daily norms had been hijacked by the rapidly multiplying elephants that filled our lives.

'Ten a.m.,' he replied curtly. 'I'm about to leave. Don't worry, I'll still be in time for *our* appointment.'

He put extra emphasis on the *our*, turning to look at me, a coldness in his eyes I hadn't seen before, as if I'd somehow questioned his right to be there.

Stuffing all his paper secrets into the envelope, he hopped down from the bar stool at the kitchen worktop and slid the envelope into his laptop case. It was a normal move. Nothing out of the ordinary, but something about the swiftness of the way he moved sparked anger in me. Everything sparked anger in me these days.

'Our appointment, my appointment. It's the same damn thing. And, quite frankly, I feel a little alone in all this. You spend your days skulking around with those damn envelopes, secretive and evasive. I know you don't like fighting, but these silent moods are worse. Just say it already, whatever it is,' I spat at him.

He spun like an ice dancer on the tiles of our kitchen floor. The indignation on his face said one thing, but his calm and measured words told a poisonous truth we were doing so well to ignore.

'*Our* appointment, not yours. *Our* child, not yours. *Our* life, not yours. I'm not being secretive and quite frankly, Stephanie, you have no idea what *alone* feels like. No idea at all.'

He stood there. Not moving. Just balled fists and a steady expression. My husband was changed. He was not himself. The anger that had been simmering and building had nowhere left to hide. With an invisible clock ticking down, it was time to face this decision once and for all.

'Alone is how I'm making this decision.' I threw my words back at him as he turned away from me, as if the louder the words the more importance they held. 'It's *my* body, James. It's *me* who has to keep this child safe until it's born. It's *my* child until it's ours. It's *my* life, *my* heartbeat, *my* pain. I don't just *feel* alone. I *am* alone. Where have you even been the last few days? Not here! Hiding at the office avoiding all this.'

My retort hit his back like a lasso and he whipped around to face me.

'Don't you dare. I have tried, *multiple times*, to talk to you. But it's on your terms, when you're ready, or not at all. You're being unfair.'

He had a point, but I wasn't about to concede it.

'Your stroppy childish silences and endless mournful looks aren't helping. It's not supportive,' I continued.

'I'm not a guide dog, Stephanie. I'm not here to blindly support you. We support each other. That's how marriage works. I need you and you need me. We work stuff out together. We plan our life. Together. Make decisions, together. That is marriage.'

I stood, arms crossed, lips pursed and readying myself for what he had stored up. I could see his thoughts crossing his mind, could hear the cogs turning.

'What if the worst happens? You might not *think* you need me right now, but I'm as much a parent as you are, Steph. Even at this early stage, I'm as involved as you. If you weren't here, I'd have to raise this baby alone. Have you even considered that?'

I had no answer for him. I kept my arms locked across my chest. Of course I'd thought about it, and then put that thought in a box and locked it away. I wasn't ready to discuss what might happen without me. I didn't see the point; I wasn't going anywhere.

'Is that what you're worried about? Will being a single parent mess up your carefully laid plans? Is that why you're being so secretive about this "Amy" woman?'

His face contorted, flushed red, and I had never seen anger fill him like that.

'You've actually lost the plot. I can't talk to you when you're like this. You're being so irrational.' He was struggling to speak through gritted teeth.

'Whatever, James. I've survived on my own and looked after everyone else all my goddamn life,' I said. 'I don't *need* you. I chose to spend my life with you. My choice. So is this.'

He stopped dead in his tracks, one foot over the threshold of the kitchen and his palm flat on the side of the doorframe. His head dropped. 'You don't *need* me; you don't *want* me. Strong words, Stephanie.'

He wasn't facing me, but he didn't need to for me to know the look that was on his face: passive defeat.

'I am not having an affair,' he said, head still bowed. 'I'm devastated that you even think I would. I'm trying to keep the love of my life alive. I would have thought that much was obvious.' His shoulders sank as he let out a sigh. 'I'll see you at the hospital,' he muttered before leaving me alone in the kitchen surrounded by my own anger and self-righteousness.

He opened the front door before pausing for a moment. He couldn't leave this house without saying it. It wasn't his way. I decided to give him an out.

'You don't have to come to the hospital, James. If you don't agree, don't come.'

I knew I was being unreasonable. It hurt the rational side of my heart to hear myself being so unnecessarily cruel to him. Something in me knew he didn't deserve it, but I needed to be cruel to someone. I didn't deserve this, and I was so sick and tired of being alone in this anger. I wanted him to be angry with me, or at me if that was what he was feeling, at the world even. I wanted him to be as angry with someone as I was. I wanted him to fight, not walk away.

'I love you, Stephanie. I'll see you later.'

The rest of the morning went by in a blur. I had coffee, threw it up. Made breakfast, threw it up. Got dressed, then undressed and dressed in something that didn't make me feel restricted and therefore nauseous. Then I threw up anyway.

In the end I picked a pair of black leggings and a loose-fitting black pinafore. I was dressing like a mother already, like my mother.

At almost seventeen weeks, my bump was slowly growing, but the cut of the dress exaggerated it. It's why I chose it. I didn't want them to look at me with that tilted-head expression. Just for one day, I wanted to be an 'expectant mother'. For the looks to be filled with hope and happiness, not sadness.

I scrolled through my phone to find the message I had sent to the Macmillan nurse. No reply yet. I sent another asking if she was still free, but I secretly hoped that she was fully booked. A reply came back almost instantly: she apologised for the slow response, but she had in fact, just had a cancellation. We arranged to have a chat before my consultation.

I had been circling the hospital car park for almost half an hour when a space finally freed up. An elderly woman guiding a frail gentleman nodded to me and pointed to a car just across from where I hovered. The man looked battered and bruised and walked with a limp. The poor old woman could barely hold up her own handbag as she supported her husband into the car. I noticed her flushed cheeks as she glanced towards me, apologetically holding up her hand. I put my own car in park and got out.

'Here, let me help,' I said while cupping her elbow, feeling the rough skin on an arm that had clearly nursed many worries over the years.

'Oh dear, thank you so much, sweetheart.'

Her voice was like silk, smooth and delicate. I imagined this beautiful lady sat in front of a fire reading grandchildren bedtime stories like some old-fashioned version of *Jackanory*. She looked so familiar. I recognised her kind eyes. It was the same lady who had helped me when I was sick outside the hospital. It seemed we'd traded places; this time it was her who was close to tears.

'Time sneaks up on you, you know. One day you're guiding them around the dance floor at your wedding and the next you are manoeuvring them through a hospital car park. I don't know where the time went.'

I was dumbstruck, with no idea how to respond to such an honest and emotional outpouring. I wasn't sure if she recognised me, but I couldn't help but wonder what twist of fate had engineered us to be in the same place again.

'It took him forty years to learn to lean on me, and when he finally does, I'm too weak to hold him up alone. With that new hip of his, he has no choice now. I guess neither do I.'

She chuckled as she closed the door on her husband. She took my hand in hers, her skin slipping over the top of her bones, wrinkling under the pressure of our combined fingertips.

'Are you visiting, dear?'

'No. No, I'm not.'

I wasn't sure what else to say. I waited to see if the memory of me would kick in, but it seemed to pass her by like a fleeting déjà vu.

'Then I truly hope you have someone to lean on, my dear. It makes the journey much more bearable when you have someone to share the load with.'

I couldn't do much more than smile.

The Macmillan Centre wasn't far from the main entrance to the hospital. I liked the idea that it wasn't simply a room next to the oncology ward, removed from the clinical white walls and bleach smells. As I walked in, friendly faces greeted me, from staff with name badges to family members sat next to loved ones sporting vibrant bandanas.

'Stephanie? Hi, I'm Sarah.'

A woman in her early forties put her hand out to shake mine, and as she did, I felt my emotions boil over.

'Sorry, yes. I'm Stephanie. Sorry . . . this is all just . . .' I couldn't find the words.

'Don't worry, I understand. Most people feel a little out of sorts when they walk in here for the first time. Everyone expects this place to look like a doctor's office. Thankfully – I hope, at least – it's far from that.'

Sarah guided me towards a table with bright-coloured chairs surrounding it.

'Take a seat here. Can I get you a tea or coffee? Glass of water?'

'Tea, please. Ever so British, I know, but a good cup of tea would help,' I replied.

Something about her manner put me instantly at ease. The comfortable surroundings helped. It was the first time during the whole ordeal that I hadn't felt like a lab rat being shuttled from cage to cage.

As I waited for her to return, I stood and browsed the library of leaflets. It felt peculiar to see the words written so brazenly in front of me.

'Don't let it overwhelm you,' came the voice once more, as I replaced the booklet that outlined how to speak to family members about diagnosis.

'This place is so calm, not at all what I was expecting,' I said.

'It never is. But then I don't think many people think about what they expect a cancer centre to look like. Most hope they'll never see the inside of one.'

Sarah guided me away from the central meeting area and motioned for me to follow her down the corridor.

'We have a range of facilities here. We run regular fitness classes for those dealing with various stages of cancer. We have massage and alternative therapy rooms for patients and their families, even a small salon that offers advice on hair loss and treatments.'

She pointed to the various rooms as we walked past.

'Let's sit in here, shall we?' She guided me into a low-lit room, a bright orange feature wall painted on one side and comfortable couches and chairs at its centre.

I spent the next half-hour explaining my situation to her, in a way that I hadn't done until now. We choose our words carefully with the ones we love, but with Sarah I didn't need to. She'd heard them all before, and much worse besides. She knew all the stats and clinical jargon, so my late-night googling sessions sprang forth and I let the questions flow. We talked about my test results, the diagnosis and the prognosis, and she asked about my support system.

Then came the one question I was terrified of.

'So, you have a meeting with Dr Li today. Have you and your husband talked about what you might do?'

I hadn't said the words out loud yet, but the truth was that in a matter of hours, I would have to give the same answer to the consultant.

'I think I've decided to keep the baby. I'm not sure what that means yet for treatment, but I know that I don't want to give up my baby without a fight.'

Sarah didn't judge. Or if she did, her face didn't show it. She paused and waited a little while longer before saying anything.

'OK. Well, I'm glad you feel like you've made a decision, but you said that *you* have decided. How does your husband feel?'

'We've talked a little and he doesn't exactly feel the same way. He can't seem to move past the thought of losing me, to see any other ways this could play out. But honestly, this is my decision. I know I can handle it and as much as James loves me, I know my body better than he does.'

Sarah stood up and joined me on the sofa. Taking my hands in hers, she looked at me and waited. She didn't fill the air with her opinions, she just sat there and waited.

'He is in a lose-lose situation, so I have to make this decision. I'm the fixer; I need to fix this. It's what I do.'

The words caught in my throat, the edges cutting me as they were voiced.

'Why do you feel like you have to be the one to fix

this alone?' Sarah's eyes were soft, and her voice was calm, but the question sent a shiver down my spine.

'I don't feel like I have to. That's how I approach everything. It's who I am.' I could hear the defensiveness in my own words, and as Sarah slowly closed her eyes in an exaggerated blink, I could hear the cogs turning in her mind as she tried to form her words delicately.

'You're not the first, and certainly won't be the last, to think they can and should tackle this alone. It's a fairly common reaction to the diagnosis. Emotions around something like this are incredibly complex.'

Sarah squeezed my hands in hers and I fought hard not to break down.

'But you can't fight this alone. No one ever can. You'll have a team of people around you doing their very best to help and you need someone to lean on. Have you spoken to anyone else about this?'

I couldn't help but laugh. My reaction obviously caught her a little off-guard, and I found myself apologising and hastening to explain. 'Everyone who cares about me has voiced their opinion. My dad, my best friend . . . they're all lovely and supportive, and they care *so* much.' My voice broke as a knot of emotion grew. 'They're all so understanding, but it's not them who'll have to live with this guilt hanging around their shoulders. I will.'

'That guilt will morph over the years into a different emotion. Most of the time, it's gratitude. You become more grateful for the memories you were able to make, rather than guilty for the decisions you took.'

We spent over an hour talking about my options. We talked through what treatment could and would look like if I wanted to carry on. What the side effects would be and how the pregnancy might be impacted; we even discussed egg freezing and IVF. But mostly, we talked about James.

It hadn't taken her long to cotton on to the idea that I was struggling with his role in all of this.

As I stood to leave, she embraced me, and without pulling away said, 'This is going to be a long and windy road, with ups and downs along the way. Our doors are always open, and we'll help you through this as much as we can.' She stroked my upper arm, and the sympathetic head tilt finally made an appearance.

'Cancer will test even the best of friendships, and will most certainly test your relationship. Remember that you can both come here, together or separately, to talk through your worries.'

We said our goodbyes and I made an appointment for the following week, once we'd made final decisions on a course of treatment.

Nothing had been resolved as such but talking through the muddy mess that consumed my mind, without having to worry about the emotional impact it would have on the other person, was freeing. I felt brave, liberated and ready to make myself heard.

As I walked down to the hospital corridor, I couldn't help but take in the unsettling image of people lined up along the walls. Like lambs to slaughter.

As I neared the consultation office, I caught sight of him. The nervous twitch of his leg was a dead give-away. Not that I needed it. There were days I could honestly say I felt his presence before I laid eyes on him. My heart always felt calmer and my vision clearer when he was in the room. The world felt heavy with the weight of my decision, but he made it feel lighter. Until I remembered what I was about to do. How I was about to change his world.

He stared at the blank wall in front of him, his right leg jumping up and down to the rhythm of his heart-beat.

He spent his life on the positive side of calm as often as possible, but everyone has their moments of stress. For James, if his world got out of control it would manifest in physical form.

We measured it once, spent an hour measuring the speed of his tapping, which seemed to mirror his rising heart rate. It was as if his body itched to run, but an internal voice kept him rooted. A battle between fight and flight.

The tapping was quick today. Much quicker than I'd seen in a long time. I took the seat next to his and, without looking at him, placed my hand on his knee and tapped out a slightly slower heartbeat. Gradually his rhythm changed to meet mine, and as it did, he wrapped his hand in mine and knotted our fingers together.

I glanced up towards the clock again, and the slivers of gold tinsel were now gone. No remnants of sticky tape, celebration or joy left behind. Maybe I shouldn't have said anything – I almost missed having a silent cheerleader.

'About earlier . . .' His voice broke through my thoughts.

'Not now,' I replied, not looking at him but squeezing his hand in reply. 'We can talk about it after.'

'OK,' he said, his voice low, meek, dripping with worry.

I turned to him, and his eyes broke my heart. I loved

this man, with all my being, and I was about to break him.

'Why don't we go up to Devil's Dyke after. Get some fresh air, a drink maybe. Talk. Properly.'

Before he could reply, Dr Li joined us in the corridor.

'Stephanie, nice to see you again. Would you like to follow me?'

He showed us back into his office. A room that was becoming far too familiar for all the wrong reasons.

'Thanks for coming. Take a seat, both of you,' he said as he shuffled around the papers on his desk.

Thanks for coming? What a redundant sentence. Like we had any choice in the matter. Would there really be anyone who would be given this kind of news and not return to find a solution? I didn't *want* to be here. It wasn't a choice.

'Thank you, Dr Li.' James was being overly polite again.

I watched as he shook hands with the white-coated man and took a glass of water from him, smiling. My fight-or-flight was kicking in. I was ready to fight. The anger rose in my chest, ready to challenge anyone who might disagree with me.

Would they gang up on me when I announced my decision? I looked between the two men sat either side of the desk, my results the only thing between them, and wondered when my life had slipped into a universe where two men were discussing my fate.

'Did he just say "thank you for coming in"?' I mumbled to James as I lowered myself into the chair. I hoped Dr Li hadn't heard me, but as I turned in his direction, I saw the flicker of his eyebrow. I raised my voice a notch, enough to know that he definitely would hear me as I turned to look directly into my husband's eyes. 'It's not like we had a choice in the matter. A parasitic cluster of cells are trying to kill me and my baby. I couldn't very well sit at home, could I?' I finished as I shrugged. If Dr Li looked at me and only ever saw an angry woman who probably wouldn't make the most patient mother, I didn't care. I had to play the part of the angry woman to have the gravitas to fight these men alone; that was what I planned to do.

I turned my attention back to the doctor, crossing my arms and daring him to say anything, but he didn't take the bait.

Instead, he clicked his pen, the same bloody pen. He wasn't writing anything, but clickety-click, clickety-click. Clickety-fucking-click.

'Our baby,' James muttered. Just loud enough for the doctor to hear and more than loud enough to light the fuse.

'My child. My cancer. My body,' I shot back, looking deadpan into the eyes of the man who held my future in his hands rather than the man who once held my dreams.

'Ms Jackson, I can understand how you're feeling, and you have all the reason in the world to feel anxious. But I can assure you that we're here to help you *all* through this.'

I turned to look at my husband, my poisonous words written all over his face.

'Our child,' James said. 'My wife.' His voice rose. 'Our decision.'

That was the most assertive I had ever seen him. His face was stern, and his eyes tore holes in my resistance.

I wanted to hug him, to tell him I would fix this; I could do this. I would do this. I would fight and win. But that wasn't the part I was playing today.

'We can't keep going over this, James. I'm not going to change my mind. I have thought about it. I even spoke to Helen, and Dad, and Julie, and a support worker. This isn't a snap decision. There's nothing left to say.'

No one moved. I'm not sure any of us even took a breath.

'OK, Ms Jackson,' Dr Li started, but he didn't get far before my husband held up his hands to pause him in his tracks.

'How about,' James began, his palms clasped between his knees and tears pooling ready to fall, 'I don't want to lose my wife. How about, I have loved you since the moment we met, and I want to see a mini version of you running around our house, but not at the expense of losing the person I love.'

His words had started slow, but were gaining speed, like a horse cantering across the field desperately searching for freedom.

'Or, Stephanie, how about, we decided to have a baby together. To raise a family together. We talked about how we would bring up our babies together. We never once discussed how I would bring up a child as a single father. That wasn't in the plan.' His voice broke, each word cracked and splintered.

'How about, I don't want to raise a child alone. I'm not even sure I would want to be in this world without you, let alone raise a child alone that reminds me every day of what I've lost. Does any of that make you think twice? Have you even thought about how it would affect those you'd leave behind if you don't fight to save yourself?'

I reached out to take his hand, but he didn't release them from the vice grip between his knees, so I laid my hand on his leg, hoping he could feel my warmth.

'James, I know you think I'm doing this because I'm stubborn, and maybe I am, but I can't think about what might happen if this doesn't work. I don't have that luxury. I don't have the luxury of thinking of the future because I know I might not have one, and I have absolutely zero control. Think about it, what if I get the treatment and it doesn't work? Then what? Then you lose me anyway, and you lose the chance to have the child you always wanted. Is that better? Or, what if the treatment works . . . what if everything aligns and the treatment works, and we spend the rest of our life wondering "what if?" about trying to keep the baby. I can't live my life by what-ifs, James. So, I'm making a decision that I have control over. In what could be my last ever chance to have any control over my own life, I'm choosing.'

My words came at him like a freight train. I saw the realisation as it settled in his brain, I had given this more thought than he realised. His face now looked less angry and more mournful.

'Steph, I can't do any of this without you. I don't want to.'

I moved my hand, peeling his from his knees and locking our fingers together. I needed him to feel the quickening of my pulse as I said the words.

'I'm not sure I'll survive making any other decision, and I'm not sure *we* would survive if you made me make that decision.'

He dropped his head and the tears held back now fell freely, his shoulders shuddering with the outpouring of emotion.

'Why don't we start with talking about what your options are at this stage and how quickly we can proceed with treatment once we've decided?' Dr Li took control of the situation. For a moment I'd forgotten he was there. He flicked through the pages in front of him, each one filled with words, numbers and charts. None of them meaning anything to me, but every single one of them affecting my life sentence.

'Well, actually. We have, well, *I* have made *my* decision.'

James lifted his heavyset deep brown pools of disappointment and looked deep into my soul.

'I'm keeping *our* baby.'

Dr Li placed his pen on the desk with a final click. I jumped right back in before he had a chance to respond.

'Let's talk about what treatment can be done while I'm pregnant that will still keep the baby safe and how soon after the birth I'll need to start more aggressive treatment.'

My words came out strong and I gave myself a mental pat on the back. I was a woman who knew her own mind and I wouldn't be swayed.

'I'm not interested in statistics at this stage. I don't want to know how quickly you think this will kill me. I want to know how long you think you can keep my baby safe.'

With that, as if the mention of peanut was the last chip that split the dam, James put his head in his hands; let out a low, stifled scream.

I had broken him. Maybe even broken us. I'd made a decision that I knew deep down would surely destroy our marriage. But what other choice did I really have?

As the doctor talked numbers and treatments, I stared at the broken pieces of shell that made up my husband; the glinting of the wedding band tangled in his salt and pepper hair. I wondered what he must think of me. If one day, he might find it in his heart to forgive me.

I wanted to tell him that *he* was the reason I wasn't scared. He was the reason I was strong enough to make this decision. He would be the most amazing father and I trusted him to carry our dreams forward if I wasn't there to complete them.

He would need time to heal, but as long as I hadn't pushed him too far away from me, we'd have time to heal together before our child arrived. I had work to do, but I had enough strength to fight for both of us until he was ready.

# CHAPTER NINETEEN

We didn't talk as we left the hospital grounds. James followed me dutifully to the car, a beat behind me the whole way. We were out of step with each other for the first time in our relationship and it felt so strange.

As I pulled the car keys out of my bag, he slipped his hand into mine, but instead of a comforting squeeze, he took the keys from my fingers and pressed the button.

'I'll drive.'

His tone was so abrupt, his voice low and gruff with emotion. If it wasn't for the fact that I felt so completely numb, I would have argued with him, but my brain was still dissecting the information Dr Li had given us.

I slipped into the car, clicked my seatbelt and pulled a bunch of leaflets from my bag. As James started up the engine, I let out what genuinely felt like the first breath since I'd made my decision clear.

'Where did you get those?' James asked, motioning

to the pile of papers sat in my lap. I flicked through and picked out the one titled 'Cancer during pregnancy'.

'From the support worker at the Macmillan Centre before the appointment.'

He didn't respond.

'Her name was Sarah. She's lovely, actually. She just listened, didn't judge. It was nice to be able to talk.'

I was filling the space with words.

'She talked about the three categories of cancer.'

I paused. Waiting for him to respond or show interest.

It was hypocritical of me to expect him to talk about it only when I wanted him to, but I pushed anyway.

'Do you know them?'

'No. No I don't. But then it seems I don't know a lot about anything. I had no idea that while I was sat tearing my hair out, you were making a decision about our lives with a total stranger. Why wasn't I there? I would have appreciated speaking to someone too!'

His tone was curt, cutting into me like shards of glass.

'Because I wanted to know I was making a decision without being swayed by everyone else's emotions and expectations.'

'Fine, Stephanie. I'm not arguing about it anymore. Seems pointless now that it's a done deal. Would you like to explain to me what role I'm supposed to play? Seeing as you're the one calling the shots.' He tutted and tapped on the steering wheel as the traffic came to a slow crawl in front of us.

I tried to lighten my voice again. I wanted to move forward, in a constructive manner, if that was even possible. He was right, the deal was done. Time to start the hard fight.

'Right. I'll explain then. The three categories. It's generally used to describe prostate cancer, or cancer screenings, but the way she explained it really helped me understand.' I shifted in my seat, adjusted the belt across my stomach and looked at the side of his face while he concentrated on the traffic in front.

'Cancers, in general, fall into three categories. The rabbit, the bird and the turtle.'

I flicked through the pages of the brochure, not looking for anything in particular, just to steady my shaking hands.

'Turtles are the slow-growing cancers. They grow so slowly that often people with turtle cancers will die of a totally unrelated cause, unaware they ever had an underlying cancer.' I looked up and caught him biting and tugging at the skin on his lower lip. No response.

'The bird is the opposite side of the scale.' I took a deep breath, the air in my lungs not able to last a full sentence, weighed down by anticipation and fear. 'Once diagnosed with a bird, it's often already too late for treatment to have an impact. Once it's released, it flies free, spreads, can't be slowed down and is impossible to contain.'

That did it, he turned to look at me briefly as the traffic lights sat on red.

'The rabbit,' I added hurriedly before he jumped to conclusions, 'sits in that golden sweet spot between the two.' I nodded to the lights as they changed to green. 'The rabbit is quite content in its surroundings, but it has the potential to jump at any point. To any part of the body. It has the potential to reproduce quickly and in large numbers.'

I took a deep breath and prepared myself. 'The

problem with ovarian cancer is that it's a fluffy bunny rabbit.' I giggled at the absurdity that I was now imagining a cluster of cells as a cute white bunny with a fluffy tail. His expression stopped my giggling bunny dead in its tracks.

'As much as we now know it's there and can build a fence around it, even contain it for a while, we never know just how high or far it can jump. I have no idea if my fabulous little fluffy bunny will hitch a ride with a bird and become impossible to catch.'

I stopped talking, picking at the corner of the brochure.

'Then why on earth would you risk it, Steph?'

'You know why.'

'No, I don't. What's the point of us starting a family if half of that family unit could be gone before our child even takes its first steps?'

I didn't reply. He already knew my answer to that.

'I know that you think this means I don't want our baby as much as you do . . .' His words shocked me and I reached out quickly and put my hand on his on the steering wheel.

'I never said that. I know you want this baby,' I said.

'I have wanted every baby. I have loved them all, the moment they were conceived and even before. But I know that you think I love this one less because it could take you from me and so I've been quick to make the opposite decision. But I don't, Steph. I don't love it less.'

He was biting his lip again. Who was he trying to convince? Me or himself?

As we drove towards the South Downs, I looked out

the window and wondered how many rabbits were hiding in their warrens. How many were jumping around? How many of these strangers with their hiking boots and walking sticks were unaware that they were carrying around a turtle? How many had built a protective wall around their fluffy bunny . . . and were any of them aware that there may well be a bird making a nest in their chest, waiting to take flight and catch them unaware?

Fifty per cent. That's the statistic that sticks. One person out of every two in the UK will be touched or affected by cancer in their lifetime. We can't get away from that figure; it's plastered all over the TV adverts. We all know it; we just never think it will be us. We might like to think we're getting closer to curing cancer, but in fact, it seems to be multiplying. Too many birds and rabbits.

Funny really, so many of us believe the hand that points out of the screen each week telling us *It could be you* . . . who wins the lottery. Odds sit at close to one in forty-five million, yet each week we stare eagerly as the balls spin in the machine and believe it could be us. Why do we put such little stock in a warning with much higher odds? It's easier to believe the nice things in life, far easier to ignore the danger, I guess. Until it comes knocking on your door.

I scanned the hills and the car park in front of me. At least fifteen cars parked, two people per car at a guess, and at least another twenty roaming the hills beyond. Fifty strangers plus us. Twenty-five of those innocent lives would be touched by cancer at some point. Twenty-six if you counted me, of course.

If we really thought about it, would it change the way

we lived? If we knew we had a rabbit inside us, just waiting to jump, would we jump first? How many women, put in my position, would have made the decision I had?

'Fifty per cent,' I uttered.

'What?' James responded.

'Fifty per cent,' I repeated. 'Fifty per cent of us will be affected by or diagnosed with cancer in our lifetime. How do I protect my child in a world where one of these animals lives inside at least fifty per cent of us?'

James didn't respond. He just sighed as he turned into the pub car park at the top of the hill.

As I swung open the pub door, I was hit with a cacophony of familiar sights and smells. I couldn't suppress a smile as I immersed myself in the memories of a room that held such happiness for us. We had our first date here. I knew before I left here that night that James would be the man I would marry. He proposed to me on the brow of the hill opposite the bay window I sat at. We held our engagement party here. Would our marriage come to an end in the same place it all started?

'So,' I began, looking down at the orange juice he had gingerly placed in front of me.

James reached under the table and placed his briefcase carefully on the chair next to him, delicately, as if it contained a bomb about to explode. Then I saw it, the envelope sticking out the side.

Just as he was about to speak, I could hear the unmistakable sound of my dad's personal ringtone. I scrambled in my jacket pocket to retrieve the device.

'Hang on. It's Dad. I won't be a minute.'

James let out the air he was holding on to and a note of resignation passed over his face.

'Dad?'

The conversation was short and abrupt, and when I ended the call, I turned to my husband.

'Can this wait 'til later? Dad's really sick. He's spiked a fever and is too dizzy to leave the house. He desperately needs meds. Can we pop by and drop them off and then we can go home and talk properly?'

'Steph . . .' he let out in between exasperated sighs. 'You can't be serious!'

'Look, we have a lot to talk about; that much is obvious. Maybe, after such a tough day, we should see this as a sign not to get into a conversation that might be more hostile than it needs to be. We can talk about what happened earlier – about Amy, whatever – later.'

He took a large gulp from his glass, stood up and put his briefcase over his shoulder. The grenade pin replaced for a little while longer.

'Fine,' he said.

One word, a million emotions.

# CHAPTER TWENTY

This wasn't a normal virus. Dad looked pale and sweaty, yet his skin was burning; but it wasn't his temperature that was bothering me. It was him. The way he was holding himself. My father had never been someone who would let sickness dictate his life.

For years after Alex died, he would fight through every cold and headache. Sickness had infiltrated every crack in this house for years – you could feel it seeping out of the plaster on the walls – but one day he just decided enough was enough. He would say, *If your brother can battle this awful disease, then my body can fight off a stupid cold.*

We had built small rituals into our lives since I'd moved out. Our tea ritual was my favourite. He would exclaim that I made *the best cup of tea in the world*. Because obviously it was incredibly hard to stir a Yorkshire teabag in a pot of boiling water. I always made it the way my mother taught me. China cups, teapot, and milk jug on a tray.

I knew he never bothered with the pomp and ceremony when I wasn't around, because when I called round, I'd find a teabag staining the white porcelain sink and the teaspoon leaving a ring of tea on the countertop. He would laugh at me as I cleaned up his mess. He had remarked, wistfully and often, how much I reminded him of my mother. Bittersweet notes in each word.

I was the tea lady; he only ever made tea for me when *he* was sick. He would jump up from the sofa, hiding the tissues in the bin, and fuss around making a pot. Overcompensating, every single time. As if the steam rising from the spout would cloud the truth. It never did, but I humoured him anyway.

I could predict, almost down to the second, the roar of *Darling, where did you put the milk jug?*

It was a comforting ritual.

This time, he didn't get up when I walked in.

He was lying on the sofa, his head propped on the pillow precariously balanced on the arm, my mother's blanket pulled right up and tucked protectively under his chin. He looked so childlike, and pale and thin. When had he gotten so thin?

'Hey, pal, thanks for poppin' in. Can you stick the heating up for me?'

His voice was shaky and breathless, his words straining against the pain clutching at his body.

'Dad, you look terrible. I'll call a doctor.'

I rushed towards the mantelpiece and grabbed the cordless phone. I never used a landline at home; in fact, I wasn't even sure we had one. Dad's still sat next to the empty space where their wedding picture had been. Never replaced.

James stood in the doorway with a bag of generic cold meds from the supermarket.

'No, dear. Don't do that. Just stick the heating up and pour me a hot toddy. I'll be fine – a touch of the old Willy Whisky and I'll be right as rain again.'

My fingers hovered over the buttons; our GP surgery number was etched on the inside of my eyelids like a permanent tattoo.

'Dad, you're really sick. I can see you sweating from here.'

Replacing the phone, I wandered over to the French dresser at the side of the room. Avoiding the bottom drawer, where Dad hid all the photos of Mum, I opened the side cupboard and pulled out the medicine box. The one I had sat and labelled and compartmentalised a week before I moved in with James.

The paracetamol was gone, and the ibuprofen.

Dad hated taking pills. In the years since I'd left home, I'd never once replaced the paracetamol.

I slid the thermometer out of its protective casing.

'Dad.' I steadied the concern in my voice. 'Where are all the paracetamol and ibuprofen?'

I saw it, that flicker in his face. Always a dead give-away. He chewed the inside of his cheek. His tells were so blindingly obvious, not that I ever told him that. I'd never win against him at cards if I did.

'Oh, are there none left, pal? I took a couple yesterday for a headache. Stacy must have taken the rest. You know she is always having "lady issues".'

Stacy was a part-time cleaner I'd hired. I helped with the practical things but he was never the type to do the hoovering or mopping, and I just didn't have the time. Stacy came in twice a week to make sure the dust bunnies were kept at bay.

'She must have been taking them from you every time she came around. Didn't you ask her to replace them?'

I wasn't convinced that Stacy was the culprit, but my father was clearly too sick to have any kind of meaningful discussion. I wondered if he'd taken some then forgotten.

Was he forgetting things?

Maybe that's why he was getting thinner, maybe he was forgetting to eat too? I made a mental note to check the freezer.

'James, stick the kettle on, please. I'll pop through and make tea.'

Dad tried to employ his best puppy dog look. 'Oh . . . spoilsport. I really hoped you'd make me a hot toddy.'

'Not on cold meds, Dad. I'd like you to make it through the night!' I joked, a note of seriousness hidden beneath my smile.

A sadness crept across him as his jaw tightened.

I squeezed past James and pulled him by the cuff of his shirt into the kitchen.

'Something's not right. I think I need to stay here a few nights. I want to make sure he's eating. Have you seen how thin he is? And all those pills gone? If he's not better by the morning, I'll take him to A and E.'

James closed his eyes. I hated when he did that. I couldn't see his thoughts when he shut me off from them.

'Steph, I know he's not well, but we have to talk.' He looked at me, pleading, like a lost boy.

'This is more important. Our issues aren't going anywhere, but Dad is sick now.'

He stepped back from me and the lost boy transformed into an angry adult.

'*You* are sick now.' He raised his voice. His eyes squeezed together tightly. Even through the thickness of his glasses I could see the creasing of his eyelids and the whitening of his tightened skin.

I didn't say anything, just stared at him. Stunned by his aggression.

'You. *You* are sick.' He pointed at me, then at my belly. At our baby. 'And it *is* going somewhere. Every single moment that you stand here, it's spreading. Every moment you're breathing, all I can hear is the ticking of a time bomb. Yes, your dad has flu . . .' he paused, closed his eyes again then said, 'but *you* have CANCER.'

His chest rose and as he pulled his shoulders back, his five-nine frame doubled in size.

'You have cancer,' he shouted. 'You have fucking CANCER,' he screamed again. At no one and everyone. His body shook and his face reddened. Gone was the calm and sympathetic man I loved.

With his hands over his face, he spoke through the confines of his spread fingers. 'I'm sick and tired of pretending this is OK. I'm sick of you thinking only about yourself and not how this is affecting *all* of us.' He dropped his hands and grabbed my shoulders. 'I'm sick of you burying your head in the sand. You're ill. Your dad has the flu and you have CANCER.'

I broke away from him but found myself rooted to the spot; stuck in the concrete he was pouring around me.

'You're dying. He has man flu. YOU ARE DYING, Stephanie, and you won't do a damn thing about it.'

He fell to the floor, as if his outburst had used up all the air he had ever consumed. Like an empty discarded balloon, he was spent.

'This is ridiculous, and I can't take it anymore. What you're doing is reckless and selfish and I can't take it anymore.'

With a sudden surge of defiance, I pulled him up from the floor and stood an inch from him, my eyes as close to his as I could get without losing focus. 'Selfish. How fucking dare you,' I hissed at him, determined not to let my father hear me.

He slid away from me, back through the kitchen door, along the wall and towards the front door. I followed him like an angry terrier nipping at his heels.

'How dare you tell me how I'm supposed to feel and what I'm supposed to do.' I took my shot at his back, challenging him to face me.

'Oh, take your bra off and burn it while you're at it, why don't you,' he uttered as he slid his feet back into his loafers at the bottom of the stairs. 'This isn't about me, or anyone else, trying to take ownership of your body. This isn't me trying to make you have an abortion because the condom broke, or we forgot to take the pill.'

He looked back at me, paused, took a breath and calmly spoke the words I had almost pushed him to the very edge of saying.

'This is me TELLING you to have an abortion so we can fight this thing and you can LIVE to try again.'

'You insensitive arsehole.' I shoved him. Hard. In the chest. Clearly caught off-guard, he stumbled back into the front door. 'You think this is about me being feminist? You think this is about me deciding you don't have a choice? You're the most delusional child I've ever met.'

My anger had nowhere else to go. Tears burned tracks of pain down my cheeks, like lava melting my eyelashes. I no longer had control of my emotions.

'I'm being selfish because this is happening to *me*. I'm being selfish because it's *my* body that will have to go through the pain. Because it's *my* mind that will have to come to terms with the loss, because it's *my* life and the life of a child that I'm carrying inside of *my body* that is at risk. When it's *your* body and your life you get a say. This is *not* your decision.'

All the words said between me and Helen were screaming at the back of my mind, each of them wanting to leap forward and take back my rash words. Each one wanting to jump at my husband and scream 'she doesn't mean it', but they were being held back. Fear and anger are fierce competitors and they were winning the war.

The silence said more than any of the words we'd hurled at each other.

'If you don't come home tonight . . .' he started, his voice now low and controlled. He had remembered himself. Calm restored. 'If we can't sit down and talk this through rationally,' he continued, 'if you can't listen and understand my point of view, then I don't know what the hell I'm doing here. I don't know why we're married if we're choosing not to make these life-changing decisions together.'

The canvas of our lives was ripping. I could feel the stitches straining and hear the fabric tearing. I couldn't hold on; I wasn't sure what to hold on to.

'I'm not coming home, James. My dad is sick and needs me right now.'

'Stephanie, *you* are sick and need *me* right now.'

I tried not to say it. I knew it would be the end. I knew that if I said it, I couldn't take it back.

'No. No, James. I don't think I do.'

His jaw fell slack. 'Fine.' The word seemed to be less said than breathed. 'You win. I can't do this. I can't stand around and watch you kill yourself.'

I had steered him to the edge of the cliff and there was nowhere else to go but jump or be pushed. He passed me the bag of medication, the plastic handles now wet from the sweat of his balled-up fists. He opened the front door, walked through it and left me stood there as he disappeared from view.

I turned to find my father behind me, wrapped tightly in a blanket and staring, eyes wet with tears, at the closed door. Not looking at me, but past me, through me. He seemed as shocked as I was.

'He didn't say I love you,' I said, feeling more bereft by the words left unsaid than pained at the ones we'd shared.

'He does. You know he does,' said my dad as he wrapped me in his embrace.

'I pushed him too far,' I confessed against his heart.

'Shhhhh,' he whispered, his arms tightening around me. We sat on the bottom stair and I clung to him like a baby koala and begged for his hug to be strong enough to stick all my broken and damaged pieces back together.

After a while, I wasn't sure if the wet patches I could feel on his chest were from my tears, or the sweat from his overheating body.

'Dad, you're really sick. Come on, let's get you into the living room,' I said as I wiped the tears from my face.

Just like that, the world righted itself.

I shook off the pain and fear and kicked into motherly mode. I tucked him up in the blanket and switched the TV from the gruesome daily news to *Cash in the Attic*.

As I walked back into the kitchen to mix up a flu remedy, I gave myself a stern talking-to. If James wasn't strong enough to help me battle this, if he wouldn't support me while I saved our child, I would do it on my own.

Tomorrow. Not today. Tomorrow I would fight. Tonight, I was already a mother to my father, and I had a job to do.

# CHAPTER TWENTY-ONE

I woke before the sun rose from its cosy blanket. As the room slowly lit, rays hit the edges of my childhood desk. Dust danced in the air above the split and marked wood where memories were etched in every dent. My workspace was littered with folders and books still stuffed with notes taken during my university years, a small cheap snapshot of Helen and me eating chips on the pier like tourists before our final exams sat snug against the mirror. A red ribbon hung above it; the same one James had tied our first house key to the day he asked me to move in with him.

I hadn't been ready to leave my father alone and it had all moved so quickly with James. He anticipated my fear that day and bought a ribbon to hang the key until I made my mind up. At first, the weight of it was like a symbol of how heavy the decision was, but after wearing it around university that day, when I took it off and hung it on my mirror that night, the absence of it, of him, made me wonder if I could ever live without him around me. I had turned up the next day to meet him with a suitcase in my hand.

My hand drifted to my belly, the smallest bump the biggest reminder that I'd been naïve to think I could escape him. He was everywhere, and like the weight of that first key, this weight was just as symbolic. I would be lost without it, empty. But I would be lost without him too. I missed him.

I pulled back the duvet and winced as the cold bare wood cooled the pads of my feet. James and I had decided on plush carpets for our first home. I'd insisted on it. My mother had pulled up the carpets in our bedrooms when we were young. It was easier to keep them clean when Alex was sick so often. I wasn't sure if the goose bumps spreading over my skin were to do with the cold or the memories, but neither felt pleasant.

The wooden floor creaked below me as I tiptoed to the bedroom window. I stared out into the garden and watched as the golden light shone a spotlight on all my dad's hard work.

It used to be so well tended. He could never find the milk jug, was useless at paying bills and couldn't cook a roast dinner for love nor money but give him a hoe and a spade and he could breathe life into any patch of green; but his normally manicured grass looked more rugged than radiant.

His prize-winning delphiniums stood proud against the back wall, lined up like soldiers. Dad planted them for Alex when he was sick. He called them 'his protectors', standing guard at the end of the house to make sure he was safe. They were the only part of the garden that remained proud even as they fought nature's desire to start the decaying process. The rest of his garden was losing its zest for life. I had never seen it this bad, ever.

I dressed quietly and paused before turning the door handle, running my fingers down the bumps and undulations of paint that created the massive dragon on the back of my bedroom door. The tail snaked its way up the white gloss finish, each scale a mark of my height growing up.

We'd shared this room as children. We'd shared our dragon friend too, from tail to tip of the wings, from where only my markings continued.

I wondered how tall my own baby would be. Wondered if my father would paint the same dragon on my child's wall. Maybe the two men I loved would paint it together, bond as father and grandfather, if I hadn't pushed James away for good. I could sit in the rocking chair and take pictures of their progress as they laughed and chatted about how their lives would change.

I crept past my dad's room, the door still open a crack from when I checked on him. He was sleeping, out like a light, his chest rising and falling heavily with the duvet straining against the fight with gravity.

The dangling red ribbon on my mirror played on my mind. The emptiness I felt was growing. I needed to go home. I needed to see James, explain, apologise.

It was a Saturday morning and without me there to drag him to yet another antique shop, he was likely to be tucked up warm in our bed.

I began plotting my monologue. Helen's words echoed in my mind *It's not what he's said, hon. It's what he's not saying.* There were too many words between us that had not been said. The angry ones had pushed past the fear first. We were both holding on to words unsaid, and maybe the words left unsaid would be the ones to save us.

He had taken my car when he left, which I had forgotten of course as I searched my dad's house silently for keys that didn't exist.

As the taxi pulled up in front of our home, something didn't feel right. The taxi driver coughed and repeated the price, eager to have me vacate his space.

'Sorry. A million miles away,' I apologised as I handed him a bundle of coins.

I walked slowly up the driveway. Something was wrong. His car was missing. The sun was barely warming the world and he was never up and out early unless I dragged him out by the earlobes.

I pushed the front door, still half expecting to see his shoes at the foot of the stairs and his keys hanging on the hook. But the stairs and the hook were both empty.

'James? James, are you here?'

I don't know why I shouted for him. Like some kind of horror movie scene when you know full well you would never shout up the stairs to find a person you know fine well is not in the house.

He never went anywhere at the weekend without me.

Hanging my jacket up, I noticed that not only was his jacket gone, but his waterproofs too.

I took the stairs two at a time, noticing that my breathing was not so easy today and the pains in my stomach were back. I gripped on to the ball at the top of the banister and spun around it.

I threw open the bedroom door and was confronted with the crisply made bed.

He never made the bed. He hated the extra throw pillows and the order I demanded they were placed in but each jacquard print sat precisely where I'd placed them before I left for the hospital yesterday. The wardrobe doors were open and bald hangers swung in the breeze created by my abrupt entrance. Pulling open the top drawer my fears were confirmed. All his underwear was gone, so was the suitcase from the top of the wardrobe.

He was gone. All of him. Gone.

I hurtled towards the bathroom, just reaching the sink before the relief of letting go.

Splashing water on my face and washing away the bitter taste from my tongue, I looked up through wet eyelashes to find a folded piece of paper propped up against my little dragon friend.

*Steph,*

*I need some time. I've taken some time off work and I'll be staying at Steve and Julie's.*

*I can't wrap my head around all of this. You have it figured out in your own head, but I can't think straight.*

*I'll be back in a few days.*

*J x*

I'd pushed him too far and I knew it, but I never imagined he would disappear like this without telling me. He hadn't called, or texted. He had just Dear John'd me and left. At the very moment he should be standing strong by my side and supporting me, he'd gone off to lick his wounds. I didn't know if I felt more angry or terrified. Had I put a nail in the coffin of our marriage?

I read the words over and over again, the letters swimming in front of my eyes, but none of them held their meaning anymore.

My anger rose, heat from my palms burning the paper, wetting the page with my frustration. If he couldn't cope, if we couldn't stick together now, I would have to do it alone. I would if I had to, if I had no choice. But I didn't want to. I wanted him to fight for us, for our baby.

I drifted back downstairs and retrieved my phone, typing out a text message to the only person who would understand.

*James is gone. I stayed at Dad's last night, got home and he's gone. Left a letter to say he needed some 'space'.*

I hit send and watched as the message delivered to Helen's phone. I waited, but nothing. What could she say? There was nothing to say.

I scrolled back through my contacts and found the number for the Macmillan nurse – Sarah.

*I think I could do with another chat. Would you be free later today? Stephanie*

As I hit send, a reply came through from Helen.

*Where? Are you sure? Did you fight? I tried to call him, but his phone is switched off.*

I put aside my anger at her getting in touch with him

first and considered the question. Did we fight? Yes. I pushed him. I pushed us too far, right over the cliff and into this space of not knowing, but I wasn't ready to tell her that yet.

I tried to call him, but it clicked straight to answer machine. I hit call again. No luck. Still voicemail. I opened my messages, the last from him still visible, telling me he loved me and would see me at the hospital. Before the doctor broke us in two. Before I broke us.

As I stared at the screen trying to compose a message in my head, it vibrated and caught me off-guard. A picture of my dad's face lit up the screen, his smile so vibrant, his face fuller, healthier, happier.

'Dad?' I asked, before he could say anything on the other end.

'No. It's me. Stacy. Your dad. He's— Um, Stephanie, the ambulance is here.'

It took a moment for me to recognise the voice at first, and a second longer than that for me to process the words.

'What? Stacy? Why? What's going on?'

I collected my things from the heap on the floor, grabbed the keys to the other car and prayed the beaten-up heap we rarely used would still run, or at least get me to the hospital before breaking down.

With my ear stuck to the phone, I listened as Stacy explained how she'd arrived to do the cleaning to find my dad at the bottom of the stairs. He was being rushed to hospital.

In the background, I could hear the paramedics working on him. I turned the key in the ignition and thanked God as the engine roared into life. I was sure I heard them ask if he was on any medication, then

Stacy answering that yes, he was and that it was all in the box in the bottom drawer. I slammed on the brakes before I even left the drive and shouted down the phone.

'Stacy, did you tell them he's taking meds? What for?'

The line went quiet as I heard what I assumed was the slamming of ambulance doors.

'I'm going with him, Stephanie. I'll meet you there.'

Then the line went dead.

The drive to the hospital was excruciating. Traffic along the coast road was impossible and I was paranoid that at any moment, some jobsworth police officer would pull me over for dangerous driving. I didn't care. I needed to get to Dad. The pains in my stomach were back again, but I couldn't focus on anything other than the road and getting us both to the hospital in one piece.

'Hold tight, little peanut. This might be a bumpy ride.'

# CHAPTER TWENTY-TWO

When I arrived at the hospital, Stacy was inconsolable. She was trying to explain to the doctor that she really didn't know anything, that she only cleaned for us once or twice a week. She only knew he was taking *them* because she'd tidied them away last week when she'd popped in and found him asleep on the couch.

As I neared them, the doctor was pulled away by a woman in blue scrubs and given a folder of notes.

'OK, great, thanks. It's fine, thank you. I have his notes now. Take a seat, I'll take it from here,' he said as he tried to turn his back and walk through the heavy double doors.

'WAIT. That's my dad,' I shouted as I rushed towards him. 'Someone tell me what's going on!'

'I'm sorry, you are?' he asked as I reached him.

'Stephanie. I'm his daughter. What's going on?'

The doctor turned and gave some medical instructions to a colleague before returning his attention to me.

'It seems your father may have developed pneumonia. It's a common side effect when the immune system is compromised. The chemo will have lowered his defences. We need to try and get the fluid off his lungs and stabilise his breathing.'

I waved my hands in front of him, trying to get him to stop talking. 'Wait. Wait. He's not having chemo. I have cancer; he doesn't have cancer. Have you got the notes mixed up?'

'I'm sorry? No. Were you aware your father was on medication?' He flicked through the notes in his hand, the file thick with pieces of paper filled with charts and numbers, words and scrawled doctors' notes.

'No. He hates even taking a paracetamol. He only took the cold meds last night when I forced him to. Are you sure you haven't made a mistake?'

Stacy held a box in her hands, looking sheepish.

'I think you need to speak to your dad. Right now, I need to get him stabilised. I'll come and let you know as soon as you can see him.'

The doctor turned and walked away, not realising he'd left me stood with a million questions and no answers.

I looked towards Stacy, her face as white and fragile as fine-bone china. We both took a seat in the waiting room and I felt another twinge of pain as I reached towards her to take the box.

'Can I have that, please? I've never seen this before.' I felt like I was opening Pandora's box.

Stacy left soon after that. I sat for hours waiting to be told any news. When I was finally taken to see him, he was settled on a ward, fast asleep and surrounded by starched white sheets and beeping machines. He'd been wrapped up soundly in my mother's blanket only hours ago, sleeping peacefully. Now he was hooked up to monitors and nothing in my world made sense.

His secret sat in my lap. A small wooden box with an ornate carved lid. I'd never seen it before. But then why would I? I hadn't been in that bottom drawer since the day he'd filled it with envelopes stuffed with photos of her. I rolled my fingers over the little pill packets with odd-sounding names scribed on them, my father's name and date of birth printed on the labels.

The doctor hadn't explained anything. He said I should wait until Dad was awake and speak with him first.

I sat and listened to the beeping of the heart-rate monitor, staring at the dripping of fluids as they travelled down a tube and disappeared under his paper-thin skin. Skin that only a few days ago looked white or grey, but today, under these harsh lights, seemed to be glowing yellow or pale orange.

The dripping of the fluid in the bag gave me something to focus on. I counted every single drop. Three hundred and twenty-six droplets before my father stirred.

'Dad. Dad . . . it's me. Are you OK? Dad, you're in hospital.' I stroked his temples and pushed his hair away from his forehead.

'Water. Grab me some water, pal,' he mumbled.

I took a jug from the table, poured a cup and carefully helped him sip the liquid. His lips were cracked and white with sores on the inside that I hadn't noticed before.

'Dad. You have cancer.'

I saw his eyes flicker as the thought crossed his mind to lie to me. He stopped sipping and stared at me.

'Snap,' he finally replied.

And with that, the straw fell on the camel's back and shattered it. Tears rolled down my cheeks and I lowered my head onto Dad's chest.

'Why the hell didn't you tell me? How long did you think you could keep this secret?'

I pulled the chair closer to the bed and took his hand in mine.

'Oh, Stephanie, sweetheart, you have enough on your plate. There's nothing they can do for me, what was the point in worrying you when you have your own health to worry about.'

I carefully stroked his wrist, trying to avoid the wires. 'Tell me everything, Dad.'

He took a deep breath, and instead of looking at me, he stared at the wall and recited all the details he'd been given only a few weeks before.

It was stage four. He had gone to the doctor's last month when he'd noticed stomach pains and bloating but had no appetite. Tests confirmed pancreatic cancer. It had spread to his liver and lungs now and any treatment was palliative. His liver was shutting down, which is why he looked jaundiced. His lungs were affected now too, which explained the pneumonia.

'Why didn't you tell me? I would have brought you straight to the hospital last night.'

I was angry that he'd kept all this from me. That I hadn't noticed. That I'd ignored the obvious signs and allowed myself to get distracted from taking care of him.

'Because, my darling girl, you needed looking after last night. Don't think for a moment I haven't noticed just how little you let anyone help you.' He patted my hand

and smiled that sympathetic, knowing smile that only fathers can give you. 'You're going through the hardest time of your life, and I know that more than most. I wanted to sit on that floor with you and hold you. I wanted to be the parent in this relationship for once.'

His words wounded me. Had he simply been letting me play that role?

'But, Dad. We could have helped. I could have helped.'

'My beautiful girl, listen to me. I watched your brother fight leukaemia until every single cell in his body had given everything it had and more. I watched and could do nothing but hold him as he hurt.'

It seemed cruel that he had to say these words, least of all a day after the anniversary.

'I am a father. That's my job. It's my job to be there to wipe away the tears and make you feel safe in this scary world. You need me to be a dad; you don't need to help me fight my battle. I need to help you fight yours. I just thought I had more time.'

The world spun, and I couldn't feel the floor.

'They can't do anything for me now, pal, but I can be here to help you. You need to listen to me, and you need to truly hear the words I'm saying.'

He shifted in the hospital bed. But his skin seemed to ripple and sag from his bones as he tried to sit tall.

'This nasty disease took everything away from me. It took my son, it took my wife, my marriage, my hopes and dreams. It stripped everything away from everyone in my life and left my whole family changed. And I did nothing to stop it.'

I tried to cut him off, but he raised a hand to silence me.

'It stripped me of everything I had, and I let it. I didn't fight for my family. I didn't fight to keep us together. I let it change you. I allowed you to take over the role your mum left behind and the shell of a man that grief left behind was too weak to fight.'

I watched as the man I had loved since my very first breath crumbled in front of me. This strong giant who had stayed silent all these years was pouring out his every thought onto the overly starched sheets between us and for the first time in my life I had no idea where to place myself.

'Dad.'

He patted my hand. 'Stephanie. I've had time to think about this and you need to let me get it out.' He took my hands in his and squeezed. 'Don't make the same mistake I did, Steph love. Don't push away the only person in this world who can help you fight this, because you'll only spend the rest of your life surrounded by the ghosts of the bad decisions you've made.' He looked wistful and I didn't like the tone of his voice. He sounded defeated.

'You didn't make bad decisions, Dad; you did what you could. She didn't. She left. You're still here.' I was furious that he still seemed to carry the guilt of her abandonment on his shoulders.

'Stephanie, sweetheart, she left because I couldn't live. She left because I couldn't face any of it. Because I wouldn't help her. Because I couldn't let her help me. By the time your mum packed her bags, I'd already checked out. That's why I was so upset. Not because she'd left, but because I didn't stop her when I had the chance. I didn't fight for her. She was hurting too – for her son.'

He stopped talking, but the look in his eyes said it all and I knew exactly what was coming next.

'It's James's child too. And you're his wife. He's terrified, Stephanie. Trust me, I know how that feels. He's utterly terrified and angry and confused, and you're pushing him away to protect yourself, the very same way I did. If you do that, you'll end up alone, my baby girl. Just like me.'

'You're not alone, Dad. You have me. You've always had me.'

'Oh, sweet girl, I know that. And you've been the best and most important decision I ever made in my life. But I made that decision with a woman I truly loved. I made you, with the most perfect woman in the world. I made a life with her, two children and a home. And I threw it all away because I didn't know how to support her. Because I couldn't see her pain. Don't do the same thing I did.'

A nurse walked in, disrupting the flow of conversation. She seemed oblivious to the gaping hole appearing in the floor beneath us as she fussed with cables and readings. We of course sat there, typically British, pausing our drama for the politeness of small talk and chitchat.

The nurse asked Dad how bad the pain in his stomach was.

'Ah, not that bad, love. I can cope,' he replied, but the nurse wasn't having any of it.

'Now, if we're going to be friends, we need to build a net of trust between us. I can't help you if you don't tell me the truth.'

I didn't want them to be friends. I didn't want him to be in here long enough to know any of their names.

I wanted him home and well and for everything to go back to normal.

'Well, if you insist. I'm about a seven today. I think the coughing made it worse,' Dad explained.

'OK, I'll speak to the doctor and see what pain meds we can get you on to make you more comfortable. Do you still feel nauseous?'

'A little, yes. But I am sat in a hospital surrounded by sick people, so I could be feeling sick by proxy.'

Had he been feeling this level of pain the whole time and not told me? I felt like a failure. I dropped my head into my hands as I tried to work out when everything started to fall apart.

I heard them chuckling together and looked up, determined to focus on him rather than my own worries. I marvelled at how my dad still managed to see the light in these situations. He'd been the same when Alex was sick. Always smiling and trying to keep everyone happy. Maybe that's what he meant. He'd buried his true feelings for so long he was never able to tell Mum what he thought or how he felt. Did cancer really sever the connection between them? Would it wreak more havoc in my own marriage? How had all of this gone on under my nose without me seeing it? I was so sure that I knew everything about the men I loved, but as I looked at my dad, I wondered what other secrets he was keeping. My mind wandered to James and the secrets I'd not yet confronted with him. The ones we were both running away from.

The nurse chatted away to Dad, asking him a tonne of technical questions. How the chemo was going. What side effects he'd been having. While he was distracted, I took out my phone and tapped a quick message.

*Dad's in hospital. It's serious.*

I paused, hovering over the send button. I wanted to tell him I was scared. Tell him it was cancer, that I needed him, but I couldn't bring myself to type the words. I deleted the message and retyped.

*Please call me, James. Dad's in hospital and it's serious.*

I hit send. No kisses, no *I miss you*. I needed to find a way to tell him. My dad was as much of a father figure to James as me. He'd lived so long without parents in his life that Dad had taken him under his wing and helped fill that hole.

I stared at the screen, only one tick, grey. It hadn't even delivered to his phone.

'Hey, Dad, I'm going to pop to the cafeteria and grab a coffee. You interrupted my morning routine. I'm surprised I haven't turned into a grizzly bear yet!'

I tried to make light of the situation, inject some humour.

'Caffeine isn't good for the baby.'

No humour, his fatherly tone fully engaged.

'You know what, Dad? It's one coffee. I don't think one coffee is going to change anything. Today, I'm gonna drink a single cup of strong coffee, because life isn't fair at the best of times, and my dad and I both have cancer at the same time. I'm pretty sure I can survive one Americano, I'll go back to decaf tomorrow.'

Small acts of rebellion. That was how we would get through this. Minute acts of rebellion to challenge this shitty, unfair world. I had been the good girl for far too long and look where it had left me. No mother, no brother, a dying father, a parasite trying to kill both me and my baby and a marriage on the way to the gallows. One sodding coffee was not going to change anything.

I left the room in search of liquid resilience, and as I did, my phone buzzed. My heart jumped and I prayed it was James.

*I'm around later today in the clinic if you want to stop by. Sarah*

I'd forgotten I'd even messaged the Macmillan nurse.

*Seems it's not just my illness I need to think of now. My dad is in hospital, pneumonia complications thanks to stage-four pancreatic cancer. I didn't know. I'll be here until he's released. I'll get in touch when things settle down.*

I wasn't in the mood to talk now. I wasn't even sure what I would say to her. Everything felt so jumbled.

*Let me know what ward you're on and I'll pop and see you both. Stay strong, remember you're not alone. Sarah*

I replied with the ward number. I'd need a coffee before seeing her again. My emotions were all over the place and I needed to prepare myself.

I refreshed my messages but there was still only a solitary grey tick next to James's message.

Apparently, I *was* alone. I would need to get used to that.

# CHAPTER TWENTY-THREE

I paused at the door as I left his room, terrified that each time I walked away from him might be the last. I had spoken to the doctor while he was sleeping. There was nothing they could do, and quite frankly they were surprised he'd lasted this long without being hospitalised. He was declining rapidly, his organs were shutting down and his body was finding it harder to fight off infections. I couldn't get my head around it.

My mind wandered back through the memories of the last few weeks. How long had he known that all these small moments were the last for us? Had he known when he took that spoonful of my apple pie or when he kissed Alex's headstone goodbye? He knew he was sick, and these were all 'lasts' for him, but they weren't for me. I wasn't prepared. I would have cherished them more. Taken more pictures, said more words, made more memories. I would have appreciated the small things.

I was so angry with him. Those stolen glances, the extra hugs, the small hand squeezes; they all made more sense. I was furious that he didn't once think to tell me. Warn me. I was so angry with him, but I wasn't allowed to be. Because he was dying. I wasn't allowed to be frustrated with his deceit because he did it for me. But he would never understand that he stole the chance for me to make those final memories with him.

Now, I would forever remember that the last night I spent at home with him was only because I was being petulant and hiding from my own fears. I didn't stay because I was worried about Dad; I stayed because I didn't want to face my own life. If I'd known, we could have curled up and watched one more Bond movie together. What if this was it? What if we never got one more movie night? I wasn't ready for any of this.

I wanted one more game night, enjoying an expensive bottle of brandy while watching the fairies spark and dance in the fireplace. If only he'd told me.

My body was on autopilot as I walked down the corridor. Before I realised how far I'd gone, I found myself at the door to the chapel.

It had been years since I'd stepped foot inside a church.

I fiddled with the chain around my neck but resisted the urge to stroke the etching.

My fingers hovered over the door handle. I could feel a buzzing vibration under my fingertips; the room itself seemed charged.

My heart thumped against my rib cage, but I couldn't push the doors open. I wasn't ready to face that final hurdle. Talking to Him felt like defeat. It felt like begging, and what good would that do? He didn't listen when I begged for Alex's life, and He didn't listen when I screamed on the doorstep of our house the day Mum left. What good would crying at his feet do?

I lowered my hand and fished around in my bag to retrieve my mobile.

One solitary grey tick taunted me from the phone screen, mocking my pain and desperation. He hadn't even read the message.

I continued towards the canteen. The pain behind my eyes was worsening and I knew I'd soon be in the clutches of another migraine. I needed to try and stave it off long enough to get through this, for Dad.

In the canteen, I spun the empty coffee cup in circles on the saucer and stared at the intricate patterns the bitter substance marked on the cheap porcelain. Small grains of sugar glistened at the bottom of the cup, a whispered promise of sweetness in a cruel world.

I zoomed in on the sugar granules, the hospital logo marked on the table just out of shot.

*Trying to find the sweetness at the bottom of the darkness . . . #thesmallmoments*

Within a few seconds I was already getting likes on my Instagram page. One comment, from Helen.

*Hope you're OK, darling girl. Call me if you need me.*

I opened up a new message window.

*I'm at the hospital. Not me, don't worry – it's Dad. Pneumonia (brought on by terminal pancreatic cancer). Doctor says he doesn't have long. Still no sign of James. If you hear from him, tell him to get here as quick as he can.*

I watched as the rotating dots appeared and disappeared again in quick succession.

*Steph, I'm so sorry. I'll swing by once my shift is over. Let me know what ward you're on. I'll try James again.*

I replied with the details and felt almost immediately lighter. Helen offered no platitudes. No 'it'll be OK – he'll make it'. She knew I was not good at being pandered to.

As I made my way back to my father's room, the world around me felt less in focus and I stumbled over a child who was running full tilt down the corridor towards me. He looked up at me and laughed. I smiled back and helped him to his feet as his frazzled mother arrived by my side. She thanked me and took his hand, her other palm resting softly on a large bump. My heart hurt. I would likely never feel that – one child in my arms and another on its way.

As I waved the cheeky young chap goodbye, I noticed a familiar figure over his shoulder in the distance. I only caught a glimpse from the back, but she wore a long skirt and sandals, greying hair swept up high on her head in a messy bun, the same as the woman in the graveyard. I didn't see her face, but there was something about the way she walked.

Before I could shout after her, she disappeared, and I found myself at the door to my father's room. Through the window I could see tears on his cheeks. His tired eyes were closed, and his body heavy against the sheets. A breathing mask covered his mouth and nose and his monitors beeped as the nurse by his side checked his vitals and wrote notes on his chart.

The whole scene unfolding in front of me felt so surreal. It made no sense that this strong, healthy man, who had always been my confidant, was fading away. It made no sense that this man, who had rolled down hills with me as a child, run around the park chasing butterflies and endured more than his fair share of hangovers with me, was suddenly being taken from me. Would this world even feel real without him in it? What was it in our cells that decided today would be the day? When did our bodies determine that they'd had enough?

It struck me, in that moment, that my body was doing exactly the same. For the last twenty-four hours, I hadn't once attributed the C-word to myself. I was slowly but painfully coming to terms with its attachment to my dad, but hadn't yet fully come to terms with it being attached to me.

As I stared at my father, in the bed hooked up to monitors, I wondered how long my body would give me before it chose the same fate, and just how much control I really had.

I wanted my family first. I wanted my life, my loves and my passions. I wanted more sunsets and all the birthday parties. I wanted the terrible twos and the toddler tantrums. I wanted the sick days with a duvet on the sofa and the explorations in the forests. I was risking never doing that bear hunt.

Were they all right? Had I not been seeing things clearly after all? If I did what they were asking, I might never be able to have my own child, but if I didn't, I put myself at risk of repeating the scenes unfolding with my father.

This shouldn't be a choice anyone ever had to make. Ever. How did they expect anyone to ever make that decision? I was starting to hear it all. All those worries they had for me, the ones I'd so easily dismissed. I had them all now, those fears, for my dad. It seemed like the cruellest way for the universe to prove a point, point out a lesson I was stubbornly trying to ignore.

I was crying again, sobbing. All I seemed to do these days was cry. A strong smell of chemicals and antibacterial hand gel overwhelmed me, and just like a switch being flicked, the smells burst open the door in my head that let the migraine through. It smacked me in the face like a baseball bat and my knees gave way.

The arms of a kind nurse rescued me from the floor and guided me towards a chair at the side of the room.

'I'm sorry, I have the most terrible migraine. I suffer from them . . . but today . . . with all this . . . it's really bad,' I tried to explain as she checked my pulse.

'I can get you something for that if you like?'

Her voice was soft and caring. Full of love and kindness. Her long dark hair was plaited carefully and thrown over her shoulder like a Disney princess. Her Scottish accent made her cadence almost angelic, and my migraine was causing auras around her head, colours and distortions fogging my vision and creating a halo around her. I searched the girl's chest for a name badge.

'Jenny. Thanks. But I'm pregnant. I'm not sure what I can take. I'm seventeen weeks.'

'Right. Congratulations. Migraines in pregnancy are quite common actually; it's the hormones, you see. Why don't I get you a cold compress and a paracetamol?'

She turned away and grabbed a blanket from the bottom of the bed and placed it over my knees.

'You stay here, keep your eyes closed,' she said as she stood and pulled the curtains in the room closed. 'I'll grab you a glass of water and a cold pack for the back of your neck.'

'Um. I have cancer too,' I blurted out.

I'm not sure what made me say it, and by the look on the girl's face, it wasn't the response she'd expected either. Her doe-like brown eyes filled with tears.

'I'm so sorry.'

She came back over and bent down next to the chair, talking to me as if I were a child who had lost her favourite toy.

'Let's tackle one thing at a time, shall we? I'll get you a cold press. Your dad is stable for now, so why don't you sit back here and try to nap while he's asleep. I'll wake you if there are any changes. Back in a wee minute, OK? Do you need another blanket?'

In this cruel and painful world, with all the sickness that surrounded me, it lifted my heart that this striking young girl with the heart of a saint and the face of a model had chosen to dedicate herself to saving the lives of others.

'Thank you, Jenny. For everything. For my father too.'

Each word that formed on my tongue hurt more as I breathed them into life.

'Don't be silly.' She smiled. 'It's my job. Anyway, your dad's lovely. Patients like him break my heart and give me hope at the same time.'

I put my head back against the cold headrest and closed my eyes as the nurse left the room, flicking the main lights as she softly closed the door. The only sounds I could hear were the beeping of the machines and my dad's rhythmic breathing.

I had spent weeks obsessed with the idea of my baby. I'd been putting my little nugget first, refusing to see that James would have to watch me go through all of this. Seeing the consequences, touching them, smelling them and tasting them. It changed all the shapes of the picture I'd painted of my own story. The bravado was slinking away from me and I wondered if I'd been wrong all along.

With the pain striking axe-like blows inside my head, I squeezed at my temples and tried to focus on the white noise around me. As I did, I swore I could feel the smallest of pressures on my shoulder. A warmth radiating through my skin. Comfort. I hoped it was Alex. Here with us at the end. Here to help me, and to help Dad.

# CHAPTER TWENTY-FOUR

I had no idea how long I'd been here. I wasn't able to nap. The tears seemed to flow no matter if I kept my eyes open or closed but in between the tears I focused on the sound of his heart and felt the slowing of his breathing as I rested my head next to his.

I knew the end wasn't far away. The doctor said he would be less and less 'aware' the closer he got to the end. The drugs were making him hallucinate in between brief moments of lucidity. His body was shutting down. I wanted to beat his chest and tell him that for once in his life, this was when he needed to fight. That I would forgive him for not fighting for our family back then, if he promised to fight now. I needed him.

Everything in my life had been so controlled but as I lay beside him, I was highly aware of how little control I had over anything.

Morning sickness, migraine, stress and impending grief were having a particularly disagreeable effect on my body. Pain radiated across my stomach, like tightening belts at various places across my torso, and I struggled to fill my lungs with air. My heart rate was spiking, and my watch buzzed to remind me to breathe.

I couldn't breathe. I couldn't see. That damn elephant was sat on my chest causing all the pain it could to make me recognise and acknowledge its presence. I gripped at my chest as I ran into the corridor to look for help.

My eyesight blurred and I could barely make out the faces of those in front of me, just shapes, shadows and mumbling. I clutched at my chest, my necklace pulling on the back of my neck and scratching at my skin as I slid down the wall of my father's room.

Just as the world faded from view, I recognised the face of the kind nurse.

When I opened my eyes again, I was sat on a chair outside my father's room, Nurse Jenny and a colleague were kneeling at my feet. Jenny held a cold flannel to my neck.

'You're OK, Stephanie. You had a panic attack. It's normal in these situations. Just breathe in deep. Hold for three and breathe out again. We want to check you and the baby over, just because I think you may have blacked out for a moment.'

She took my pulse, her warm fingers pressed on my wrist as her big brown eyes studied the watch in her hand.

'That's it. Breathe. Stephanie, is there anyone we can call? Someone who can come and sit with you?'

'My phone,' I whispered, 'can someone please— My phone is in my bag.'

The other nurse fetched my bag from the room and opened it.

I blinked hard twice to make sure I was reading it right. A missed call, from James. I opened the message app. Two blue ticks.

'I think my husband is coming. I'll be fine. Thank you. It's been a long day.'

I took the cold flannel from Jenny and wiped my face. This wasn't the time to fall apart. My father needed me; peanut needed me. I needed to pull myself together.

Jenny walked me back into the room. I felt like an elderly lady, my body aching from a fight I wasn't aware I'd been a part of.

'I think you need to have something to eat and drink,' Jenny said as she placed a blanket over my knees. 'But first, I'm going to check you over. Make sure there's nothing else more serious going on. Don't worry though, I'm pretty sure it was a panic attack and you need to take it easy. Maybe, when your husband gets here, you can take a walk. Get some fresh air?'

It felt odd to have someone fussing over me while my dad lay helplessly in a bed hooked up to wires. I took a mug from the other nurse who had returned with a cup of tea. The liquid was too sweet with too much milk. Dad would be furious.

'Thank you,' I said, the Britishness in me reluctant to complain.

Jenny checked my heart rate, blood pressure and temperature, while I sat watching my father's chest rise and fall. It seemed to be slowing. His face yellowing almost by the hour.

The hours passed slowly and quickly simultaneously. I checked the clock every ten minutes, praying for James to arrive and tell me everything would be fine. Each time I prayed that the clock would tick away the waiting time, I got angry at the knowledge that I was trying to speed up the final hours of my dad's life.

He still hadn't uttered a word but he didn't need to say anything to me now. His eyes said it all. He wasn't really here anymore. He kept staring into the middle distance, at a spot on the wall, and every now and again he would smile. I hoped that maybe he was looking at Alex. That maybe he could see his own parents or the spirit of my brother calming him. Although his body looked broken, his face looked at peace.

I tried to keep my eyes open, scared to miss a last moment with him, but the exhaustion bit at my determination as I laid my head next to his on the bed. I prayed. I was far past the point of denying it, even to myself. I begged a faceless God, and my brother and anyone else who might be listening, to let it be peaceful.

Not once did I pray to save him. I knew it wouldn't work. All I wanted was human kindness and compassion – for him to no longer feel this pain.

Something shifted. The air seemed to thicken. My chest tightened and it wasn't a chill but a tingle that passed over me. Not a warmth, but not cold. I felt it on my skin and in my bones as the room around me changed.

I studied my dad's face as he stared off into the distance, mumbling incoherently with his gaze fixed on something on the other side of the window.

'No, not really. I feel like I should . . .' he muttered, only just loud enough for me to hear.

I moved my chair closer to the bed and tried to catch his eye.

'I'm not scared,' he continued. 'You look so familiar.'

'Dad. Dad, it's me. Are you OK? Can you see something?'

I tried to follow his eyeline, to see what held his attention, but all I could see were buildings. Could he see Alex? They say you do, before you pass: see the ones you love. I felt so conflicted; part of me hoped he could. I wanted him to have some comfort as he passed, but I also wasn't ready for this to be the end.

My dad was crying.

I watched as the tears pooled in his lower lids and, with the weight of the world held inside them, they gave up resistance and fell.

'Dad. If this is too hard . . . If you're in pain . . .'

I was terrified to say the words I was thinking, scared that giving him permission would make him give up. But I could see it in him. I could hear it in his voice.

I watched as he tried to lick his lips.

I couldn't talk. I just nodded and lowered my head onto the side of his bed, desperate to hide my selfish pain from him for one moment.

He stroked my head and I said a silent prayer. I prayed I would remember this, the way his calming touch would settle me and the way he'd played with my hair as a child. I prayed I wouldn't forget any of it.

'I'm so glad it's you. I'm so glad you're here,' he finally let out.

He was staring at the window again. I jammed my knees against the cold, hard metal frame of the bed, eager for that extra inch of closeness even if it hurt me.

'Dad. Are you OK? I'm glad I'm here too. I would never leave you. I'm here.'

I gripped his hand, tight enough that I felt like I might be able to anchor him to this world, that I could steal him from the next. Maybe if I was strong enough for both of us . . .

He opened his mouth to speak again. 'I'm so glad you're here. She'll need you. I'm not scared. Don't be scared for me. I'm not scared.'

He still couldn't look at me as he spoke. His pupils fluttered as he focused and refocused his drifting eyes.

'Who will need me, Dad? No one else needs me except you. I'm here. No one else needs me. I'm not going anywhere.'

The nurses tried to warn me about this. That the chemicals in his body would create visions, but it pained me more than I expected to see him in such a state of confusion.

I watched as another tear rolled down his face and a chill passed across my shoulders. I checked the window, but it was firmly closed so I fussed with the blanket and pulled it towards his chin, tucking him in like he used to do for me as a child. I tried to place the oxygen mask back on his face.

He pushed the mask away, his hand-eye co-ordination so off that he almost smacked himself.

He looked away from me and focused on a spot at the end of the bed, as if looking me in the eye was too painful.

'She wanted you so very much,' he rasped. 'She prayed her whole life for you. Life is short. Hold her close and tell her I love her. So much. Please. I love you.'

He turned to look at me, straight in the eye, as if he was waiting for me to respond.

'I don't understand, Dad. Who? Mum?'

It angered me that even in his last moments, she had a grip on him. Even when I was desperate for him to leave this world peacefully, the pain she covered him in had followed him until his very last breath.

'Don't cry. Not for her. Don't think about her right now. Breathe, Dad.'

He put his hand over mine, as I tried to replace his mask, and squeezed ever so slightly. Looking back towards the spot at the end of the bed, he took a deep breath, closed his eyes and as he let it out, he said, 'I'm very glad I got to meet you. I love you so very much. My hope.'

The next breath he tried to take was ragged. He opened his eyes, looked right into my soul. 'I love you. My Stephanie. More than you will ever know.'

His whole body was struggling now. He wasn't getting enough oxygen.

With the machines buzzing impatiently, I replaced his mask with shaking hands, kissed him lightly on the forehead and lingered as long as I possibly could.

'Sleep, Daddy. I'm here. I'm not going anywhere.'

His breath changed and the monitors beeped ferociously.

Jenny burst into the room and patted me on the back. She looked over the chart and checked his vitals before switching off the noise on the screens.

She didn't need to say anything. It was obvious.

'I've switched the machine monitors off, so they won't disturb you.'

His chest lifted and emptied, a sound coming from so deep it rattled his ribs. A single tear slipped silently from his left eye. I wiped it from his face and kissed his forehead as he took his final breath. The grip of his hand slackened and the weight in the room changed.

I collapsed onto Dad's chest. I wanted instantly to take it back, I wanted to pray to God to save him. How could I have even for a moment thought that he'd be at peace? He would be at peace here with me. With us. All of us. We needed to be a foursome; my peanut needed a grandad. I needed my dad.

My whole body gave up and I melted into the shell that represented the only protector I had ever known. How was it possible that he was gone?

I sat up, brushed the strands of hair from my face and tried to squeeze the pain from my eyes. I fixed his hair and crossed his hands at his chest, as the nurses fussed with the monitors and unclipped the tubes.

'Stephanie, is your husband coming?' Jenny's face was white, pained, but so full of love.

'Yes. I think so. He should be here soon. He's driving down from Yorkshire, so he should be here within the hour.'

She nodded and put her arms around me. I wasn't used to such over-familiarity from strangers and wasn't the type to hug someone I didn't know, but Jenny had been the only person to share in the most painful moment of my life. I needed to feel human touch. I needed James, but Jenny, the young nurse I had known for less than twenty-four hours, was all I had, and it seemed she understood that.

'Why don't you go and take a breather. Get some air.'

'Yes, I think I will. Thank you,' I replied. The walls seemed to pulse, and the ceiling felt lower than it had an hour ago. I needed to get out.

I stood up and brushed down my black dress with my clammy palms, trying to beat away all the invisible threads that were tying me to this room, to this bed, to Dad. I picked up my bag and bent down to kiss my father for what I could only assume would be the very last time.

'I love you, Dad. Sleep well.'

I wasn't sure what else I was supposed to say. It was the last time I would see my dad's face, yet I couldn't bring myself to say all the things that were running around in my head. The words were stuck behind a wall of pain.

As I walked down the corridor, I couldn't feel my feet on the floor. I could see the mouths of people moving, but the noises were muffled. My whole world had shifted.

I wasn't sure if I was breathing; I couldn't even tell if my own heart was beating. All I could feel was the pain in my chest, the lump in my throat and a dull aching pain deep in my stomach.

I looked up and took a deep breath as I pushed open the doors to the chapel. In front of me stood a plain room with an altar and a tall gold cross. The chairs and pews were arranged in a horseshoe shape, facing the small altar, and paint stained the glass murals on the back walls. The air left my chest as I stepped over the threshold and genuflected before taking a seat. Old habits die hard.

I wasn't sure why I was here. Not sure what I wanted to say, or how loud I wanted to scream. I was alone, no one to question me and no one to comfort me.

As I stared at the cross, I tried to go through the five stages of grief in my head. If I knew what the stages were and how I felt, I could control how I reacted to the emotions.

'Denial. Anger. Bargaining. Depression. Acceptance.'

I rehearsed the words the counsellor had drummed into me, the one I had seen when Alex died.

'Denial first. Don't skip the steps. Acknowledge them. Feel them and you can control them. But feel them,' I parroted.

I was glad there was no one in the room to hear my crazy ramblings. Pure determination and structure would get me through this, not faith. Not God. I needed to say these words out loud. Have the universe *hear* that I was not doing this again. This was my one last act of rebellion. To sit in this room and state my intention to get through this without Him. Without anyone. I got through my grief alone the last time, I guided my broken father through his and we all ended up all right in the end, until the end.

I knew that if I faced this head on, I could contain and manage my grief. I would have to move quickly through it all so I could focus on the new life growing inside me.

'Denial. Well, let's face it. I can't deny it anymore. You took him. You selfish arsehole. Why? Have you not taken enough from us, from me? There is no denial here. I'm well and truly aware of what you've done.'

The words came spilling out so fast I couldn't stop them. I didn't have any intention of stopping them. Tears charged down my cheeks and I winced at the pain as I clenched my fists and drove my nails deeper into my palms.

I closed my eyes, ready to shout about the next step, ready to launch my words at the cold metal cross that stood in front of me. Taunting me with its silence.

I drew breath, ready to propel my words at Him again.

'Anger,' I spat.

But before I could say another word, I heard a voice behind me.

'It seems like that may be where you're at right now.'

The voice was familiar. Comforting and rage-inducing at the same time. I placed my hands on the seat in front of me, afraid to face the person behind me.

'Stephanie, my darling. I'm so sorry.'

I turned around in my seat, the woman behind me dressed in a long flowing purple and blue tie-dye skirt.

'Mum.'

My voice was weak and wanting and made me sound like the small child I once was. It was the same sound that word made when I yelled it down the street the day she left.

# CHAPTER TWENTY-FIVE

'What the hell are you doing here?'

I couldn't move.

The ghost of my inner teenager begged to run forward and hug her, but that same angst-ridden child was ready to launch at her and pound her chest until she cried all the tears I shed when she left me.

I leant down to steady myself on the pew, eager to look controlled. How much had she seen? How much had she heard?

I spotted the gold cross hanging from her neck, nestled in the dip of her cleavage. I remembered the day my dad had bought it for her; I was with him. All these years later, stood in this room where I was mourning his loss, and she had the gall to wear his gift close to her heart with another man's ring on her left hand.

She spotted me staring at it and raised her painted nails to stroke it. Her hands, now wrinkled, showing telltale signs of ageing, and tan marks around her wrist gave me sneaky glimpses into her life without us. She must holiday regularly; you don't get tan lines living in Yorkshire.

'My God, you look so much like him; like both of them,' she said.

Her voice was softer. Calmer than I remembered. Heavier. She wore a familiar grief across her face, most noticeably in the wrinkles below her eyes. My father had borne those same scars. The pain was etched into her skin like a road map that linked them across the miles.

'I asked you a question,' I spat back at her, trying not to look into the familiar eyes that once lulled me back to sleep after nightmares and soothed my tears when I fell from my bike. 'Why the hell are you here?'

I stepped slowly towards her, not for comfort, not to be near her, but to hear her reply. To commit her words to memory.

I had imagined this moment all my life, the day I would confront her, make her justify herself. I never imagined that I would do so without my father's comforting hand by my side.

'Your dad called me last week. He told me he was sick. I drove down to be here in case he needed me. In case you needed me.'

She stepped towards me, reaching out her hand for me before I blocked her. One poker-straight arm created a wall between us, the other hand protecting my baby.

'*Need* you? You can't be serious. You've been gone for twenty years and not once when I needed you were you there!'

I gave myself a pat on the back mentally. I would not lose control.

'You don't get to turn up now. You don't get to swoop in and fix everything that you broke.'

I stepped towards her, my body inches from hers, my heart reaching through my chest begging to be met by its long-lost partner, but I strained to hold it back, lowered my voice and stared directly into her eyes.

'I don't need you. He didn't need you. *We* don't need you.'

I winced as the pain in my stomach began to burn once more, a deep throbbing in my pelvis. I was holding on to so much fury that my stomach muscles were struggling with the burden.

'There it is. That's anger. That's the real anger you need to feel.' She tried to reach for my hand, but I swatted it away.

'Anger I *need* to feel? My whole life has been filled with this anger. This pain.'

My voice grew louder, and as much as I tried to stop myself, the past that had been bottled for so long was ready to have its moment in the light.

'This pain, caused by *you*, has defined my life, and you show up now to tell me it's OK. You taught me not to need you. *You made me not need anyone*,' I shouted, getting the last word out before reaching to steady myself again. I would not, could not show weakness in front of her.

'Stephanie, this anger, this grief, it's different. I remember it; I live it every day. Come, let's go for a walk. We shouldn't shout in here.'

She tried to reach for me again, but I stepped back, stumbling on the wooden foot of the pew. I almost lost my balance. I slammed my fist down on the wood and stared at her as I finally let go.

'I'm not going anywhere with you,' I screamed at her, the pain ripping though me. 'I don't want you here. I don't want to see you; I don't need your help.'

The pain in my stomach shifted, radiating around my back and shooting up through my ribs and chest.

'I have wondered, for years, what I would say to you if you ever bothered your arse to come back.' Through gritted teeth I spat my words at her, everything around her losing focus and definition. 'Never, in a million years, did I think you'd wait until Dad died so you could dampen the anger of your return with my grief. How fucking dare you.'

She winced at my anger and language and I added another invisible tally to my score card.

'That's not what I'm doing, Stephanie. Your dad asked me to stay away. He told me to wait.'

She started crying. How dare she cry. Who was she crying for? Not me. Not my dad.

'We weren't enough for you to give two shits about then, but now he's gone you get to pick up the parental baton. No. Absolutely not.'

The pain grew stronger, the base of my spine felt heavy and my stomach burned, the sickness rising in my throat.

'What do you even sound like? You don't sound like a mother. You don't even look like my mum. What the hell happened to you?'

I tried to laugh at her through the pain. I wanted to make her feel small, insignificant, unloved and unwanted. I wanted her to feel like I had all those years.

I tried to look at her, but nothing was in focus.

'I don't need you. I DON'T NEED ANYONE,' I wailed at the top of my lungs before I felt it.

For one almost imperceptible moment I tried to deny it was happening, but I knew it. I think I'd known the whole time. I looked down, but the black leggings were holding my secret in tight.

I bent double and let out a howl.

'Go away. I don't NEED you. I don't want you here. GET OUT,' I screamed as I pulled my hand away from the inside of my legs to see red blood painted across my palm.

'Nooooo,' I shrieked.

A blood-curdling noise bounced off all four walls and imbedded itself into my soul. I clung to my stomach, wrapping my arms around my torso, a small part of my brain hoping that in doing so I might be able to knit my baby and my womb back together.

'Nooooooo please no. You've taken EVERYTHING from me. Don't take my baby. Not now. PLEASE.'

I was screaming at my mother, at God, at myself.

'Stephanie, you're pregnant? How far? Stephanie. Talk to me. How far along . . . NURSE – SOMEONE – HELP.'

She was shouting, but the world was fading and all I wanted was for the floor to open up and take me too; take me to my father's side, take me with my baby.

Before I knew it, she was by my side, scooping me up in her arms and leading me towards the door. The floor beneath me felt like quicksand, determined to suck me under. I wanted to fight her off and surrender. Everything was gone now. Nothing mattered anymore.

As the world slipped out of focus, I begged never to wake again.

# CHAPTER TWENTY-SIX

I woke in a white room. It looked just like the one I had lain in with my father. The same irritating flickering and buzzing of the light above my head. I turned my head slowly towards the brightness of the double window and focused on the clouds skittering by. Perfect blue skies with puffs of cotton candy.

A dragon-shaped cirrus cloud floated past, wispy wings spread wide with a large smile at its centre.

Dad. Mum. Peanut.

My heart rate spiked, but it wasn't my watch buzzing that alerted me. It was the monitors. Looking down I could see the wires; they were stuck in me. Why were they stuck in me?

My mind tripped back a few beats; memories filtering in, jumbled up and moving around trying to find their place. Then the arrow struck my heart. I ran my hand down my body and could feel a bandage across the length of my stomach, sharp pains shooting up as I traced my fingers over the foreign object that seemed to be glued to my skin.

I flicked through the filing cabinet of my mind, fuzzy images not quite forming a complete picture. My lips were dry and my forehead pulsed. I searched the room for clues, for some indication as to what had happened, refusing to acknowledge the reality under my fingertips. Not ready to believe it yet.

He was here. James. He was sat in the chair at the other side of the room. His five-o'clock shadow less of a shadow and more of a mane covering his face. Clearly, he hadn't shaved in days.

His grey-speckled locks were messed up. He had been tearing his hair out? His glasses rested precariously on his chest and his hand, under his chin, balanced him on the arm of the chair. Even sleeping he looked tired. My heart ached for him, for his arms, for his embrace.

Before I could wake him, the door opened. She breezed across the lino floor like the wind, bringing with her memories, pain and comfort all wrapped up in a ridiculous tie-dye dress.

'Darling. You're awake,' my mother exclaimed in the giddiest of voices. She raced over to the table and placed two coffee cups down before fussing with the blanket and pillows at my head.

Her frenzied shuffling woke him. His eyes were heavy. Those golden flecks still missing.

'Peanut?'

He looked at my mother. Not a word passed between them, but a world of knowledge shared.

'I'll give you both a moment,' she said, looking at James before kissing me on the forehead.

The strange sensation felt alien and too familiar.

She squeezed James's hand quickly before turning and leaving the room.

'James. Peanut?'

'I wish I'd been here sooner. I got here as they were wheeling you into surgery. I have never in my life been so terrified, Stephanie. Never in my whole life have I ever wished I could trade places more, well . . . not since . . .'

'James.' I cut him off. He was avoiding the question. This would not be one of those times when his silence was enough. I needed an answer.

'There were complications,' he started, before the door opened and in stepped the white coat, followed by Sarah, my Macmillan nurse.

Sarah rested her hand on James's shoulder. 'How are you feeling, Stephanie?'

I looked between the eyes of the audience gathered at the end of my bed, secrets and fears written all over them, my life and future painted painfully on the faces of relative strangers.

'I'm wondering why the hell I'm laid in a hospital bed. Is my baby OK?' I directed my question at James. His was the only voice I wanted to hear.

Dr Li stepped forward, his expression unwavering, but something about his eyes offered a glimmer of the human within him. Remorse maybe?

'I'm so sorry, Stephanie. We encountered a few complications.' His voice wavered, just enough.

I shook my head; I knew I needed to hear these words, but didn't want to hear them from the doctor. Anyone but him.

'Stop – don't talk to me. You've given me enough bad news. I don't want to hear it. Not from you. Not again. You should be wearing a grim reaper's cloak, not a white coat!'

Sarah reached down and took my hand. 'Stephanie, let Dr Li explain.'

I looked over her shoulder and saw my mother peering through the glass in the door, tears streaming down her face. I looked at James as he closed his eyes, unable to look at me.

'You had a miscarriage. There were a few complications and we had to rush you straight into surgery,' Dr Li continued.

'No. no. You can't tell me that. You can't. Don't you dare. You saved my baby; I know you did. I told you I wanted to keep my baby. That was my decision. I decided I was having my baby. I was very clear with you.'

Sarah looked at James and a million words were uttered without their lips moving.

The pain was more than indescribable. It was visceral.

'It's my fault. Isn't it? I shouldn't have got angry. I lost control. It's all my fault,' I wailed.

Sarah shook her head as she sat on the end of the bed and rubbed my legs. I could see my mother, still peering through the glass. Uninvited. I was tired of people being in my story that I had not invited in.

'I thought about it, you know. I really did. Like Helen said. Like you said, James.' I looked towards my husband, and he raised his pain-filled tear-stained face in my direction.

'I thought about it, like you asked. I wanted to be sure I wasn't just doing this for me. I wanted to do this for us. For our family. I tried so hard to keep our baby. I tried. I really did. But then I started thinking . . . did I do this? Is this my fault?'

Sarah stroked my hand again and tried to shush me, but the sobs were coming out faster than her calming words.

'Stephanie. Nothing you did caused this. Nothing. It's not your fault; it's not anyone's fault. There was no decision you could have made that would have changed any of this.'

'I got angry and stressed. I wasn't relaxed. Was that it? Was it my fault for getting angry?' I tried to cling on to a reason; I needed a reason. I needed some kind of explanation as to why I was now sitting here without the baby I had chosen to put ahead of my own health.

'No, Stephanie. Listen to me. It wasn't your fault. Nothing could have prevented this. It's not as simple as that. The human body doesn't work like that.'

'*She* shouldn't have been here. If I hadn't been stressed, if I'd been calm . . . If you . . .' I turned to face my husband.

'If I hadn't left you. If I was here. Is that what you were going to say?' His reply sounded sheepish, child-like.

I looked him in the eyes but couldn't finish the sentence. I knew it wasn't his fault.

Sarah placed a hand on James's shoulder again and looked between the two of us, one at a time, trying to knit us back together like a parent fixing a fight between warring siblings.

'None of this, none of any of what you guys have experienced in the last few weeks, is your fault. You couldn't have controlled any of it. You need a moment to deal with the shock of it all, but you can't blame each other.'

'No, I know. I just . . . My dad . . . Peanut . . . *Her*. And you weren't here . . .'

James bent down and wrapped me in his arms. His body, the weight of it, felt safe. He felt safe. He felt like home.

'Please don't tell me my baby is gone, James. Please don't tell me it was all for nothing.' I cried and muttered into his jumper, breathing in the fibres that now smelt less like fresh air and more like hospital chemicals and grief.

I pulled away and looked between Dr Li and Sarah

'I need to hear it all. I need you to tell me everything.'

The doctor looked at James and Sarah before pulling a chair over to the side of my bed and leaning forward. It was the first time I had noticed the colour of his eyes. The first time I noticed his hands, the ring on his wedding finger that he spun around and around as he explained how my life and dreams had all changed in one unscripted moment.

'OK, so there are a few things we need to update you on. But first, I need you to stay calm. The operation was lengthy, and you have quite a few stitches.'

Just like that. My world changed. Forever.

Sat in that room, beside the man who left me when things got tough and under the gaze of a mother who had abandoned me years before, I learned that not only had my father left me on my own, but my baby had been taken from this world with him, and any possibility of me ever having a child of my own had gone with them.

My dreams were shattered, my body broken and my heart in pieces all over the flaked floor tiles of that painfully clinical room.

# CHAPTER TWENTY-SEVEN

Nothing in my world made sense after that moment. Nothing felt real and there was such a huge part of me that was angry they hadn't let me die on the operating table.

Sarah had been an amazing comfort. She sat and talked to me and James for over an hour. Re-explaining everything Dr Li had gone through with us, but in a more human way.

I told James to tell my mother to leave. I needed to have my own world back in focus and I couldn't deal with her too. I didn't want her to be a part of this.

Sarah explained that the miscarriage had caused heavy bleeding that they couldn't stop. It helped to have her walk through all the details, even though at times I had to watch as my husband paced around the room crying tears of confusion. He begged a few times for me to stop asking questions, but I needed to know, and not only the basic details; I needed to know everything.

I needed to be sure that they had tried absolutely everything.

Due to the massive bleeding, they had operated, and once they knew that my baby was not viable, and noticed the cancer wrapped around not one, but both ovaries, they took the difficult decision to remove both. I had what had been described as stage-1B cancer in both ovaries. Hearing the definitions helped me see the situation from a different angle. I needed that space and detachment. James, however, couldn't cope with clinical jargon.

What should have been a 'simple procedure' quickly turned into a much more difficult situation, and almost four hours in surgery. I had emerged from theatre not only having lost my baby but having lost both ovaries and my womb. I would never carry a child. Our peanut had been our last chance. I couldn't help but feel responsible. It had been my job to keep our baby safe inside me, and my body had failed its job. *I* had failed. I couldn't find the emotion or the vocabulary to explain how I felt and when I tried, Sarah simply explained that it was normal for a mother to blame herself at first, but that the guilt would fade. It was a process. She didn't get it. I wasn't sure I would ever get rid of that nagging doubt.

It was becoming clear that I would never hold a baby that looked like me in my arms. I would never see myself reflected in the eyes of another.

I turned to James and shook my head. Stunned.

'This can't be happening. I can't be hearing this. I did everything right! I thought I had made the right choice. I was giving our baby a chance, and I lost her anyway.'

Even as the words formed, they felt wrong, sounded wrong.

'No. I didn't lose our baby. Our child was not like a set of keys that you drop one day and can't find again. Why do they say lose?'

I waited for Sarah to give me an answer to an impossible question. She couldn't; instead, she comforted us, told us our choices and gave us leaflets on grief counselling.

We talked through the options of burial. I was only seventeen weeks pregnant. They don't register a baby before twenty weeks. My darling baby would never be registered. As far as the world was concerned, my beautiful peanut was never here, never existed. Didn't live and didn't die. But it did. I felt my peanut living inside me. Saw the heartbeat, felt its presence. Now all I could do was hold my invisible child in my memory and no one would ever know the impact this tiny almost-life had on me.

Once all the facts had been aired and Sarah had left the room, I lost my ability to cry anymore. I was spent.

I was kept in for a few days. The doctors wanted to talk over treatment options now that the cancer had been removed. I winced as they spoke of it, as if an obstacle they were trying to navigate was no longer there, so the path ahead was easier, clearer. A cruel absurdity.

Dr Li's face had lifted a little as he neared the end of his explanation. Despite losing the baby, they'd managed to clear all the cancer from me by removing the womb. Although regular tests and monitoring would be required, he was confident they had gotten it all. For ovarian cancer, it was as close to a miracle as he'd seen in his career. A chance to take the entire mass and leave nothing behind.

Even as he said those words, my heart lurched. They left nothing behind. That was the emptiness I felt. They took my baby, my dreams, my wishes and left me empty.

It was a win for them, but I'd lost everything.

I would be offered preventative chemo, after the initial tests of course, to make sure it didn't return, regular and more frequent monitoring would become a part of normal life for me, and the C-word would never fully leave our lives. I was at risk, but right now, I was lucky. That was the general consensus, anyway.

I didn't feel lucky.

It felt strange that I'd arrived at this hospital less than two days ago with everything and, as I lay in that room, staring at the same four walls, I realised I would be leaving with nothing.

James left a few hours later. He wanted to grab a few things to make me feel more comfortable, so he said. There was more to it; I knew that. I could see it in his nervousness and need to escape the building. As he slipped out of the room, my mother replaced his presence.

'I don't know if I can do this, Mum. I don't think I can bear talking to you.'

I wasn't bothered about my abruptness. I didn't care if her feelings were hurt. She hadn't been around long enough for me to worry about how this was affecting her. All I knew was that she brought pain and memories, and my head couldn't focus on right now, let alone start dissecting the past.

'I know, darling. I understand. But I think you need me more than you realise.'

I shook my head at her in utter disbelief. 'What messed-up part of your high-and-mighty mind thinks that of all the people in my life, I'd choose you to be the person to lean on?'

It was cruel; I knew that. But what did she expect?

'I think you might believe I deserve that, and you're grieving, so I'll let it go. But I'm still your mother, and the only mother you'll ever have. No matter how much I've hurt you, I deserve more than that.'

I tried to sit up, but the stitches in my stomach made it impossible, the severed muscles paralysing me. It was the most vulnerable I had ever felt, and in a moment when I needed to run away faster than ever before, I was rooted to the spot.

'You deserve what exactly? Compassion? Love? Respect? You don't deserve anything from me. I don't owe you anything.'

All the teenage journal scrawls floated through my mind, all the angry poems and shouting out song lyrics in the dark. Every mean word I had ever thought about her was sat in a queue on the end of my tongue, waiting its turn.

'Why were we not enough, Mum? Why was I not enough to make you stay? I wasn't enough, Dad wasn't enough, but now that he's gone and I'm broken, now you want to sweep in and glue all the pieces back together?'

Her hands shot to her chest, her chin slack. 'Is that what you've thought all this time? That you weren't enough? Stephanie, I never left you. I left the pain. I couldn't cope with the cruelty. I needed space and your dad—'

'Don't you dare mention him to me.' I cut her off

mid-stream 'You are not worthy to speak of him. He was a better man than you ever gave him credit for. He deserved better than you.'

She sighed and sat in the chair James had vacated. It felt too close.

'Your father is . . . was . . . the most incredible man I had ever known. He was my first love. My one true love. Losing Alex broke us beyond repair. We blamed each other. We hurt each other. I hurled words at him hoping to bruise him enough to make him feel my pain. He never once reacted, never once blamed me. Never once took the bait.'

She took a long deep breath in and held it for a moment, her eyes closed. I could feel the cogs of her memory turning behind her eyelids.

'I needed him to blame me, Stephanie; I needed to blame him. I needed someone to justify why it was all happening.'

As she spoke, it angered me that I understood her words. I had done the same. I had pushed James the same way.

'Losing a child was the only thing in the world that could have broken us. We were a unit, all four of us. We were a team. I lost myself when Alex died, and your dad . . . my husband. My Robert. He couldn't help me. We couldn't help each other. I ran away, but your dad never chased me. He didn't come to find me when I was lost.'

I couldn't say anything. This woman in front of me had been my main source of pain and anger for more years than I could count, but as I watched her pour her story out, I recognised her; I recognised the pain. I was looking at myself reflected.

'I know you think you don't need me. I understand why you *believe* you can do this alone. I thought the same at first. I know you're strong; I know you'll survive. But you don't need to do this alone. Grief is a path best walked in company, and as much as you'll hate to hear it, I'm the only person on this planet who understands how you feel.'

She stood up from the chair and came closer, sat on the bed. She placed her hand at the side of my face and my head dropped into her hand, resting for a moment and lightening my load.

'I'm the only person in this world who loved your dad as much as you did, and I feel that loss more today than the day I walked out; and as much as you've spent your life hoping and praying not to be like me, we share one big thing in common – the only thing I prayed we would never share. Grief.'

I didn't want her to be there, but the soft touch on my face and the closeness of that heartbeat that my own recognised calmed me.

'How am I ever supposed to feel whole again? My baby, my only chance.' I sobbed into her hand, gripping at my hospital gown.

'I'm not going to tell you that it gets easier,' my mother replied, as she struggled through her own tears. 'Losing a child is the hardest pain you will ever feel. It never leaves you. The grief is one I would not wish on a single soul.'

I winced as I tried to sit forward, my whole being desperate for a mother to hold me.

'It doesn't leave you, Stephanie,' she whispered though my matted hair. 'Your brother is as much with me today as he was the day he was born. That little peanut will have a corner of your heart you'll never give to another. But you have to learn from me, from us. Keep James close – he seems like a truly lovely man and he loves you so much.' She pulled away and wiped the tears from my cheeks before wiping her own. 'Don't push him away, Stephanie. This grief is the hardest thing you'll ever face. Face it together. It's so much harder to face it alone.'

'I want my dad,' I cried, the pain ripping apart my body. 'I want my dad and I want my baby. It's just not fair.'

'I know,' she whispered.

The pain of the stitches in my stomach was not even close to the pain the rest of me was feeling.

'I know, my beautiful girl. I am so sorry. I'm here. Shhhh, I'm here.'

She rocked me back and forth, like a babe in arms.

We sat on that bed for what felt like a lifetime. It didn't fix anything, I didn't feel lighter, but for the first time in weeks I felt understood. Seen. Heard. I felt a little less alone.

# CHAPTER TWENTY-EIGHT

## SIX MONTHS LATER

Recovering from the surgery was tough. The scars on my body healed about as quickly as the scars left behind on my heart. I didn't talk much. I was assigned an assessment counsellor while I was in the hospital recovering, but I knew what I needed to say to get the all-clear. They were looking for signs of depression. I wasn't depressed; I was broken. There was a big difference in my mind.

There was no checklist for what it was I was feeling. In the space of a few weeks I had felt every spectrum of emotion. Joy at finally being pregnant with the child we always wanted, fear at the potential of losing it, determination to win the fight, anger at my father's betrayal, fear of losing him. I had screamed at God for taking him, begged him not to take my child and mourned the death of my baby as well as the death of every dream that tiny cluster of cells stole from me.

Sarah helped. She became a friend over the following months. Our regular chats about treatment turned into mini counselling sessions. First over coffee, and then a small glass of wine. She became the person I could be most honest with. On the days when James wasn't able to give me what I needed, I turned to her. She, in response, would turn me back towards my husband, helping us both through a grief she could never understand.

My mother found her stubborn side again and refused to leave. She rented a house in nearby Hove and split her time between visiting me as often as she could and popping home to Yorkshire to recharge. Some moments were tough, and arguments happened regularly. Things started to feel a little more normal when she fought back, challenging my childish attitude. Just like when I was young, the arguments were generally followed by a calmer discussion, tears and tea. We slowly started to get to know each other again.

I noticed her struggle, often. This wasn't home for her anymore. She struggled with the memories that were painted on the pavements all around us. The days when it got too tough, she would disappear for long walks on the South Downs. The rolling hills reminded her of her true 'home'.

Hearing Yorkshire described as home bit at me for a while, but she'd lived a whole life without us, and I could see the stress on her face as she battled with the traffic and busy city noise. I learned that the pain and grief had caused her so much anxiety, retreating to small-village life was the only thing that saved her.

I had never considered leaving the coast, but as I walked the streets of my hometown, memories pained each step. The noise, which I once found a comfort to get lost among, now made me itch. I found myself drawn to the hills, searching for peace, begging for silence. Grief had pushed her towards God's own country, and I was beginning to understand why.

She had explained that when the grief and memories clawed their way back to the surface, she would travel. Greece, Spain, Italy. She would take cruises around the Med, and once even around the Caribbean, which is where she'd been with her husband when she got the call from Dad. She had travelled all the countries Alex had wanted to visit. When the grief got too much, when the pain resurfaced, she made happy memories to replace the hard ones. She threw away her dark, mournful clothes and embraced a new life that she hoped Alex would smile down on her for. It was her coping mechanism. I knew it wouldn't be mine, but we each have to find our own. At least, that's what Sarah kept telling me. I might not don a maxi dress and trip around the Colosseum, but I would find a way to channel my emotions somehow.

Every day was a learning curve, and it was far from easy. There were days when I hated my mother being anywhere near me, like the day she served me up a bowl of risotto, and seemed utterly confused when I screamed at her. The memory of Dad was still so fresh in my mind. I didn't explain why; I couldn't find the words.

There were days too when I couldn't have been more grateful for her presence. Like the day when I was searching for my comfy jumper from university, the one

I'd stored in the back of the cupboard, and she walked into my room to see me staring at a small white bag, unable to open it and knowing that the beautiful little silver baby rattle from North Laine sat inside. Memories covered in delicate tissue paper at the back of my wardrobe.

She took the bag from me without even opening it, without asking a single question, and put it back, lifting me into her arms without saying a word.

Leaving the house had been hard at first. Mothers and their babies seemed to explode on the streets like some kind of baby revolution. Panic attacks were coming thick and fast but a tight motherly squeeze of my hand kept my head from spinning.

Everywhere I turned I saw my father; every child I saw took my breath away.

James tried hard to cope, but there was something that held him back. I caught him often staring at the picture of the three of us on our mantelpiece. The wedding picture that said it all, the three of us stood at the top of the aisle, my father passing my hand into James's. I could still hear his soft voice that day: *Protect her; she's all I have.*

James had made a solemn vow to us both that day, but the promise he made to my father created an unbreakable bond. Two men knitted together by a common love.

We were finding our way back to each other day by day, but something still sat in my peripheral vision, something I wasn't quite sure was there, but I felt it all the same.

It wasn't until I saw a tiny corner of an envelope sticking out of his briefcase that I was reminded of the secrets he'd been keeping from me. In all this pain and grief, I had completely forgotten about the clandestine meetings, whispered words in the darkness and knowing looks in Yorkshire.

It was almost six months since we'd lost our little peanut, and James had organised a trip back to Yorkshire. With so many memories in each and every corner of Brighton, maybe some space would do us good.

Dad's funeral had taken it out of us all. The organisation for something so morbid seemed odd. There was as much paperwork and finer details to arrange as there had been for our wedding. The priest, the church, the flowers, the speeches; the only difference seemed the difficult choice of casket rather than cake.

We held a small memorial for peanut on the same day. James had thought it would be too much, but I wanted it all done together. It felt less lonely to send them off together.

Mum had offered to help, of course. She was utterly devastated. Her not-so-new husband, Bill, accompanied her. It seemed unnecessarily cruel to deny her a chance of having someone to lean on. Things between us were not by any means fixed, but we were working on them and as much as I had fought against it initially, she seemed genuinely torn apart at losing the love of her life. Pained that they hadn't finished their lives together, the way they'd planned.

Bill was a lovely guy, and it was second time around for both of them. It was clear he loved her, but that day, it had been very clear just how much she wished she'd fixed things with my father. I guess it's easy to hide from your past but saying goodbye to someone you shared it with is a whole different kettle of fish.

I had chosen to go through one round of preventative chemo. For James's sake really. I would have taken a risk and just had regular check-ups, but I couldn't put him through that worry again. Not if I wanted us to work. The prognosis was good, and James's relief was obvious. The last set of tests were only a few weeks ago, and in yet another cruel twist of fate, we were back in the very same room again, the same doctor's office where we first heard the news.

Dr Li was fairly confident, but cautious. Apparently, I was lucky. I didn't feel lucky. I still felt empty.

I was told that if I had not fallen pregnant, the cancer would have spread before it was caught, and I wouldn't be here now. My unborn baby saved my life, despite the fact that I couldn't save it in return. The ultimate sacrifice before having even taken a breath. The cruelty seemed so wrong.

James was back at work, but I had to quit my job at the studio. Baby shoots were the furthest thing from possible. Felicity was understanding, of course; James said she broke down in tears when he told her. I couldn't even face her.

They say mothers 'nest' before a baby arrives, but I didn't come home with a baby. Just a desire to cleanse. I had James rip up and replace the carpet in our bedroom, the stain from the dropped coffee that one blissful morning now a memory rather than a permanent reminder. I couldn't sleep in our room until every trace of that moment had been removed. If I couldn't look at a stained carpet, I wasn't sure I'd be able to photograph a sleeping baby, or an expectant mother. Maybe I never would again.

A trip back to see Steve and Julie in Yorkshire

would do us both good. When I told Mum we were heading up there for a break, her body seemed to react to the relief and I was beginning to understand why. The idea of spending time in the hills, the fresh air and never-ending sky filled me with longing. I had always been a city girl, but now I wanted to be as far away from frenetic energy as possible. I wanted to be where my world would stop spinning for a while. Where the pace of life moved at the same speed as the roaming cattle and the windswept clouds. I wanted to breathe in new life and feel Mother Nature at my fingertips.

James and I both needed time and space to talk; to figure out if we'd be able to navigate this new changed world together – if we even wanted to.

They say acceptance is the final stage of grief, but I didn't feel it.

I would never feel a life inside me again. I accepted that.

I would never know what it felt like to have those small feet kick from the inside. I accepted that.

Never again would I know the feeling of carrying another heartbeat. Again I accepted that.

So why didn't it feel over? I didn't feel healed. I had reached the end of the 'grief ladder' but something was still wrong and I felt like I'd missed a step. I just wasn't sure which one.

It took a while for me to see how all of this would change James's world too. It wasn't until I caught him watching a group of children play on the beach that I realised: James would never have a child of his own, not if he stayed with me. I couldn't help but question, were we enough? Was I enough? Could we survive in a marriage together now that we'd never have a child to complete our family?

I wasn't sure we'd be able to navigate this world together now that our one common goal had been ripped from us. Who were we before we wanted children? What did we love about each other that didn't include the idea of creating our perfect family unit?

The trip had been on the cards for a while, but with James taking so much time off work over the funeral, we had to wait until work would free up again. The days blurred one into the next and I barely recognised the seasons changing, so I was caught off-guard the morning he arrived at my bedside with a cautious smile and a package in his hand.

'What's this?' I asked as I started unwrapping the small box.

'Well,' he started, sheepishly shifting from foot to foot like a child justifying a handmade card. 'It's our anniversary today. It felt wrong celebrating it like we normally do, but I couldn't let it go by without doing something.'

I had counted the days since I'd lost them both, counted how many consecutive days I had managed without breaking down in tears, but I had no idea what the actual date was. Half the time I wasn't sure what day of the week it was. It didn't seem to matter anymore.

I opened the box, and tucked neatly into a bed of comfortable velvet were two tiny charms. A peanut and a small dragon.

'Our peanut and its protector.' His voice cracked and instead of replying I simply pulled him close as he relaxed into my shoulder. 'I miss them too, Steph.'

I'd been grieving alone for so long that it shocked

me that his pain could be so physical too. My beautiful strong man had lost his parents, then had lost his surrogate father in mine, and then our peanut, our child. We had both lost so much.

I gripped him tighter. We lay back on the bed in each other's arms, our grief and tears for the first time mixing with each other's.

'Yorkshire will do us good,' he finally muttered. 'There's something about the moors – they seem to renew life. It'll do us both good.'

'I know it will,' I said, shifting and sitting up, brushing my hair from my face and resetting my internal counter.

I had made it seven days this time. Next time I might make it eight.

'Come on. Let's get ready and hit the road. The quicker I get a lungful of fresh air, the better.'

I swung the duvet back. It was time to start moving forward. We had a future to try and paint. We had a brand-new sketchpad and we both needed to see what we wanted to draw on it, and if we were even on the same page.

That elephant in the room may have changed shape, but it was still there, just as big and intrusive as always. We weren't us anymore. Would we ever be again?

# CHAPTER TWENTY-NINE

The drive up was tough. The only sound that broke the awkward silence was the radio as it crackled between stations. Trees sped past, giving me more excuses to count the long pauses between breaths and even longer sighs.

It wasn't as if we weren't speaking – we had found it a little easier to talk to each other in the past few weeks – but we never spoke about anything of substance. We stopped working on the house; our passion to create a family home had waned.

Instead, we sat curled on the sofa watching reruns on Netflix and tucking into countless boxes of Maltesers. We talked about the shows we were watching, politics, even the weather. We were co-existing, and I was fine with that. The substantive conversations were on hold, being kept under the heavy foot of our new long-term lodger, always lurking, always watching: the ivory beast I couldn't shake from my shadow.

I had been working on my anger, determined that the stages of grief would not keep me held prisoner. I bit my tongue when he complained about a colleague at work, desperate to scream that at least the world still turned for him.

I tried not to be angry every time I walked into my bathroom and saw the empty space left by the dragon that used to watch over me brushing my teeth. James had moved it, the small statue and the pregnancy test. He had placed them both in a box and put the box in the ottoman at the foot of our bed.

He didn't know I'd noticed. But I had.

I knew because he hadn't cleaned the surface after he moved it. He'd simply removed it, leaving a calc mark behind on the marble bathroom top.

The small ring was barely visible, but I could see it. Each time I brushed my teeth, I would stare at this almost invisible mark left behind by my dreams and would run my fingers over the scar on my stomach. Unseen by so many, but the pain underneath felt so visceral.

I tried not to be jealous when I saw Mum kiss Bill in the car before she walked up the path to our door. I would try not to be jealous of their tenderness, something James and I were lacking. But I was jealous. I was angry and jealous of everyone. Jealous that she'd found such tender love after she left my dad, my wonderful dad. Angry that she was able to move on after the loss of a child, and I couldn't ever imagine sharing that space with her.

I bit my tongue and tried not to be angry because as much as everyone enjoyed telling me that 'she understands more than anyone', she didn't understand. Not really.

My mum had memories. She had moments to cling to and smells that reminded her. Photos and videos of her beautiful boy, of their perfect life before it was ripped apart.

I had a scar. That was it. A scar and a small calcium wrinkle on my otherwise perfect marble bathroom shelf. I didn't have the memories. Did that mean my grief meant less, or more?

I felt my shoulders loosen as we drove further and further away from everything in our life that brought me such pain. The salty sea air that tasted like the tears I had shed would soon be replaced by fresh air and the smells of new life. That was what I needed. A small village where no one knew me. Not a town where a familiar face on each street corner would do the head tilt and sympathetic smile.

I looked at the alarm clock, the morning hours slowly drifting past, numbers clicking over. I mentally patted myself on the back for another moment of me surviving another day, just about. I reached for my phone, careful not to wake my sleeping husband. Helen had messaged again, but I cleared the notification without opening it.

I had wondered at first if it was Helen's idea for us to go away. We'd been due to go for a drink, all four of us, last week. Helen and her husband, me and James. But in the end, I couldn't go. I sat in the bathroom all dressed up, makeup on and my black dress pressed, my unruly red waves tamed and knotted at the top of my head. I looked in the mirror and almost passed for a regular human being; but my eyes were dead. Soulless.

I couldn't face it. Panic had risen in my chest and breathing became impossible. The panic attacks were yet another uninvited guest that took up residence in the space left behind. With my back against the bathroom door, I told James I wasn't feeling well enough. I ran a bath and had an early night. He went without me.

I was existing in a home filled with the ghosts of people who walked the earth and those who never got the chance.

It was after that night in the pub that he mentioned Yorkshire. Told me that his work had offered him some time off. He'd found a cottage not far from Steve and Julie and rented it for a week.

When we arrived at the farm cottage, I was taken aback by the familiarity of it all. I couldn't put my finger on it at first. That evening, after a few hours of feeling unsettled, the sense of déjà vu bubbled over. Halfway down my second brandy by the fire, it struck me.

'I've seen this place before. I thought I had when we drove up the driveway, but I'm sure of it now. Have we been here before?'

James looked up from his sketchpad. He'd been doing that more since we lost peanut. He normally kept his scratchings hidden from me. He thought I didn't know, but I did. A whole stack of sketched dreams hidden in the bottom drawer in his office. These days, he said, he couldn't concentrate on a book long enough to read a full chapter and his brain wandered; so, he sketched.

He rarely shared them with me, keener to show me the buildings he designed than the memories he sketched, but then we all had our secrets.

He'd never seen my Instagram pictures. Those small moments that caught my breath. This was his thing. His moments.

He put the sketchpad down and picked up the glass of whisky from the side table. I watched as he drained the amber liquid, leaving silky trails down the side of the sharp-cut crystal.

'No. *We* haven't been here before,' he said, taking in air between his gritted teeth as he continued. 'I have. I lived here.'

He said it so matter-of-factly. So quickly that the words didn't even pause. I had to replay them in my mind to make sure I'd heard them correctly.

'You lived here? When?' I shifted, readjusting the blanket over my knees.

'When I was a child. This was my childhood home.' He stared at me, his eyes bigger than anything I'd ever seen. I thought I caught a glimmer of the amber flecks returning to them, but I couldn't be sure; it could have been the reflection of the embers in the fireplace.

He didn't move or expand on his explanation. He just looked at me, his eyes steady, waiting for me to make the first move.

'You mean. This is the house . . . this was your house?'

I looked around, everything in it suddenly carrying more meaning.

His face dropped. Shoulders slumped as if carrying the weight of the world.

'I'm not sure about you, but I might need a double for this conversation.' He topped up my glass with a large glug of expensive whisky, before pouring one for himself.

'No no no. If you're about to open Pandora's box in the middle of this room, I want you within striking distance. Come sit here.'

I meant it in jest, but he looked like a deer caught in headlights. Before coming over, he reached down the side of the sofa and pulled an envelope from his bag.

I recognised it straight away, those curled edges. It was the same envelope that had been passed around and hidden away from me the last time I was in Yorkshire.

He gently lowered himself onto the sofa, tucking his back into the corner, as far away from my touch as possible.

The envelope burned a hole of curiosity into the sofa between us.

'OK. So, I guess we should probably start at the beginning.' I sounded like a teacher, like a parent, like a mother.

I looked at him and pulled the blanket up further, wrapping my arms around my stomach, subconsciously stroking my scar with my ring finger.

I reminded myself that I'd gotten through the worst pain anyone could endure. I had lost my dream of a family and continued to battle against a nasty parasite that could attach itself onto the final threads in my body at any time. I tried to remind myself that if I could get through all of that without men in white jackets locking me in a padded cell, I could get through anything.

This wasn't quite the way I expected my marriage to implode, but I was ready for it. I braced myself, ready to hear about his other life, other family, other lover even? It would all make sense now – especially given his revelation about the house.

We both stared at the envelope, each one begging the other to speak first.

'It's not what you think, Stephanie. I promise. I've never talked about any of this. It never really seemed important, although I think now that I was hiding. There's been so much pain, so much grief. I need it to all stop. I need it out of my head. I need to talk. So . . .'

He picked at his nails, ripping at the edges, leaving them ragged and torn, spots of blood emerging as he pulled a little too far.

'James. Stop stepping on eggshells and rip the plaster off already, will you.'

He looked wounded. Hurt. 'Stephanie, please understand me when I say I never wanted to keep any of this a secret. It just got harder to tell you. The issues with your mum, then the pregnancy and your dad . . . then peanut. It all got . . . It felt easy to ignore it in the early days. Maybe I was in denial. These last few days and weeks . . . the finality of everything. I feel like I need to stop hiding. I need to face all of this.'

He shifted awkwardly, pulling a piece of paper from the bulging envelope and looking at it before closing his eyes, taking a deep breath and placing it in the space between us.

'It's not that this house *was* my childhood home. This house . . . is my home. I own it.'

# CHAPTER THIRTY

I stared at the deed papers in front of me, his name clearly visible. He owned a house. A house I didn't know about. I thought he was about to pass me divorce proceedings, and instead I was looking at something entirely different. Deeds, to this house. His name on the deeds. We'd battled with rot, squeaky floorboards and ill-fitting doors in a run-down house in Brighton, robbing Peter to pay Paul just to fit a new carpet . . . and he'd owned a farmhouse in Yorkshire this whole time?

'I don't understand, James. I . . .' I struggled to find my words, tripping over syllables as they fought to find life. 'We've scrimped and saved to build a home, but you already had one? Why wouldn't you tell me? Why keep this a secret? I don't understand.'

James pulled another piece of paper from the envelope. A newspaper article.

*Yorkshire Teen Loses Both Parents in Tragic Farm Accident*

'I've spent years running from this. I love Steve and Julie, but coming back here always hurts. It was too painful to remember them, and then as I got older, it got more painful because I *couldn't* remember them. I couldn't live here, but selling it – it felt too final.'

His face was ashen with a grief I hadn't seen since we lost our baby.

'You made it easy not to come back here, but when you got pregnant, something about the whole situation made me want to come home.'

The pain and emotion I had noticed in his eyes that night we met so many years ago, the melancholy I could never explain, it was all there. Crawling over every inch of his skin.

'I may not have killed them myself. But for years I lived as if I might as well have done. It was all my fault. My parents died and it was my fault. I couldn't come back to this house. Then, you showed me that test, our little peanut . . . I needed to grow up. Face things. Be a responsible person. Face my past so I could be a good dad.'

I'd never seen this side of him. In all our years together, I'd never felt his conflict with this place.

'I loved my mum,' he started, as he brushed away emotion from his cheeks and pulled back his shoulders. He stared past me at the wall behind, unable to focus on my face.

'She was the most amazing woman. We would sit in this room for hours and talk. About everything, about books, about literature, about the worlds created with the written word. We would read passages from dusty books, talk about language and how it shaped us. The fire would crackle away, and I'd watch as she sat mending Dad's work clothes.'

His eyes grew warmer as he spoke of her.

When we first met, we never talked about the ins and outs of our separate grief. We had other people to talk to about that. I had my dad to talk to about Alex and he had Steve and Julie.

We both had lives before each other. Both had personalities altered by our challenges. I recognised that going back over who we were 'before' wouldn't change who we were now, so what was the point? We lived in the here and now and accepted that anything that happened before us was just that – before *us*. But now as I watched him struggling to find the words, I wondered if I'd left it too long.

There's a window, you see. A window in a relationship when it becomes about more than a sneaky kiss in a club, or a quiet night curled on the sofa watching endless *Friends* reruns. There is always that moment when you ask each other about what came before.

I remembered that day. I remembered asking him if he missed his parents. I remembered him answering that he did, but he was young, and life goes on.

There is a moment in a relationship, at least in most relationships, when you start opening up about your feelings. Retelling memories. I did, sometimes, about Alex. He would listen and engage but it would go no further. It's hard to explain to someone new, how much someone from your past, who they will never meet, meant to you. I guess I knew that of Alex, so I suspected James felt the same about his parents. It was hard to connect with his loss of them when to me, they've only ever been pictures in a frame and names on his lips, not memories in my mind.

If I was honest with myself, when we first met, I'd been so wrapped up in my own grief that I hadn't felt ready to take on his. Then, as time passed, we became engrossed in our new life, together.

'Hold on a minute,' I said, as I stood up and walked towards the kitchen. He'd been right, of course, this was more than a small whisky kind of night, but I needed water. I needed to be a little more sober for this conversation. 'Wait, I'll be right back.'

As I walked through to the kitchen, the shape of the house meant something new to me. I tried to picture James by the fridge as a child, his mother cooking dinner over the Aga that dominated the room.

As I ran the tap, my mind wandered back to when we were planning the wedding. We'd both decided we didn't want a big affair. His parents weren't around, and my mother was not welcome. A registry office wedding was perfect for two people who did all they could to stay out of the spotlight.

Our lives had ticked along for so many years, simply accepting that there were questions left unanswered and unasked. Neither of us wanted to open a box that we couldn't close again. So we didn't. Now that box had been blown wide open and the fragments scattered across the room, no hope of ever putting it back together. He'd lived his entire life shrouded in a painful grief he couldn't even bring himself to talk about.

I returned to the sofa, placed the heavy blanket over my lap and looked up at him.

'I was so sure you had a woman and a whole other life up here. I heard you, before we came up here last time, talking to someone on the phone in the hallway. In the dark, all secretive, and then the last time we were up here, talking about 'her'. Amy. I even saw a message on your phone from her, and Steve said that you needed to sort the whole thing out before I found out. Shuffling around this bloody envelope. I thought these were divorce papers.'

The whole idea sounded so ridiculous now that the words were spoken out loud.

'I thought you were about to tell me you were leaving me,' I finished.

Grabbing my hands, he pulled me to him, the paperwork crushed between our broken bodies.

'No. My God, no.' He kissed me hard on the lips, briefly, but it was all I needed. 'Well, I was worried that these secrets might end us. But not because I was hiding an affair. But because . . . there's so much I need to tell you.' He looked down at the lies in black and white between us.

'Amy wasn't a torrid affair; she was the tenant. She and her husband lived here; they loved it here. It devastated them when I told them my plans. Steve and Julie were so great with them, helped with any issues. So obviously they were a little concerned about how I was handling the whole situation.'

'What plans? What situation?'

'Well . . .' he replied, twisting knots into the fabric of the blanket between us. 'I told them that I wasn't renewing their rental contract. I wanted this place to be somewhere we could come. Get away from it all.'

He reached over and knotted his fingers in with mine,

but there was still an awkwardness between the gaps. All these lies, all the deceit. None of this felt like the man I knew, like the man I loved. What else was he hiding?

'I don't understand. Why keep this from me for so long? How is it possible that I didn't know? I assumed it had long been sold off. It never occurred to me . . .'

I dropped his hands and picked up the papers.

'You've lied to me for all these years. How did you keep this from me? Why didn't you tell me? This isn't a small thing, James – you know that, right? You hid an entire house from me! What else are you hiding?'

His shoulders sagged and he tried to stuff the papers back in the envelope, as if shutting them away again would reverse time.

'I tried to tell you. Each time we talked about having a family, every time you told me how much children meant to you. But you hated visiting Yorkshire, and I was convinced you'd make me sell the place and I wasn't ready to let it go. I sold off the land – well, Steve did. I asked him to. I sold that off the first time we . . . well, I put the money in a savings account ready for our baby and was going to tell you and then . . . Well, it didn't seem like the right time. Then it never did. Then all this happened and all I could think was that this money could help us fight and save you. I knew I'd have to tell you. It's why I brought us here the first time, to tell you, and to say that we could fight it all the way, but you just . . . it wasn't . . . It never seemed like the right moment and you were so determined you'd made your mind up.'

I didn't respond. What could I say? I was more stunned with each word that left his body and I had nothing. No response.

'Aunt Susie was so angry with me for years for not selling up. I think she always hoped I'd sell and give her the money. She didn't agree with her brother passing everything down to a child, but then my father never expected to be leaving the farm to a child. Aunt Susie thought I was wasting my life and his legacy. We never spoke of what happened with my parents but I knew she blamed me for everything. It became this huge, disappointing part of my life that I wanted so much to forget.'

The words made sense; I knew those facts to be true. He'd lived with his aunt in Brighton for years before her death. She disliked him so much that he was always at our house for dinner. She didn't come to the wedding, her excuse that bingo was on at the community centre that day. Neither of us mourned her very long when she passed.

'But this house . . . it's yours.' I looked around, taking in the wooden beams and flagstone tiles, the cross-hatched windows and chipping plaster.

'How do you pay a mortgage on this house without me knowing? All those times we've struggled, and you had this house. When Dad offered to buy us our first home and all along you had this place? What happened to your parents? I don't even know how they died!' The questions were coming thick and fast now, as was my desire to finally put together a jigsaw that had been in front of me all this time.

'This house, it's paid off in full. It was passed down through the generations. Four generations, to be precise,' he said.

'But wait. How do you keep it running? You've never been up here to check on it. What the . . .' I couldn't even finish the question. I had no idea how to ask what I wanted to know.

James got up from the sofa and walked over to the drinks trolley. He picked up the whisky bottle and topped up his glass, then brought it over to top up mine.

'Calm down, Steph. I'll get to all that. You need to let me explain, OK? You need to let me talk. You need to listen and let me talk, until it's all out. Then you can ask as many questions as you like.'

I wasn't used to being the quiet one. That was his role.

I folded my arms, higher up my chest than was naturally comfortable. I pulled my legs in closer and stared right into his eyes. 'Go on then.'

I braced myself, terrified of what other secrets he might unleash.

'I was a mummy's boy. All my childhood. I was small, not athletic. I was bookish and smart. I was everything my father wasn't. Mum fell pregnant with me late in life after years of not being able to have a baby. I was the only child she managed to keep, and she always said that Dad was over the moon because I was a boy. He needed someone to help him on the farm, and obviously wanted to pass the farm down the line.'

James got up and wandered over to the dining room table. He pulled a box from underneath and I was surprised I hadn't seen it earlier. A packing box. He brought it over and placed it on the floor at our feet.

Pulling out a photo album, he opened the first page and placed the book between us.

'Mum used to call us the three musketeers. There was nothing the world could throw at us that we couldn't handle. It was the very first proper book she bought me. The only one I kept when I left.'

He reached down again, riffling through the box before pulling out a dusty paperback, edges ripped and discoloured by time.

'When we found out you were pregnant, the first time, I knew I had to come back here and get these things. I wanted to pass them on. But to pass all this on, I knew I'd have to talk about them. Then . . . well . . . it didn't feel right to top pain with pain, so I waited. I was always planning on bringing you up here after the scan and telling you everything. I hoped it would be a happy occasion, then the scan, and the cancer and then you made your decision and I just . . .' He pinched the inside corners of his eyes and the bridge of his nose. He had been going through all these emotions and never once told me.

'There never seemed to be the right moment.'

He flicked open the front cover and passed me the book.

*To my little boy. Remember that we will always be stood either side of you, fighting this world together. The three musketeers. Always, Mum xx*

I flicked through the pages absentmindedly and a piece of paper fell out of the middle. A delicate sketch of a beautiful woman and man sat at a kitchen table. I looked between the sketch and the photo album. His parents.

'Did you . . . ?' I asked gesturing at the worn memory in my hand.

He closed his eyes and nodded slowly. 'Yep. I drew that. They'd sit at that kitchen table once a month and lay out all the bills and all the paperwork and go through it together. Maybe it's why I couldn't watch you do it with your dad every month; it's so surreal sometimes, reminds me so much of them.' He shook the memory from his head, blanking his mind like an Etch-A-Sketch block before returning to the story in hand.

'Running this farm, when it was a farm, was hard work. I would sit and sketch them as they talked. Even when they talked about money, they wouldn't fight. My God they loved each other. Dad worshipped the ground my mother polished, and she made the world around him sparkle just to see him smile. They were the most formidable team.'

I traced my fingers over the lovely pencil drawing. The lines seemingly unbroken. The effort and care around their features so perfectly balanced.

'I must have been ten years old when I drew that one. There are hundreds more. I gave up drawing for a long time after they died. Mum always encouraged it, but Dad . . .' His words trailed off. Clearly, he wasn't ready to go there yet. He shook his head, and just like resetting a typewriter he pushed his emotions to one side and restarted the story on the next line.

'That's Mum. That's Dad.'

He pointed at the picture a few pages into the album now. They were grinning, both of them dressed in heavy wellies and thick wax jackets. His mother handing his father what looked like a brown paper lunch bag.

'I took that as part of a school project. Semiotics – a media project. We had to take pictures showing in a series what we thought of our parents. My parents were hard-working, always outdoors and always thinking of each other.'

In the picture, behind his parents, was a big barn. I recognised it from somewhere. Digging around in the paperwork I found a clipping.

*Tragic Farm Accident Takes Two Lives* was emblazoned across the top, with the picture of an ambulance in front of that very barn. Exactly where they'd stood in this picture. The same barn we'd parked in front of.

He saw the recognition on my face.

'It wasn't long after that was taken.' His face fell.

'Dad and I had a difficult relationship in the later years. I guess you could say he was a typical farmer. Like the ones you'd see on TV shows. What you expected to see when you met Steve and Julie. That was my dad. Up with the cocks at five a.m. every morning. Always covered in mud and never a day when there wasn't a job to do.'

James pulled out a few more pictures from the album and passed them to me. Handling them like precious china, I moved the memories between my fingers. Watching as the image of his father came to life in my mind. Stocky. A little tubby around the waist and a face that had seen more than its fair share of sun, wind and rain. Weathered, but his eyes – even in these old, faded pictures – were remarkably like James's. His smile, the way that tiny crease at the corner of his lips looked like a dimple when he smiled – there it was caught on the face of the man who made him.

'He hated that I wasn't like him. The older I got the more I loved reading with my mother at the kitchen table. I preferred sitting outside drawing the fields rather than working them. When I was choosing my options for GCSEs I was so excited. I wanted to do art and media.

I wanted to draw, write, be creative! Dad wanted me to leave school and work on the farm. This was our legacy. His life's work.' He flicked through the album, pictures of his father with the animals, on tractors and surrounded by home-grown veg in the kitchen.

'He was getting on in years, and me coming of age meant I could work the farm with him until I was ready to take over. He had my life mapped out from the moment I was born.'

He paused. A sorrowful and painful blush crossed his cheeks.

'He had a life planned out for each loss my mother had. He'd wanted a son. He'd wanted an heir to the family throne.'

I glanced down at the final image in the pile he'd given me, and the focus of the picture shifted. Suddenly I couldn't see the smile on his father's face but the separation between them. James stood with his mother's arms wrapped around his small shoulders, fingers entwined at his chest. His father stood next to them, arms crossed, hat tipped a little too low over his forehead, just that little bit too far away. Them and him.

'I was seventeen when it happened. I was impatient with Dad's insistence that I help him. Steph, I was a teenager. I wanted to go out at night to the pub with my mates, meet girls and have a laugh. But I also already knew I didn't want to be a farmer. Dad eventually gave in and let me go to college, but only on the understanding that I'd focus on working once I was done.'

He paused, long enough for me to push him to continue.

'But you didn't, did you? You didn't stay at home.

You went to uni.' I urged him on, desperate to hear the end.

'I nearly didn't.'

He pulled a smaller envelope from the box and passed it to me. Inside were dozens of fragments of torn-up pieces of paper.

'That was my acceptance letter to Leeds Uni.'

In my heart I knew it was coming. I could feel the train gaining speed and the destination coming into sight.

'Dad found out that Mum and I had applied to universities. Normally Mum would open the post. I would collect it from the box every day as part of my chores, and Mum would deal with the paperwork, filing it all away in the right places until that day of the month where they would sit at the table. I never thought he'd find it. Not like that.'

He took a deep breath and sat back on the sofa, knotting his back in between the cushions like he was settling in for the night.

'I brought the post in that day and set it on the table. My acceptance letter was there. As I was about to open it, Dad walked into the room. I shuffled the envelope in between the others and tried to act normally. He asked what I was doing, told me Mum was sick and that he'd take the post up to her in bed. I tried to insist but he wasn't having it. Even now I can remember the whole thing, beat for beat.'

His words came thick and fast, as if the quicker they were said the less they would sting.

He took a long drink and I did the same, feeling the knot in my chest rising.

'He was angry with me. I'd been slacking with the farm chores. He told me he needed help in the barn.

We'd stacked all the logs for the winter. We had so many trees on the land and after a bad storm, Dad had been forced to fell a load. We had a truck coming the following week to take them from the barn where we'd stored them, stacked in there drying. Anyway . . .'

He shook his head and ran his hands through his hair before taking his glasses off and rubbing his eyes.

'He told me he needed me to take the day off college to help him with farm stuff. Ben, a lad who helped out, was sick and he needed to shift a load of stuff in the barn so they could come and collect the logs. We got into a big fight. I told him I wasn't going to take a day off to help him. That he could get someone else to do it. I had exams coming up and I couldn't stay off just to shift a load of logs. I was rude to him.'

I couldn't imagine it. I couldn't see it. Couldn't hear it. My James being disrespectful, to anyone, let alone a parent. He cleared his throat and ran his hands though his hair again. I could see how uncomfortable he was. After all these years I never imagined he'd be uncomfortable telling me anything.

'He kept ranting about me wasting my future and that I needed to step up and remember my place in the family. That I needed to put more of an effort in to learn the trade.'

The chiming of the bells from the grandfather clock in the hallway paused us in our tracks, giving James a moment to gather himself.

'I screamed at him. I told him I wouldn't do it. I never screamed at Dad, but I did that day. I stormed off up the stairs to get ready for college and slammed the door like a petulant teenager. I still remember the sound that door made.'

He went quiet. I stared at him. That couldn't be it. That wasn't the story. That wasn't the end, surely. But he'd stopped talking.

'James?'

'Steph. That was the last time I saw Dad. The last words I uttered were that I hated him and that he was ruining my life. That he was a terrible parent and he couldn't see how much he was holding me back. I said the most horrendous things to him, and he just stood there and took it.'

He lowered his head into his palms, unable to look me in the eye.

'He knocked on my bedroom door, tried to come and talk to me, and I ignored him. I screamed at him and said I hated him. That was the last thing I ever said to him.'

'James, you were a kid. You couldn't have known. Every teenager hates their parents. It's an unwritten rule.'

I could feel his pain and wanted to pull him close, but the curiosity and confusion held me back. There were gaps in the puzzle. I bent down to collect a scrap of newspaper from the pile but James beat me to it.

'Wait. I need to tell you the full story. I need to get it out.' His voice cracked. 'I haven't spoken about this to anyone since it happened. I need to explain . . .'

His voice trailed off and I wondered how much pain this secret had caused as it ate away at him over the years. Wondered how much of his personality it claimed as it fed off his fear and guilt.

'I heard Dad go into the bedroom and the mumblings through the wall. Then I heard him get angry. He raised his voice at Mum; he'd never ever done that before. Not that I'd ever heard. He told her he would "let me go over his own cold dead body".'

I watched as the memories played out like a movie across the glazed reflections in his eyes, as if he were living it all over again.

'He slammed the bedroom door and left. A few minutes later, Mum knocked on my door. She was so sad, Steph; her and Dad never fought. But I watched her face change as she handed over the letter from the university. We opened it together and hugged and cried. It was an unconditional offer. I never in a million years expected it. She was so proud. She promised me that she'd talk to Dad and sort it out. She got dressed and went out to see him in the barn.'

A shiver ran through my body and froze my spine in place. I couldn't help but wonder what his mum was thinking as she took her final steps towards that barn. All her plans, the dreams of seeing her son graduate. All the memories she'd never get the chance to make with him.

'I was about to leave for college when I heard raised voices again. Dad's growl and my mother's pleading voice battling his. Then I heard a rumble before Mum screamed. I will never forget it, Steph. The sound haunts me at night.'

I moved the paperwork from the sofa onto the box on the floor and shifted over to meet him. Wrapping my arms around his shoulders, I pulled him in close and felt his body shaking against mine.

'Dad had lost his footing on the logs and fallen. He pulled the top one with him as he tried to balance and hit his head on the way down. The coroner said he was probably unconscious when the collapse happened and wouldn't have felt much.'

I held my breath. Every inch of my body wishing I

could spin back time and somehow take back that misstep for him, that one small move that ended in such tragedy and so much pain for the man I loved.

'Mum had been standing at the bottom of the stack and screamed as Dad fell, but as he did the unstable wood collapsed around him. The logs rolled on top of Mum and crushed her.'

I tried to lift his head from my chest so I could see his eyes, so I could hug and kiss him, but he wouldn't move.

'Don't, Steph. I can't look at you. Just let me finish.'

His head was heavy on my chest. I lay back against the sofa and let him speak his truth directly into my heart space.

'Dad was buried under the logs by the time I got into the barn. Mum was crushed but still breathing. I held her hand. She only woke briefly. I tried to keep her awake as I called the ambulance. I tried so hard; I really did. I kept telling her I was sorry. She died before they arrived.'

There it was. His big secret laid out in front of us. His pain speckled in the shape of teardrops across my chest and his regrets blanketing the space between us.

'My parents died because of me. It was my fault. When the ambulance and police arrived that was all I would say. That it was my fault. Dad wouldn't have been on that stack of wood if I'd gone out to help. Mum would have still been tucked up in bed with a Lemsip. And the very last thing I ever did was tell my father what a rotten disappointment he was as a parent. He died thinking that I hated him.'

I lifted his head and looked into his eyes, finding small traces of the flecks of amber fighting against the painful memories to shine again. They were there, buried, but with each word he spoke, more of his pain released and I could see his beautiful soul returning. It wasn't until I looked at the photograph discarded at my feet that I saw it. Those same flecks, in his father's eyes.

This small, locked door that we had for so long pretended we didn't need to open was now flung wide for the whole world to see. For the first time since we met, I looked into the eyes of the man I loved, and I could see every single inch of his soul.

Now he made sense. It all made sense.

# CHAPTER THIRTY-ONE

We sat there for the longest time. So long that the fire fairies stopped dancing and fell asleep on the burnt-out shells of the logs. The room grew colder, and I pulled the blanket from the back of the sofa to cover him.

I wasn't sure when he fell asleep, or if he was even properly asleep. All I knew was that one moment he was sobbing into my chest and the next his head was heavy, his breathing laboured, and his body finally gave in to mine.

How had I not seen it? How had I been so blind and naïve? As I stroked his hair and looked around the room, our entire lives seem to shift in front of my eyes. I had never noticed all these missing puzzle pieces or the pieces that were lodged into spaces they didn't fit.

Each day he would leave, but never without saying *I love you*. Each night he would kiss my head and say, *Sleep safe*. We messaged each other multiple times throughout the day and he never fought with me. He never raised his voice, never questioned me and now it was so obvious why. *This* was why he was who he was. This was why he wanted a child so badly; he wanted a second chance. Our family was his shot at redemption.

The room grew so cold I could barely handle it. His body kept mine warm, but the tip of my nose felt like ice. Gently shaking him from his slumber, I raised his head and sleepy eyes to meet mine.

'Let's go to bed.'

As we walked through the house towards the bedroom, I found myself wondering about the ghosts that wandered these halls. I swept my hand along the dated dado rail that ran the length of the upstairs corridor, only then noticing the rawness of the wood, the small scratches on the skirting boards and the slightly discoloured edges on the corners of the wallpaper.

We passed a smaller bedroom and I paused as I watched my husband walk through the doorway into the master bedroom with heavy shoulders and a pained gait. I peered through the open door of the smaller room. Dark wallpaper covered the walls. The same slightly uneven dado rail separated the room in half. The moonlight bounced off the walls, highlighting small imperfections I would have never noticed before now.

The window called to me as the light from the full moon poured in, and when I walked further into the room, I recognised the view. There was an exquisite painting on the wall of our office back home. Scratched out in heavy oils, a large oak tree stood tall and proud on the top of a hill, framed by a lead-framed bedroom window. A woman sat beneath the arms of the tree with a book in her hand as the day awoke around her, warm colours and the promise of a new day spread across the canvas.

James had always said that the painting was from a friend back home, but as I stared at the silhouette of the tree in the window, I realised the artist was him. A slice of his home hung secretly above his desk as a daily reminder of this place, his memories and, I now realised, his mother.

His pain hung in our home, his secret encased in glass on our walls, a daily reminder of his guilt, of his past and the secrets he hid from me. He'd never let this place go. He walked away from his mistake, but it never left him.

I wandered back into the bedroom to find my beautiful husband curled up in the master bed. He looked so small. Coiled up with the duvet tucked under his chin, his eyes softly closed. He looked like a child.

I wondered if this had been the same room they had slept in, wondered if he was lying on the same side of the bed as his mother or father. It took so much courage for him to bring me back here.

I slipped between the sheets and the heavy down duvet, feeling the weight relax my shoulders as my head hit the pillow. He turned, sleepily, and without opening his eyes, pulled me close to him. His heartbeat slow and steady, his breathing rising and falling with mine.

This was home.

I struggled with the deceit, and I still had questions. I couldn't wrap my head around these lies and omissions that had filled our lives together, but as we lay next to each other with our own pain, our own regrets, we also shared a collective grief.

'I miss our peanut. It was never ours, but I miss our baby,' I whispered into his chest.

I wasn't even sure he was awake; I didn't expect a response.

He moved one of his arms from around my body and found my hands, clutched in front of my chest, and knitted his fingers into mine.

'So do I. Always more at night. I dream of what we could have been. I miss our dreams. I miss the life we nearly had.' His voice was so low, his words so full of honesty.

'I'm so sorry, Stephanie.' He squeezed my hand ever so slightly as he kissed the top of my head, and I knew he meant it. It was an apology for nothing and an apology for everything. Our heartbeats raced against each other as we slipped into dreamless sleep, neither of us allowing our subconsciousness the chance to paint pictures of the future.

# CHAPTER THIRTY-TWO

I wasn't sure what had woken me but something in my fitful sleep made me open my eyes as the sky was beginning to brighten. The moors were calling me. My eyes rested upon the water droplets of condensation that dripped down the windowpanes, the image of the Yorkshire Moors blurred in the background, a world away from the built-up streets of Brighton.

Something drew me from my comfortable bed.

I slipped from the warmth and pulled my thick warm jumper over my pyjamas; tied my trainers tight. I had never been a runner, had never bought a pair of trainers before, but the doctors told me that running would help me overcome the panic attacks I'd been having since the day my world collapsed. More often than not, I woke in the mornings and rather than grabbing my camera, I would reach for these alien shoes and run until I felt more pain in my legs than in my chest. But today my chest was being pulled towards the hills, not for pain but for relief.

It was time for me to visit her again, the mother who had cloaked me that day on the moors. The mother who had comforted me. I'd found a partner in my pain that day but maybe I'd left an element of my grief behind.

I stood at the top of the pathway. The oil-slick pavement beneath my feet begged me to follow it down to the depths of the valley, but as much as my legs itched to be pushed past their limits, my heart was pulling me in a different direction. No longer down twisty pathways into the unknown, but towards the top of the hill where the earth met heaven's gate, to the oak tree whose roots, buried so deep, kept her strong and fortified against the harsh winter weather.

I climbed the steps carved into the moss by Mother Nature, a perfectly formed pathway towards this beacon of hope that stood atop a mountain of pain.

'God's own country,' I whispered into the silence. 'I can see what he meant now.'

I approached the sturdy oak with caution, as if scared to wake her from her winter slumber. Her leaves now dropped, but her branches stretched out as far as possible towards the sky, eager to absorb each and every moment of life. Long gone was her feathered cap, her beauty, replaced by a blanket of fuzz, hugging tightly to the bark to keep her warm.

As my fingertips touched her exposed bark, I could hear the voices of the rings of history within screaming to be heard. Could feel each groan of the bark as the wind moved it ever so slightly from side to side.

I wondered what James's mother would have felt as she sat here, wondered how often he sat here with her. I strained my ears to hear the whispers of a mother and child as they read together.

I lowered myself tentatively, careful not to disturb her repose, and knitted my spine into the crevices created by her notches – the perfect nook, waiting patiently to invite me into her embrace.

The last time I had sat on these hills, I felt abandoned by God, alone in a cruel world. The Mother of the Moors had comforted me. She had become part of me that day and it felt right to be sitting here with her as I navigated the new world that stretched out in front of me.

The cold bit at my face, and the grey dawn sky reflecting on the reservoir below made me shiver, and just as I wondered if this romantic notion was foolhardy, she opened up her eyes and once more welcomed me into her fold. The sun rose over the crest of the moors on the other side of the water's edge, and I watched as a trio of ducks argued and squawked overhead. Their screams like fighting children at the breakfast table. She had tapped her baton on the stand and ordered her followers into action. The symphony began, slowly at first, cautious then magical. The birds joined in the chorus and the bleating of the sheep provided the bass. The moors came alive as Mother herself rose to greet them. The grey morning sky transformed, the music of the surrounding nature the backdrop to a painting she was creating in front of my eyes.

I held a breath of air in my lungs and prayed for it to fill each and every part of my body, sucking down the golden light and allowing it to revive the greyest parts of my soul. If there was any darkness left within me, this light was surely fighting it.

The squawking children of the sky hit back against freezing air with their wings as they struggled overhead, bursting through the sun's rays and hitting the water with such precision that they seemed to leave a trail of glittering diamonds like a wedding veil in their wake.

Resting my head back against the cold wet moss of the tree, I turned my face towards the sky as the rays from the hillside finally reached my little corner of the world.

Golden droplets seemed to hang in the air, each one suspended in time. Each glinting and sparkling but together creating a beam of light that warmed the parts of the earth it touched below. The teardrops of dew laid down by the darkness of the night before fought hard against their victor, desperate to nestle their way between the small hairs of the moss, but she had other plans. The pain of the night before would not be dragged into this beautiful day. She was here to renew life and bring me hope.

I hadn't noticed the numbness creep down my fingers until it bit at my palms when the warmth of her rays brought pins and needles to my skin, pricking at the band of gold on my left hand. I had given my pain to her that day on the moors, cried and screamed until my heart felt nothing but empty. She had comforted me and sent me off to war. Now I was back, and this was my reward. This was her pride. She opened her heart and flooded the landscape with all the warmth she had within her. This was right.

He was right.

I needed to come back to this place to repair, to heal. So did he. This place would make us whole again.

In that moment, I understood why my mother had chosen to heal here. In every sense of the word, this place helped her breathe again. I could feel it, in the goose bumps that covered my skin and the breath releasing from my chest. This place was fixing me, sticking all my broken bits back together.

I allowed myself to truly soak in all her sounds and smells. Closing my eyes, I surrendered control.

The crunch of the leaves behind me woke from my spiritual happy place.

'Hey, beautiful.'

His hair was ruffled. Bedhead always did suit him more than the neat waves he hid himself behind for work.

I smiled at him and moved to stand up.

'No, don't. I'll sit down with you. It's strangely comforting to see you here. We used to sit in this exact spot . . . in the . . .'

'Nook . . .' I cut him off, finishing his sentence as I ran my fingertips down the bark.

'Yes. Exactly. Nook. "Shaped just for us" Mum used to say.' He lowered himself to sit by me. 'We used to read this together here. And others.'

He pulled the book from his pocket as he sat by my side.

'I always imagined that we'd sit here one day, with our third little musketeer.' Tears filled his eyes, but the smile that crossed his lips held them back. As he flicked through the book, I could feel his hunger to be here, on this hill under this tree, was fuelled by the same painful emotion as mine.

'Read it. To me. We may be two, but for now, why don't we read it to our peanut anyway.'

A flash of recognition passed between us as he opened the page. The browning paper so fragile between his fingers, the sound of the scratching pages as they turned.

I laid my head against his shoulder and watched as the clouds overhead surrendered to the wind and allowed themselves to be pushed across the sky.

We sat there for a while; his voice cracked at certain parts as he read. He wasn't reading every page but picking out passages that meant something to him, explaining memories along the way. It was like getting the Cliffs Notes according to James and his mother.

We laughed at the language and talked about his parents. We talked about how they would have felt about us, how he thought his mother would have reacted to the news of our pregnancy and how she would have used good ole Yorkshire food as comfort to help us heal.

Then he was quiet, lost in the page in front of him.

I turned my face back to the sky, watching the rolling clouds, aware that he needed his quiet moments just as I did.

One cloud caught my eye as it seemed to morph in front of us. I watched as a dragon appeared in the outline. Its head held high, and tail outstretched. The cloud moved in a way that made the head seem to drop to its chest, like he was bowing to us. Tears rolled down my cheeks as I thought of my dad and my baby peanut.

*I have nothing but memory. It is my happiness, my treasure, my hope. Every time I see you is a fresh diamond which I enclose in the casket of my heart.* James's words seemed to echo the portrait painting itself in front me as he read from the book. The cloud continued to morph; there one moment, gone the next. The outline formed a hole at its centre. A hole in its heart. Tears now tumbling down my cheeks, I tried hard to stop my shoulders from shaking, but the force from within me was so strong I couldn't hold it back.

'There are so many good souls up there now.' My words caught behind the lump in my throat as I tried to give them up to the sky.

James put the book down and turned my face to meet his. 'Yes. But they're not alone.' His eyes were questioning. He opened his mouth to say something but stopped himself.

'Say it. What is it? I can tell you want to say something.'

'I'm not sure it's the right time. But then, I don't think it ever will be.'

I shifted from my man-made seat amongst the moss and sat back on my knees. 'Go on.'

He drew breath into his lungs and readied himself. 'We can still have *our* family. We can still have *our* dream. It could look different to everything we ever planned, but maybe that's what we need. Different doesn't have to be bad.'

I didn't say anything. Scared to breathe. I was still grieving the loss of Dad, dealing with the hole left in my heart by the dream of a child that would never be.

'I came back here when you told me you were pregnant. Something drew me back and even though I knew you would never live here, I knew this needed to be our home. I think we should make this our home. I think this place could be good for both of us. For all of us.'

'What do you mean, all of us?'

He took my hand and squeezed tight. 'We can adopt. I spoke to Helen. We talked it all through. We can adopt and she can help us. We can give a child a home and love. We can build our own family from all the broken pieces that are left behind. We can move here, sell our place and start again. Do this place up and fill it with happy memories again.'

The words fell from him, fast and furious against the frozen air.

I couldn't breathe. I couldn't even think about how I was supposed to make my body function. I had never planned this. None of this was on my mental mood board. We were going to build our home close to Dad, and live near the sea. But as I looked at his face and the knots of the tree behind him, something screamed in me to listen.

I sat back against the tree but didn't let go of his hand. Staring out over the moors I let out the breath I'd been holding.

'This place, it feels so . . .' I couldn't find the words, but my pause clearly worried him. His shoulders and body tensed and his jaw tightened. 'It feels so peaceful. Dad would love it here.' I paused a beat, hearing my own words. 'Would have loved it here.'

I still wasn't used to talking about him in the past tense.

'Adopt. Would they even let us? I'm not in remission yet.'

His jaw softened and the amber flecks of hope returned to his eyes.

'Helen says it would take a little longer, but she knows couples who have been in similar situations. She can help.'

I looked back towards the sky and felt my heart flutter. I wanted so much to hold my peanut in my arms. To show a child what it felt like to be truly loved and cared for. I wanted to take care of someone.

'Could we really leave Brighton?' I wasn't really asking him; I was asking myself. Could I leave behind the place I'd called home? Could I leave Alex? My dad?

'Sometimes in life, Steph, we need to turn the page and start afresh. I can get work up here. With so many businesses moving up North, there are plenty of firms I could apply to, and loads of exciting new developments. You could do the same, maybe get back into wedding photography? We could adopt, start again, build new memories. We could still have that family life we always wanted, and give a child who needs a home a truly loving one.'

I could hear the excitement in his voice, tucked behind those notes of hesitation, but peeping there all the same. I remembered how he'd looked that day we got here, the freedom and peace on his face. I thought about the tears I'd cried and how this land had helped me breathe. The sea had always been my companion, but the rough waves and unforgiving tides had had their time. Maybe the moors would help rebuild me. Maybe the solitude of a peaceful life was exactly what we needed after years of pain and disappointment.

'OK. I am not saying yes; but let's think about it.'

I took a beat, wondered if I should say the words prickling at my tongue. We were in a different place now, a place of honesty and openness. I had to say it.

'This place . . . these hills, this sky. Something about it feels right. I feel a little more at peace. I think I'm ready to start talking about it, our options, I mean. Adoption. Maybe.' I took a deep breath and steadied myself. 'But let's not involve Helen just yet. I know she means well, but this is our journey. Let's do our own research first. We need to do this together.'

He pulled me close to his chest and hugged me. 'I agree. I just thought that maybe you needed someone else to talk this through with.'

'That's lovely, and I appreciate it. But I'm married to you. Not Helen. I think you were right: these kinds of decisions should be made together. You and me. No one else.' I smiled and kissed his lips.

'We'll take our time, and keep it between us, until you're ready. There's no rush. But you're right. There is something about this place that feels like home. At least it does again now.'

'Do you think we could be happy here?' I asked him, tentatively, because I wasn't one hundred per cent sure myself yet.

'Here.' He looked at me, shocked, but trying to hide it for fear I would change my mind. 'Maybe.'

We both looked down towards the home at the bottom of the hill, standing proud among the rolling fields. I turned my focus towards the barn that once gave him so much pain and wondered if he could live with these ghosts. I'd be leaving so many of mine behind, but he was about to make a new life surrounded by his own. The barn could be torn down, but the memories would remain.

'Maybe having your mum close by isn't such a bad thing anymore either. I know it's not perfect between you, Steph, but you would have a support system. Your mum, Steve and Julie, it's the closest we'll get to a family,' James said.

We could breathe life and love back into that home; it could be a home filled with the laughter of a child. A child we could give new hope to. That we could give a loving home to.

I had never felt less in control but so much at peace as I did in that moment. It all felt possible. A new start. A new life and a new future.

*Was* it all possible?

# CHAPTER THIRTY-THREE

It was never going to be a simple process, adoption, but then I didn't think it should be. Having a child was a commitment, and most parents would have nine months to prepare themselves. To go to the baby classes, stock up on essentials and prepare their lives for an addition. So it made sense that to adopt a child, the process would be long, complicated and emotional. It took a few years for us, with all the added complications, but I didn't mind. I could wait. I had waited this long.

Now, I was preparing the house for her arrival, and after all the years of waiting and praying, hoping and grieving, we would finally be a family. In less than twenty-four hours, our lives would be altered forever, and much like the day before I married James, there wasn't an ounce of nerves in me. Because I knew we'd made the right decision.

James was a different story. He was more nervous

than I'd ever seen him. The house had been a flurry of DIY projects all week. Fixing the 'rough banister' in case she got a splinter, reseating the stones that made up our doorstep so she didn't trip and graze her knees, and of course going to the pharmacy to stock up on all the creams in case she *did* trip and graze a knee. He was in full nesting mode, and I loved him for it.

Me, I'd spent a lovely morning with my mother, picking apples. She'd written down her recipe in a beautiful bound 'family recipe book' and given it to me as a gift the day we got the final approval. A recipe book to fill with all our memories so that our child could one day pass them on to her children. So, we'd picked the apples and bought the ingredients, and they were waiting patiently in the kitchen to be mixed together by the delicate fingers of our new three-year-old daughter, under the careful expert guidance of her 'granny', of course.

There was nothing left to do now but wait. Wait and smile and . . .

'Have you written that letter yet?' James rounded the corner, his smile written all over his face. He bounced around the place like an excitable puppy.

'No, not yet,' I replied. 'I don't know what to say.'

'Remember what Helen said: it's best to write it now, before she gets here. Life is about to get very busy, and you don't want to forget this moment.'

He blew a kiss in my direction and shut the door to my study. I sat, staring out the window at the fields beyond, and took out a plain piece of paper from my desk drawer.

Taking a deep breath, I looked at the picture in the silver frame, the three of us, our first picture together.

We looked like a family already. I couldn't wait for it to be real.

I uncapped my fountain pen, held it above the plain white paper and smiled. This was one memory I never wanted to forget, and Helen was right: one day, our little girl would want to know how this all came about.

*My darling girl,*

*We have been asked so many times already if we are ever planning on 'telling you' about your adoption, and how we intend to do it. Your lovely auntie Helen suggested that this might be the perfect way. Something for you to keep and read when you need to. Something you can hold and know that right from the very beginning, you were loved. By so many people.*

*I hope that one day, when you read this letter, it will help answer all the questions you might have about how you came to us and hopefully you will see just how much you were wanted, how much you were needed and the impact you have had on our lives.*

*I am writing this the night before the most important day of my life so far, a day I never imagined I would see, but one that fills me with so much love and excitement, and so it seems fitting that I write this letter today. Why? Because this is the last day we will be us, without you. Tomorrow, you will finally be coming home. But I think I need to start with a different day. I need to start with the day we first met.*

*It wasn't the first time we'd seen you, of*

*course, but it was the first time I got to hold you in my arms and feel the softness of your skin. I got to see your eyes, beautiful girl, and they melted my heart. Something so knowing and familiar, so innocent.*

*By now, you will know about your other mother, the one who brought you into this world. I have promised myself that we will always be honest with you. We will always tell you that we chose you, but that someone else held you in their heart first.*

*When we looked through the adoption files, I knew immediately that you were a little girl who deserved to be loved, and something about your story fitted with us so well. Your mother was beautiful, determined and independent. She decided that she wanted a child so much that she found a way to have a baby without a partner. She had never found the right man, but was determined to complete her dream of becoming a mother. Then a tragic accident took your mum from this world and, with no family and no one to turn to, your path eventually led you to us.*

*You were brought into this world the very same day my dad was taken from it. It felt like a sign from above, that on a day when I was feeling the pain of losing my dad, and my baby on that same day, you were taking your first breath and making your mother's dream come true.*

*My heart broke when I read your story. It broke for your mother. I know all too well how hard it is to want something so badly that you will do anything in the world to see your dream come true. It broke for you too, because before you had even taken your first steps, you felt your first loss. That loss is one I understand.*

*Fate had stripped us both of the families we expected to grow old with, but taking you into my arms and our hearts felt like we were patching up small holes in us both.*

*My darling girl, I will never be able to explain the feeling I had when the door swung open. I gripped your father's hand and my whole body shook.*

*Your beautiful long blonde hair seemed to float behind you as you ran towards us. Before the counsellor could even introduce us, you had your arms wrapped around my legs and for a moment I was terrified to move.*

*We were introduced formally. The counsellor bent down to your eyeline, and both your dad and I did the same. She introduced me as Stephanie, and then she said your name out loud for the first time, and just as it had the day I saw it written on the file, my heart stopped.*

*Hope. My Hope. Our Hope.*

*I thank your mother silently every single time I say that name out loud.*

*The word hit my heart hard that day in the office, but to hear your name and see you smiling at me at the same time . . . my whole world seemed to knit together. There was something so knowing and wise in your sapphire eyes and I could feel the gaping hole in my heart healing over.*

*But then, something happened that blew my world apart.*

*You didn't pause. Not for one beat. You leant forward and wrapped your arms around my neck and squeezed so tight I couldn't breathe.*

*I tried to peel you away from me and put my hand out to shake yours. I had rehearsed my words over and over again in the car on the way over.*

*'Hello, Hope. I'm Stephanie. It's lovely to meet you.'*

*Your face, your expression, it changed, and you broke into laughter. Throwing your head back and slapping your hands on the sides of your legs.*

*'Silly. I know you. You're my other mummy.'*

*It was as simple and as innocent as that. I wasn't Stephanie to you – I was your other mummy. My whole world fell into place in that moment.*

*You leant forward and left the most beautiful imprint of a kiss on my cheek and whispered into my ear, 'Don't cry anymore.' I hadn't even realised I was.*

*You patted my face before turning to your dad and giving him a hug. He stood up, lifting you into the air and spinning you around. The two of you laughing as if it was the most normal action in the entire world.*

*My world changed that day, Hope.*

*You changed our lives.*

*The three of us together. Something about our family picture just fitted. It was as if you were the small jigsaw piece that connected us all together. The three musketeers.*

*Tomorrow marks the first day of a new life for us all. I promise to write as much of our journey as possible from here on, and I pray that when you read this as a young lady, you know just how loved you are.*

*Your other mummy X*

As I placed the lid back on my pen, I stared at the cursive lettering and couldn't believe what I was looking at. Never, in a million years, did I think that I would write a letter like that. I never imagined our family coming together in any other way than the traditional route, but as I folded the paper and slipped it into an envelope, I wasn't sure it was ever supposed to be any other way. This was our story. This was our family. We had fought hard to get here, but it was worth every painful step.

I slipped the envelope into the ornate carved wooden box, which had once sheltered my father's secrets for me. Now, it was filled with ticket stubs from our train journeys. Car park stubs from the day we first met her, and of course, the tiny little ceramic dragon. I might not have bought it with her in mind, but that dragon started a series of events that ended with us all finding our 'forever homes'.

The door to my study squeaked and gave away the intruder lurking beyond.

'I'm done,' I said, as my husband sidled into the room.

'Me too,' he said, a cheeky grin on his face. 'I decided

to write a little thing too.' He blushed slightly as he passed over the envelope. 'Not a lot. Just something for her to read and know how excited I was. I am. You know what I mean.'

He tucked the envelope in next to mine before pulling a little sketch from his pocket. 'Maybe we can put this in too?' he said cautiously.

I looked at the pencil markings and my heart leapt. He had sketched, from memory, the moment Hope clung to my neck. We might not have a photo to remember that moment, but to me, that pencil sketch meant so much more.

I closed the lid, took his hand and left the office. This time tomorrow, our house would be far from quiet, and I couldn't wait.

# EPILOGUE

Our daughter now feels as much a piece of this place as she is a part of us. Of me.

She walks these floors and these rooms as if she has always known the footprint of this home. She fits into our lives as if she has always been a part of us.

Life has been an adventure. We have watched as she begins to grow more into her own personality. Her stubborn nature is obvious, but there's something ethereal about her. She feels everything very deeply. I caught her once staring at the sky with bewilderment written all over her face. I asked what she was thinking, and she smiled and said, *Nothing really. I'm just remembering*.

She feels the life in everything she touches. Savours the smells of fresh-cut grass. She once woke me on the first day of the changing of the seasons to tell me she could 'smell it'. She knows when the snow is about to fall and blanket the hills and will sit for hours watching each snowflake drift and settle on the panes of the same window her father once looked out of as a child.

Her voice softens rooms. It melts even the coldest hearts. When James and I get frustrated with each other, she will come and lay her hand on our legs and tell us that we shouldn't fight. That we love each other really. Her favourite phrase is *Don't forget, Mummy, you love Daddy. Don't fight.* She is the tiniest old soul I have ever met.

My mother visits us frequently. She lives an hour's drive away in a different area of the county, so we don't live on top of each other, but it's nice to have family nearby. We have tried hard to repair our relationship. Losing my father made me realise just how important family is, not only for me, but for Hope too. We still have a lot to work through, but watching Mum play with her granddaughter brings me a peace I was never sure I would feel.

I catch her with a small look of sadness on her face sometimes and I recognise it. I know she's thinking of Alex. Grief doesn't go away – we both know that – but it shape-shifts. Sometimes it is big and overwhelming, and at other times I find myself feeling grateful.

My beautiful Hope is gluing all of our broken pieces back together. Mum often remarks that we may have given her a home, but she gave us life, and I couldn't agree with her more.

It wasn't long until she started asking about a brother or sister. She would sit at night and listen to James reading her *The Three Musketeers* and would say, *Daddy, you say we are the three musketeers, but there are four in the book. We need to be four. We are not finished yet.*

She seemed desperate to mother something other than the sheep on the farm. Pepper, our ever-patient puppy, follows her around like a shadow but a dog was never going to be enough for her. She needed a sibling.

When we had word from the agency that our second adoption had been processed, we couldn't wait to tell her.

The moment we told her that she would be getting a baby brother, she seemed less excited and more nonchalant about the whole thing. I won't deny I felt a pang of disappointment. I expected her to scream to the heavens – instead she acted as if it was an inevitability.

*See, I told you. I knew I was getting a brother soon.*

We laughed at her matter-of-fact tone, but as I sit here now, watching her with her baby brother, I can see what she meant. We were never meant to be three, we were always meant to be four.

Today was a special day. Four years since that dreadful day. We had long ago decided to celebrate the happiness of this day rather than fester in the pain of the memories. Less sad and more of a celebration. The pain of that day and the tragedy of the situation had brought us to where we are now and in a strange way, brought us the children we now simply couldn't imagine living without.

I had invited Mum and Bill to stay for the weekend to celebrate with us, and Steve and Julie were due to join us for the barbecue later. We had spent so long renovating the house and it was time to show it off. With special memories preserved and other areas given a new lease of life, this house now felt like a home.

The pain held within the walls of the barn was buried deep the day we tore the structure down. James didn't need a constant reminder of that day, and with the barn gone, the space it opened up was perfect for a good old-fashioned kids' playground.

Although I looked forward to seeing Mum, and to the day we had planned, I hadn't slept a wink all night preparing for it. On the face of it, we would all smile, but deep down we knew it was a day tinged with bittersweet memories.

I woke sleepily, my dozing eyes falling softly on the sight of droplets of condensation as they chased each other like excited children down the frosted glass. I couldn't help but think back to that day when we travelled up here, and I'd counted the droplets like tears as they trailed down the train window. It's funny how the small things look so different depending on the stage of life you find yourself in.

Adam had been sleeping soundly in the cot at the side of the bedroom. Cocooned in a blanket knitted by my mother with small dragons sewn into the thick band around the top.

I counted each of his slow rising breaths as his chest pulsed against the heavy knit.

I turned over to find a little intruder had found her way in between me and my husband. Her peaceful face soft and smiling in her dreams, curls framing her flawless face and her father's large protective hand wrapped around his little girl's chest.

I watched as she took in the warm air from the room and with each exhalation gave back just as much to the world as she was taking from it.

It seemed like only yesterday and at the same time

a million years ago that I'd lain in this bed staring at the pained face of my grieving husband, wondering how we would ever get over our secrets and lies. The pain that consumed our bodies threatened to leave physical scars. My fingertips pulsed at the thought.

I edged my way out of bed, feet hovering over the tiles, bracing myself for the shock of the cold on my bare skin.

James's eyes were barely closed. In this restful pose he looked so peaceful, in a land where no pain entered without invitation.

I could see him in her, so easily. I knew it wasn't possible, but something about the way they lay together made it seem like they were always supposed to share the same space. The way they slept mirrored each other, both sucking in the air and expelling it with such force the noise rattled their ribcages. Two peas in a pod.

She had fixed him. She fixed me.

I dressed quietly and picked up my running shoes. A morning like this should not go unnoticed.

Control had always been my biggest downfall. I had learnt that over the last few years. I was so used to being able to control life, but letting life take over gave me everything I'd ever wanted. When I'd first stepped into the clutches of the moors, these hills and pastures mocked my fears, reflecting my heavy heart in the unforgiving mist. Shielding knowledge from me.

That day that I had poured out my soul on these grassy carpets, I had been hidden from the world, at least that's what I'd thought. But looking back now, it wasn't me who was being hidden, it was my life that was being hidden from me. It had taken so long to realise that in order to see my own future, I had to let someone else move the mist.

Now as I took each step towards the heavens, tracing the footsteps of the ghosts gone before, this land offered me forgiveness and promise. My teardrops once like the dew that had blanketed the tall grass now evaporated, taking my pain and maybe an inch of my fear along with them.

Each morning, I return to the oak tree, come rain or shine. Greeting her like an old friend and welcoming the memories that I share with her.

Today would be a special day. The ashes of my father and James's parents would now rest under this tree together. As I sat watching the sun rise, I took in the breath Mother Nature allowed me and prayed that Dad would like it here. That from up here he could watch his grandchildren play in the grounds of our home. That he and James's parents would feel peace in the place that opened up our hearts again.

I watched them play for hours today, watched them laugh and giggle as they played make-believe. Hope as the mother, cradling her baby in her arms and acting maternal towards a plastic lifeless doll, desperate to get her baby brother to join in. He rocked back and forth on his knees like a runner on the starter block, just waiting for the days his chubby little legs would move him through the long grass.

My mother sat on the blanket with them both, fussing with plastic cutlery and pretending to eat the imaginary 'apple cake' Hope served her.

Hope would only drag herself from her make-believe world when her brother put something in his mouth that he wasn't allowed. She was doggedly determined to keep him safe.

She caught me watching her.

Sat on my bench, tea by my side and my notepad on my lap, I had managed to go undetected for at least an hour before she caught my eye. Each year on her birthday I write another letter to put in her box next to the envelope containing her 'story'. But today I was also writing his story, for his box. He had only been with us for a week, but already it felt as if he had lived our whole life with us. Today, I would write how he came to us and how his big sister predicted the whole thing. Their bond was already so strong, and the love between them melted my heart. Her eyes lit up, and she checked her brother quickly, making sure Nana was watching him before leaving him. She ran towards me, arms wide open and a smile that seemed bigger than the heavens.

'Mummy . . .'

She launched her tiny frame at me and wrapped her arms around my neck just as tight as she had done that first day.

'I love you, Mummy.'

'I love you too, sweetheart. How does it feel to be a whole four years old?' I replied, feeling like the words didn't really do my feelings justice. Her giggle escaped her lips as I tickled her ribs.

'Today is the best birthday ever.' She beamed. 'Sorry you are sad about Gramps, but it was nice that he was with us too. I like sharing my special day with him.'

She glanced towards the tree on the top of the hill where we'd said goodbye before untying her birthday balloons from the branches and letting them float to the sky towards her grandpa. I think she thinks it's his birthday too, but she's too young to understand. It was so hard to celebrate her birthday on the same day that brought us so much pain at first, but when I saw the date in her file, I made the decision there and then that my dad would have wanted that. She seemed fated for us. A present from my dad to help us get through the tough times.

'Gramps doesn't want you to be sad,' she said, wiping an imaginary tear from my cheek. My heart ached at her spooky ability to understand my hidden feelings. It was a sweet thing to say, pure and so full of love.

'I know he wouldn't. I'm not sad,' I said back, pulling her onto my lap. 'Remembering people is good. It means they're still alive in your heart. He would have loved you. Very much.'

I choked a little as the words left my lips.

'I know,' she replied, with a flick of her hair and a wink in my direction.

She was so very matter-of-fact all the time, it made me chuckle. There were moments I questioned how she seemed so self-assured in her views so young.

She wrapped her arms around my neck and squeezed again.

'I love you, my darling girl. All the way to the moon and stars and back.'

'I know, Mummy. But I love you most,' she said as she sat back and looked at me.

'I'm pretty sure I love you the most,' I joked.

She bent down, cupped both hands around her perfectly formed pink lips and whispered, 'But I loved you first.' A cheeky grin spread wide across her face.

She sat back and looked me deadpan in the eyes, as if daring me to argue with her. Unwavering and unflinching.

'Oh, baby girl. I am pretty sure I loved *you* first.'

My heart thumped in my throat. There was something in her stare that unnerved me.

'Nope,' she said curtly, crossing her arms over her chest. 'I always loved you. You and Daddy. I chose you because I loved you the most.'

Her words stung my ears.

'What do you mean, sweetie?'

'I chose you. Gramps knew, too. Then I waited. I knew you would find me. Because I knew you and Daddy were good . . . and because I promised Gramps.'

And with that she jumped off my lap and ran off back into the garden.

I stared at her as she twirled around in circles holding my mother's hands, her baby brother at her feet. In a fit of giggles, she fell to the ground.

'Don't worry, Adam. I chose you too,' I heard her say to her brother, fussing with the blanket as she passed him one of the new baby rattles. 'I told you I would bring you home. Peekaboo, Adam.' She hid behind her hands before reappearing to cackling laughter. The seriousness of her tone was gone just as quickly as it had arrived.

I looked towards James, sat at the table under the shade with his sketchbook in front of him.

He'd heard it too and looked at me, a note of confusion mixed with a smile I couldn't quite place. Understanding, maybe.

I stood and placed my notebook on the bench before taking the seat next to him. I traced my fingers over the sketch he was finishing to put in the box with the other keepsakes.

Our two babies on the grass, grandmother playing with them, the old oak tree behind them and the faded shadow figures of four people all holding hands looking on from a distance, a ghosted-out set of angel wings hovering over their heads. My family, and his, and the one we never met.

I stared at the figures and couldn't help but go over those last words of my father, ringing in my ears.

*I'm very glad I got to meet you. I love you so very much. My hope.*

This child of mine, she chose us.

It made sense somewhere deep down. It might not have made sense to anyone else and as the thoughts whipped around in my mind, I looked at the sketch in front of me and wondered if it was possible. No one would ever believe me. But it made sense.

She chose us. She was meant for us. She may not have been born of us, but she watched and waited for us. She just had to follow a different path to get to us. Could my father have known it? Yes, I really think he did.

It was possible. Wasn't it?

# AUTHOR NOTE

Many people have asked this question throughout my publishing journey, so it felt only right to address it here. *This Child of Mine* is a work of fiction, yes, but there are many aspects of this book that have been born of personal experience. Fears and questions played out in this book are fears I have lived with myself, and know far too many women who have lived with the same, or worse.

However, this is *not* my story, this is Stephanie's story. She is all of us. All the women who have feared this choice, all the women who made this choice. She is the black terror that lives in the souls of those who are followed by the 'Big C' on a daily basis, worried about the affects it can have on their futures. She is also every woman who has ever felt like the choice was being taken out of their hands for one reason or another.

# *Acknowledgements*

It's true what they say, bringing a book into the world takes a team and getting to the 'end' often takes a whole village of support. So, I have *just a few* people to thank for helping me bring this book baby into the world.

It's safe to say that this book wouldn't be out in the world if it hadn't been for my agent Kate Nash, who picked this emotional rollercoaster from the slush pile and championed it all the way to the finish line. Subbing such an emotional book during a pandemic was no easy task, but Kate never doubted for a moment that she could find it the perfect home.

Thanks then of course must go to Thorne Ryan, who acquired my book for Avon, and my editor Elisha Lundin. Thank you for believing in Stephanie's story and for holding my hand on this crazy publishing ride, for understanding how much this story meant to me, but also how much it might mean to others. Thanks of course must go to the whole team at Avon, who had so much faith – without you, stories like this wouldn't see the light of day, and important conversations would go unheard. I will be forever grateful to those who took a chance on me.

At the age of 19, an editor by the name of Laura Wood took a chance on a young, naïve writer and gave her a job in journalism. Laura taught me everything I needed to know and pushed me to be better than I ever thought I could be.

Nearly ten years ago, three nervous strangers sat in a room full of aspiring writers ready to be taught by the fabulous Lorraine Mace. We entered as strangers and came out lifelong friends. Over the next decade, we would launch The Glass House Online Magazine, help each other through the query trenches and wipe away each other's frustrations with each rejection. I have since had the joy of watching you both achieve your dreams and shoot for even bigger ones. Natali Simmonds, you are and always will be my 'sanity wrapped in chaos', and I am forever grateful to have your fire and passion in my life. I wouldn't be without you. Samantha Curtis, on the days when the world feels too much to cope with, you steady me and bring me back down to earth. Forever my Pollyanna. I am SO proud of how much you have both achieved and so happy to have you by my side. Forever The Glass House Girls!

This book came to life over 5 years ago, thanks in part to some amazing authors. I had always been too scared to write the 'emotional' novel that lived in my head. A party in London (held by the Queen herself, Tracy Fenton of TBC fame) saw me mingling with authors I respected. John Marrs, Susie Lynes, Callie Langridge, Cally Taylor and Rowan Coleman all 'kicked me up the bum' that night and told me to get the words on paper. When I returned home, I read *How to be Brave* by Louise Beech and if I was ever going to be brave, it was now. Amanda Prowse, I don't even think I know where to start thanking you. Your books inspired me, your friendship pushed me, your faith that I would one day make it kept me battling through the fear. I will always be grateful for your support. Without the support of these amazing authors (and more), I wouldn't have written the first chapter.

A massive thank you needs to go to Rowan Coleman and Julie Cohen. A retreat with Rowan at Ponden Hall in Yorkshire changed my life and gave me the confidence to lean in and embrace the emotion in my writing. Julie made me cry during a retreat in Devon when she warned me I might need to start from scratch. She was right, and those tears on the sofa that day pushed me to find the 'real' story underneath.

Alison May – my mentor, my friend, my saviour. Where would I be without you. One piece of advice I can give new writers: 'find your Alison'. Find one person who can help hold your hand, be strict and tell you to 'stop spinning and write all the words.' Someone whose advice you appreciate, and opinion you value, then hold them close – because publishing is a rollercoaster.

My BarBabes. My 'tribe'. There are no words. Since meeting at our very first RNA Conference, you ladies have been my daily dose of normality. Julie Morris, Kate Baker, Jenny Kennedy, Sandra Forder, Katie Wells and Emma Jackson – being stuck on the naughty table in the bar was the start of a friendship I will forever protect. Love you all.

Special thanks need to go to Selina Ralph and Sarah Homer for their help and guidance when researching and Luke Allnutt for talking to me about his process when writing *We Own the Sky*. The advice given allowed me to write Stephanie's story in the most authentic way possible.

There are, no doubt, a million other people I should and could say thank you to, for helping me on this journey, for offering advice. All those in the RNA who championed me, gave me advice and calmed my nerves during panic attacks (here's looking at you Liz Fenwick) – and I know I am bound to forget a few, so this is a thank you to EVERYONE who has ever given me encouraging words, a consolation hug after a rejection or even just listened to me ramble about the stories in my head. Thank you.

Avril and Brian. Thank you for being some of the first readers of this book. Thank you for loving me unconditionally and being there for me every step of the way. Regan, for keeping me real, Mary for being the mother-in-law of dreams and helping far too many times with the kids while I powered through writing this. To my nana whose support never wavers, and for my grandad who I miss terribly – I hope I did you proud. My granny Doris, who always pushed me to walk with the stars, I wish you were here to see this.

Now for the biggest and most important thank yous.

My biggest thanks goes to the amazing heroes that helped me bring my own little miracles into the world. Specifically, those in the NICU unit at Aberdeen Maternity Hospital. Lauren and Emma – angels in scrubs! You saved us, in more ways than one. Lou-Lou and Dave, you guys kept us breathing even when I thought I would never breathe again. To the Li family, you know how much you mean to me, you are my 'chosen family'.

But the most important people in the world for me to thank – my amazing girls, Tabitha and Matilda. My two 'little witches'. Tabby, you were and always will be my 'dream come true'. You are already stronger and braver than I ever was and watching you grow has been the biggest privilege of my life. I want to be more like *you* when I am 'older'. I love you, my little *cacahuetita.* Tilly – thank you for 'choosing' me. For choosing us. Thank you for being always unapologetically you and teaching me that the most important thing in this world, is love. Your hugs heal, and wisdom inspires and your compassion for others always restores my faith in humanity, even on my darkest days. You girls are my whole world and there will never be a day where I am anything less than proud and privileged to be your mum. To my amazing husband. My man, my 'dude'. Thank you for not laughing at me when I told you I wanted to write a book. Thank you for believing in me. I am so fortunate to be married to a man who not only supports my dreams but pushes me the entire way. *None* of this would have been possible without you and even on my darkest days, you bring light into my life. When my heart races with fear, you steady me. You are, and always will be my rock, my red string. Te amo, siempre.